Hot Chances

JOEY W. HILL
RHYANNON BYRD

Ellora's Cave
Romantica Publishing

What the critics are saying...

ಸಿ

CHANCE OF A LIFETIME

5 Roses "If you are looking for a story which is sexy, fun and endearing, then this story is for you. While they may be strangers, every scene is filled with emotion and respect. Jake has been given the role of dominating her, but does so with a gentle hand and with her pleasure his main goal. I was sad to see the story end, but oh so happy with it from beginning to finish. What a gift to read this book!" ~ *A Romance Review*

5 Blue Ribbons "Ms. Hill writes a poignant story that touched me from the opening chapter. It's about the heart's ability to reach out for those amazing experiences in life, especially when you are drowning in everyday responsibilities. It's about taking that one chance that comes your way; that one CHANCE OF A LIFETIME, and seeing where fate may take you. CHANCE OF A LIFETIME will tap into your emotions and yank on your heartstrings, even as it leaves you breathless and panting for air. Ms. Hill has penned a winner!" ~ *Romance Junkies Reviews*

5 Stars "Hurry up and get this book! As usual, Ms. Hill has created a story that is complex, emotional and erotic as can be. The characters are so real that you'll feel like you truly know them. […] The sex is as sizzling and so perfect for each of them. This story is most definitely a *Chance of a Lifetime* read." ~ *Sensual EcataRomance Reviews*

A Little Less Conversation

5 Stars "Rhyannon Byrd has done such a fabulous job! I wish I had more stars to give, but I gave the most there were. I found myself laughing and stirred up and absolutely in love with Mark and Melanie, wishing it would never end. This is a love story that can not, and should not, be missed!"
~ *EcataRomance Reviews*

"*A Little Less Conversation* is a wildly erotic story. [...] The sexual action is intense! The author certainly knows how to write some very powerful and highly erotic scenes. [...] *A Little Less Conversation* is another arousing product from Ms. Byrd's imagination. [...] It is a well written and action packed story that readers' of Ellora's Cave have come to love and expect. This reader looks forward to the next book from Ms. Byrd."
~ *The Road to Romance Reviews*

4 Cupids "A LITTLE LESS CONVERSATION is a very hot read. [...] I thoroughly enjoyed this book. The erotic scenes between Mark and Melanie are wonderful and very steamy. I am curious if MS. BYRD is planning a follow-up book about Melanie's boss and Mark's brother kindling a relationship. So many hints of an explosive relationship are revealed throughout this book. [...] I would be so excited to see a second book featuring these characters." ~ *Cupid's Library Reviews*

An Ellora's Cave Romantica Publication

www.ellorascave.com

Hot Chances

ISBN 9781419955808
ALL RIGHTS RESERVED.
Chance of a Lifetime Copyright © 2006 Joey W. Hill
A Little Less Conversation Copyright © 2006 Rhyannon Byrd
Edited by Briana St. James and Pamela Campbell.
Cover art by Syneca.

This book printed in the U.S.A. by Jasmine-Jade Enterprises, LLC.

Trade paperback Publication September 2008

With the exception of quotes used in reviews, this book may not be reproduced or used in whole or in part by any means existing without written permission from the publisher, Ellora's Cave Publishing, Inc.® 1056 Home Avenue, Akron OH 44310-3502.

Warning: The unauthorized reproduction or distribution of this copyrighted work is illegal. Criminal copyright infringement, including infringement without monetary gain, is investigated by the FBI and is punishable by up to 5 years in federal prison and a fine of $250,000.
(http://www.fbi.gov/ipr/)

This book is a work of fiction and any resemblance to persons, living or dead, or places, events or locales is purely coincidental. The characters are productions of the author's imagination and used fictitiously.

HOT CHANCES
ಸಂ

CHANCE OF A LIFETIME
By Joey W. Hill
~11~

A LITTLE LESS CONVERSATION
By Rhyannon Byrd
~97~

CHANCE OF A LIFETIME
By Joey W. Hill

ഖ

Trademarks Acknowledgement

The author acknowledges the trademarked status and trademark owners of the following wordmarks mentioned in this work of fiction:

Glock : Glock Gesellschaft M.B.H. Ltd Liab JT ST CO

Mustang : Ford Motor Company

NASCAR : National Association for Stock Car Auto Racing, Inc.

NBA : NBA Properties, Inc.

NFL : National Football League

Porsche : Dr. Ing. H.C.F. Porsche Aktiengesellschaft Corporation

Sig Sauer : SIG Swiss Industrial Company

Trans Am : Sports Car Club of America, Incorporated

Chapter One

∞

"Stacie, that was inappropriate behavior. I expected more from you than that."

Inappropriate behavior.

She'd laughed at a joke. The wife of one of John's co-workers had made the observation, not unkindly, that John's boss looked like a giraffe. The likeness had been so obvious, she couldn't help the snort of laughter.

Maybe it had been too loud. Maybe a couple heads had turned. But all she'd done was laugh, for heaven's sake.

On Monday, her father had freaked out on his new meds and thrown her into a china cabinet. On Wednesday, her mother had needed her diaper changed. When she'd cried through the indignity of it, Stacie had cried too. She'd made multiple calls to the insurance company about a ten-thousand-dollar charge her brother insisted was incorrect and therefore refused to pay. Finally, to top off this terrific week, she'd been roped into being John's arm candy for this business party, the annual "Summer Fling" for which he *had* to have a date.

God, she was so sick of worrying about what she said, how she did things. Maybe she'd overreacted. But seeing John's face when she'd told him to "go to hell" had been worth it. She'd even taken his car, a car that certainly shouldn't belong to a stuffy corporate ass kisser who color-organized his sock drawer.

"Aarggh!" She pushed her foot down on the accelerator. The Porsche leaped forward. God...it felt so good. On these quiet rural roads, nothing around for miles and miles but corn and a rosy summer sky getting ready for sunset, it felt incredible, like riding a horse. Or riding a man. Maybe both were a form of running, but she didn't care.

Though she hadn't been out of nursing school more than a year, at the time it had made sense for her to leave her hospital job to serve as a home health care nurse to her parents. Fate had struck a cruel blow, inflicting Alzheimer's on her father within a month of when her mother was diagnosed with terminal cancer. As they worsened, she knew they needed a good long-term care facility that could be supplemented by her care.

Her two older brothers had moved north and joined a New York firm, an important career move they said they couldn't turn down, several months after she moved in with their parents. Both successful CPAs, Carl and Tom saw no reason why she couldn't provide their parents everything they needed at home. As the eldest child, Tom held power of attorney for their parents. At first, she'd tried to believe their reasoning was emotional, based on love. The "we're not putting Mom and Dad in a home" mentality, lingering from a time when the only choice was a brick box structure on the side of the highway with a few rocking chairs out front. As time progressed, her opinion changed bitterly. They insisted they would take care of the finances insurance didn't cover and her living expenses, but everything was a fight and grudgingly given.

Her dating life in the past couple years had been John. It wasn't dating she cared about, however. She'd asked Tom to pay for a relief nurse to give her a night away from the house once every couple of weeks. He'd hung up on her after calling her a selfish bitch trying to drain his children's college fund. An hour later, she'd been called by John. A former colleague of her brother's, he needed an attractive armpiece for his business dinners and didn't have much time to devote to developing a relationship. Tom said he'd pay for an overnight relief nurse whenever she chose to go out with John, as long as it didn't exceed once a month. In return, she suspected John gave him a discount on his brokerage services.

At first, she'd been insulted by the whole situation, including her brother's assumption she'd need an overnight nurse. After giving it some thought, however, she decided to take advantage of it. On her first date with John, she'd planned to have an early night and spend the rest of her evening elsewhere. She'd take a few dollars she'd put aside to check into a cheap motel and read or sleep for the night, enjoy some solitude.

But for reasons she was ashamed to examine too closely, she'd let John coax her into going home with him and succumbing to some perfunctory sex she'd actually been grateful to him for initiating. A weak moment where she'd needed comfort, someone's sheltering arms.

After that it had become a monthly habit. Go to some idiotic business function, go home with John. At least he fell asleep quickly. She could then slide out of bed and sit by the window, listening to rain patter on the glass or watching the moon. Sometimes she read whatever paperback novel she'd picked up for escapism, knowing the dream it spun would be uninterrupted for a little while. While she was embarrassed at herself, at the whole revolting situation, she knew she didn't have enough energy left at the end of the day to walk away from it. Her mother was sliding fast toward the end and her father was losing his mind, and she couldn't give them everything she knew they needed. She was so desperate for that one day a month where she'd get a few hours away from that reality, she was willing to be whored out to get it.

Imagining John's arms around her now was smothering. Intolerable. Like a dog trying to wriggle under a fence, stuck in the hole he'd dug, she understood why he'd strangle himself to death trying to escape.

Perhaps she'd spend the night just doing this. In college she'd had a Mustang. This car had a lot more power, but it was easy to get used to the difference. She pushed the gas pedal down even farther. It was just her out here, on a silver ribbon of road with hills to give her stomach the thrill of a roller coaster. It was like the feel of first love, the first bite of lust. For once she was going faster than the demons chasing her soul.

Two days ago she'd turned twenty-five. Her mother had hugged her and looked at her with tears in her eyes. She didn't want her mother to worry about her. Worry about anything. Damn her brothers. Stacie vowed her parents would never see anything but her love. Her mother would *not* pass out of this world thinking she or Dad were a burden to Stacie. Never. They'd cared for her eighteen years and then some.

She'd been a wild child. Not a bad girl, just carefree enough to blow her shot at a scholarship, unlike her brothers. But she'd found her focus in her senior year and Dad had believed in her enough to sell his treasured restored Chevy and pay for her first year of tuition in nursing school. She'd worked her ass off to pay for the rest and make the grades to get the degree.

The two years she'd spent caring for them was nothing.

Just an eternity when she was watching her mother die while her father slowly forgot who his wife and daughter were. When she learned that no matter how hard she tried, one person alone, even medically trained, couldn't give optimal care to two adults with such disparately different serious long-term illnesses. She was afraid something in her own mind was going to crack wide open soon, like Humpty-Dumpty on his wall. She put the gas pedal all the way to the floor, trying to push all of that away and the panicked desperation that went with it.

She let out a short yip of alarm at a sharp blast of noise. Glancing up in the mirror, she saw flashing blue lights about a quarter mile back.

"You have got to be fuc...KIDDING!" She rolled her eyes. "Stop it. You're alone, Stacie. You can swear. *Say it*. F-fuck. You've got to be FUCKING kidding!" She glared at the rearview mirror in triumph. She'd cussed. Not one of those weak everybody-used-them words like damn or hell. She wished John had been here to hear it, just for a moment. His mouth would have hung open like he'd just been hit in the head by a flounder. *Inappropriate behavior.*

Bite me.

What in hell was a cop doing out here in a county area so remote the radio stations had static? She'd no idea how fast she was going, but she was sure it was at least twenty miles over the speed limit. It wasn't fair. Had she been like her self-absorbed brothers in a previous life, and this was karma?

Fine. Taking a deep breath, she pulled over. She could handle one cop. The threat of jail had all the appeal to her of a weekend spa session. *With* a full body massage.

She glanced in the side view mirror as the cop's car door opened. If she hadn't been used to seeing refitted drug dealer cars used in the city all the time by the police, she might have suffered a fleeting worry about a blue light bandit posing as a police officer. The car was a sleek and deadly-looking black Trans Am. It didn't answer what a city cop was doing way out here, though. Then he unfolded and straightened from the car and she lost the desire to wonder about anything.

Holy God.

As if she'd been going so fast the world had spun on its axis and now was going way, blissfully slow, his first few steps toward her were like the movies where the hero's initial walk-on scene was in slow motion.

He wasn't wearing a uniform. With her earlier thought of a sexual predator posing as a policeman, that should have alarmed her. But when dormant hormones surged to life as they did now, like a pack of wild dogs out of control, it sort of cancelled out brain cells.

His well-creased jeans moved with his hips just right, the badge flashing at her from where it was clipped to his belt. He wore a shoulder holster and his snug dark T-shirt was tucked in, capturing the sharp, authentic look of a cop, despite the casual wear. It also emphasized a broad chest, wide shoulders and flat abdomen that drew the eye back past his waist down to other things the jeans held well. He had a black baseball cap with gold PD lettering pulled down low on his brow and wore concealing sunglasses against the setting sun. His jaw line was hard and clean as creek rock, just a hint of five o'clock shadow that went with the dark close-cropped hair she could see beneath the cap. His arms. My God, she'd just dwell on those arms for days, the sinewy strength they conveyed.

If she could program this moment like her DVR, she'd pause and rewind so he could walk toward her forever. She'd worship the cable company like gods.

The baseball field. She remembered now. As she was headed out of town, there'd been a mixture of cop cars and vehicles with police and fire association bumper stickers. The police and firemen ran a series of six games every year, a benefit for the children's center. This guy was likely off duty, heading home. So why did he mind if she was doing a little careless joyriding? Was he one of those tight-assed sticklers for the rules?

He's a cop, Stacie. They enforce laws. That's kind of their job.

But he wasn't on duty. The whine, even in her own head, made her wince. It just wasn't fair.

From the way he approached the car, she knew he was doing that quick assessment police people did to ensure she wasn't going to pose a threat. Or pull a gun from her micro-sized evening bag.

Oh *hell*. She had no license with her. She'd left it and her wallet at home because she was with John. She had a clutch purse with a few toiletries in it and that was it. The thought came to her a moment before he made that final step to the window. Tapped on the glass.

Reluctantly she turned the key and let the window roll down.

"Ma'am, were you aware you were going a hundred and thirty miles an hour?"

Holy shit. She couldn't help it. A giggle burst from her. She clapped her hand over her mouth. Well, no wonder he'd stopped her, even if he was off duty. She might as well have sauntered past his window and waved a bag of cocaine.

When he frowned, she had a sudden, explosive urge to nibble on his firm lips. What was the matter with her? She bit back more of that inappropriate laughter. Seems all the men in her life, including this newest addition, didn't approve of her laughing. Well...f-fuck them. In fact... Her gaze coursed over him. That would be a really good idea. Those jeans looked like they contained something quite capable of inappropriate behavior.

"Ma'am, is something funny? Have you been drinking?"

"No. No." She shook her head, smothered another nearly hysterical hiccup of laughter. "I should though. I should drink *a lot.*"

His brow raised, that stern expression deepening, and oh my Lord. Her panties dampened, a shocking reaction. She couldn't remember the last time she'd let herself think about the possibility of good sex. When she and John did it, she tried not to think about what they were doing at all because that would make her realize exactly how horribly unsatisfying it was. His touch barely roused her. He knew enough to get her lubricated so they could accomplish the act. She preferred to call it that versus "wet" because "wet" implied excitement, emotional involvement.

When he finished, he never even asked her if she had reached climax. Which she didn't mind actually, because if he thought she expected that, he might try doing it longer. God help her.

Was this cop really masterful like this? Or was it just a trained persona, something he took off like his badge and gun at the end of the day? Did he become a man as lackluster as John, an unimaginative couch potato?

"Ma'am, I need you to get out of the car."

The laughter faded from her mind, leaving a sense of hopeless desolation. Reality had intruded and the gorgeous cop was going to give her a ticket. Another thing to deal with, another thing she'd have to resolve with her brothers because she'd wanted one frigging moment to breathe. Something surged up in her so fast and hard it was like a bad reaction to the evening's hors d'oeuvres and just as alarming. Much worse than vomit.

A muscle flexed in her jaw. "Officer, I..." She swallowed. "Can you go back to your car just a moment, please?"

He lifted a brow.

"I'm going to cry now. I don't want to cry. It actually...d-doesn't...help anything. And...and...I'm not a crier!" She blurted it out as she felt the first tears start to well from her eyes. "I don't...try to get out of tickets and...I d-don't w-want...please. I'll take the t-ticket. Just... Oh hell. Go away."

She hit the window control. She needed a "Come back in five minutes" sign like they had at the bank. Why couldn't she have had this one thing? Why did it have to be this way, always? What had she done wrong?

* * * * *

Jake Chance blinked as glass whirred back up, shutting him out. She turned away from him, burying her face in her hands.

Well, that was a first.

When he'd told her how fast she was going, he'd wanted to add she'd been handling the car damn well at that speed. He'd pulled up to the road right as she passed. If not for that and the fact he'd immediately pulled out behind her and turned on his siren to get her attention, she likely would have been over the crest of the next hill and out of his sight before he could react.

He'd expected a face shellacked with wealth and was surprised the pale countenance staring back at him was lightly touched with makeup, though not enough to cover shadows and worry lines she was too young to have. Her shoulder-length hair was pushed back in a simple style. The dress she wore, what there was of it, was an elegant black short thing with spaghetti straps, the kind cut to show off a delicate nape, the fine line of the shoulders, a modest but intriguing amount of bare breast. It was the type of dress that teased a man with a lot of leg.

Her change in expression had alerted him, made him draw his attention away from enjoyment of her body. Her face was too thin, and suddenly it was thinner, drawn in on itself. He knew the signs of stress. He'd had women do all sorts of things to dodge a ticket, but his gut told him that wasn't what was happening here. The circumstances were wrong. A pretty woman all by herself in the middle of nowhere, eating the pavement like she was outrunning the fires of hell. Going nowhere as fast as she could. She wasn't trying to play him.

In fact, the look in her eyes roused a protectiveness in him, a second sense he had when he knew someone needed him. But even with that, it had been a long time since a woman had made him want to do the asinine thing he did now.

She hadn't locked her door. Opening it, he unbuckled her seat belt, his fingers brushing her silky hip. She smelled like one of those light floral body sprays with a hint of talcum powder. Gently he took her elbow, went to one knee. Because the Porsche was so low to the ground, it was simple to turn her and find she fit perfectly against his chest.

She hardly reacted. No jump, no stiffening. She was having a full-out flood, and it was the easiest thing in the world to wrap his arms around her.

"It's okay," he murmured.

Stacie knew she should have been shocked, but she no longer had the energy to do what was right or proper. The arms around her felt good. Strong. Able to hold her together so she wouldn't break. Until he'd put them around her, she hadn't realized how fragile she felt. He smelled of sweat from the baseball game, a faint soap and aftershave smell.

"No...it's...not. But it doesn't matter. I still have to keep on going, and I'm s-so af-fraid I c-can't. That I'll l-let them d-down."

"Sshh...sshh... Just let it out." She had her arms folded between them, protecting herself. Pushing her head onto his shoulder, Jake tightened his hold on her and let her sob. Her words struck him oddly. Here she was, pretty as a picture and driving a Porsche, and yet her words reminded him starkly of his own job. It wasn't okay, but you still had to keep doing it. Battered wives, homicides over old grudges, kidnappings, robberies, kids gunning each other down in the street...

She had a lot built up and he found he didn't mind holding her through it. So often he couldn't reach out, couldn't help. She might be crying over something utterly shallow, like she'd run up too much credit card debt, but somehow he didn't think so. The shoulders quivering under his hands were even now trying to snap back to regain control, to reel it back in. He watched for the signs, ready to ease up. When she lifted her head at last to look at him, or rather to hastily wipe her eyes before he could see her, he caught her wrist. While he didn't have a kerchief, he supposed the hem of his T-shirt would do. Pulling it loose, he brought the edge up to her face. As he did, her hand fluttered down, landed soft as a summer butterfly on his bare stomach, just above the belt holding his jeans.

Rather than jerking away, she went still. Carefully, he kept dabbing under her eyes, but he could feel every ounce of pressure from her fingers. *Christ, Chance, she's upset about something. Give her a break.*

He was rock-hard muscle, was Stacie's thought. She fought the irresistible urge to spread out her fingers, enjoy the flat stomach, the silken trail of hair she knew would arrow straight down toward his groin. Her thumb was on his belt. She should feel emotionally drained after such a cry. Embarrassed and ready for ice cream and female-only solitude. However, as her hand made that intimate contact, hard want pulsed between her thighs, telling her exactly what she was ready for.

Like her desire to speed in the Porsche, she wanted to ride fast and hard, as fast as she could, higher and higher. She didn't want to have sex. She'd given up on making love. She wanted to fuck. Like she'd read about, dreamed about. She wanted to fuck this sexy, gorgeous cop with gentle hands and hard muscles, who'd been enough of a good guy to know when she needed a shoulder. Something John wouldn't recognize if her parents dropped dead, her house burned down and she discovered she'd gained twenty pounds—all in the same day.

With his arms bent like this, his biceps swelled into nice firm curves. His hands were long-fingered and looked rough, strong. Well, lackluster and unimaginative he might be, but a couch potato he wasn't. She didn't care that a man might be a little soft, but right now she wanted a man the way a fantasy demanded him to be. A man who would spread her legs with relentless determination and sheathe himself, drowning her in pleasure. Take her over, allow her to think only about his cock and the climax he'd send screaming through her every nerve ending.

Okay, she was taking this fantasy way too far. He'd straightened to his feet and extended an open palm. He could be kind, but he was still going to do his job, make sure she wasn't intoxicated.

Taking his hand, she put her heel to the pavement. Getting out of a Porsche in a short dress didn't allow modesty.

She hesitated as he tightened his grip on her. Insisting she was going to get out of that car.

Well, why not? The speed she'd been going, the exhilaration she'd felt at the sheer freedom of it, came surging back through her. What was she worried about?

Clasping his fingers, she let his leverage bring her to her feet. Her slender fingers and wrist looked consumed by his grip. The skirt hiked up past the lace top of her thigh highs briefly before she rose. While she couldn't tell for sure, she thought he'd looked.

Suddenly her protective cop had the intimidating look of a pissed-off Clint Eastwood. Before she could step back, startled by the shift in his expression, his hands slid to her upper arms, holding her fast.

"Baby, who left those bruises on your neck?"

She blinked. The cop had just...he'd just used a possessive endearment, and heat rushed up through her at the way his jaw hardened, telling her he damn well expected an answer. It was like a sign. He wanted her too. Or was she having a delusion?

"Oh—no. It's not what you think. My father has dementia. His current meds aren't working so well, and he flies into rages. He caught me unprepared." Would have strangled her if she hadn't been able to use an umbrella to break his grip. She thought she'd patted on enough makeup to disguise it. "I take care of him."

"Sounds like you need some help. Isn't there a nurse?"

"I am a nurse."

Stacie gave him the information distractedly, already not thinking about that anymore. She moistened her lips. If she acted like this *was* a fantasy, then if she made a fool of herself tomorrow she could pretend it had all been a dream, right? Unless she woke up in jail, of course.

When he removed his glasses and hooked them in his shirt collar, she saw he had flinty gray eyes to go with his dark hair streaked with brown.

She cleared her throat. "I think you were going to determine if I'd been drinking."

"Have you?"

"One glass of wine at the dullest party that's ever been held in the history of corporate America." She stepped backward two steps while he watched her closely.

"Let's be sure. Just walk down the center line, ma'am. One foot in front of the other."

A straight line, no stepping off right or left. She'd been doing that for the past seven years. Mom and Dad had believed in her, and she'd tamed the wildness. But tonight she wanted to let it loose. She'd have the control to rein it back in. Tomorrow.

"Mind if I take my shoes off first?" She gestured to the shiny three-inch heels. "I wouldn't want to catch one on the pavement and make you think I was something I wasn't."

He inclined his head. Holding onto the car, she took off one shoe then switched her grip to do the other. Now he was even taller. Dropping the shoes behind the seat through the open door, she turned, propped one foot on the back wheel. Reaching up a few inches under the skirt, she unhooked the garter and rolled down the stocking deliberately, knowing she was revealing her leg from the side almost to the hip.

Let's see how far we can take this. The sheer stocking came off like a dandelion's seeds at a puff from her lips, blowing lightly in the air. After she did the other, she turned to find him watching. Avidly, a man's desire in his eyes. His jaw flexed. Smiling, Stacie approached and draped the stockings over one of his broad shoulders, coming close enough she could feel his heat. Since something in his eyes told her she should be cautious about coming too close, she took a step closer.

"Thanks," she said simply. "That's the best compliment I've gotten in months."

As she moved by him, she made sure her hip brushed his before she walked toward the center line.

Chapter Two
∞

Jake Chance had dealt with countless women who tried to use their wiles to get out of punishment for their crimes. But this one... He wasn't sure what she was up to, but it was almost like she was enjoying herself, not in the slightest bit interested in how much trouble she could be in. She was a knockout, a girl-next-door innocence in a fuck-me elegant black cocktail dress.

It had a low back held together with one horizontal strip that passed just beneath her bare shoulder blades, just wide enough to cover a bra strap. Below it, the cut of the dress dipped to the small of her back, increasing his focus on a perfectly shaped pert ass that he'd like to grip with both hands as he bent her over the hood of his car.

Hell. Though he was getting harder by the minute, he was just going to have to grit his teeth and bear it. This wasn't his jurisdiction, but he lived out here. The county sheriff wouldn't mind him putting a little fear of God into a reckless driver. He *would* mind him fucking her senseless up against the side of his car.

The lacy dangling strap of her garters he'd glimpsed teased his imagination. A man could slide his fingers under hooked garters, feel the silky elastic stretch over his knuckles as he gripped her hips, drove into her. Her stockinged legs would tighten over his back, heels to his ass as he buried himself into wet, blissful pussy.

The deft way she'd taken off her shoes told him she wasn't drunk. He might be the intoxicated one at this point. Having her walk the center of the road put a few feet of space between them, which he desperately needed.

Stepping onto the white line, she placed one foot before the other, deliberate as a deer. Those bruises he'd seen at her neck continued down her back. They'd been concealed by makeup but became more obvious in the play of the dying sunlight on her skin. Women lied about things like that, but the genuine surprise she'd shown at his question, the fact she displayed none of the familiar defensive wariness around a cop, told him she was telling the truth about how she'd gotten them. It still pissed him off though. There was more to this story. A woman shouldn't be handling a grown man with dementia by herself.

Putting her hands out to either side like a bird, she looked back and gave him a mischievous, thorough look with midnight sky blue eyes. "My, that's a very big gun you're carrying, Officer. You're scaring me."

His lips twitched. *Then you better get your ass down that line before I decide to pull it out and use it.*

Had he lost his mind? He cleared his throat. "Just walk the line, ma'am."

As she put one foot in front of the other, her hips swayed. He could swear she was exaggerating the motion. It taunted the part of him that enjoyed a little fight out of a woman before he overpowered her and made her scream with pleasure. It'd been a while since he'd let a woman get that close. Women now were too jaded and distrusting, thanks to the bastards men could be. But this one…

She did the walk with perfect precision, executing a graceful pirouette at the end that made the skirt swish around her thighs.

"And touch my toes?" As she went down, that short skirt inched up, close to showing him what was beneath it. When she rose, she cast an innocent look over her shoulder. "Did I do it right, or should I do it again?"

She was not going to make him laugh. But his lips had to press hard together to resist it. "We actually require you to touch your nose, not your toes."

"Oh." She dimpled. "My fault." Dropping her head back on her shoulders, she brought one pale limb up, one slender finger touching her nose, then the other. As she lowered her arms, the spaghetti strap tumbled off the curve of one shoulder.

The bra she was wearing had to be one of those strapless demi-cup things that held breasts up on a shelf, as inviting as cold beer sitting at easy gripping level in the fridge. If she was one of those trashy types willing to give him a blow to evade a ticket, maybe he would have taken advantage of it. No. No, he wouldn't. He was a good cop. But something about the feverish quality in her eye intrigued him. She wasn't drunk or on drugs, but something was driving her, a need so powerful he could feel it pulsing off her. Something in him was responding to it full force.

Padding across the asphalt in her bare feet, she came back to him. The wind caught wisps of hair to caress her neck in a way he'd like to do. This was a woman who should belong to someone, who should be cared for. She wasn't promiscuous or irresponsible. Despite catching her in a situation that suggested otherwise, he knew the difference between chronic irresponsibility and the need to run from something, to cut loose because the rubber band elasticity of her soul was stretched to breaking.

"I need your license and registration."

She bit her lip. "I don't have them. I mean, John may keep the registration in the car, but—"

"This isn't your car."

"No." She shook her head.

"Is that your boyfriend?" He tried to keep it professional, authoritative, a voice that would compel her to tell him the truth the way a doctor's authority compelled a patient to tell him anything.

"John?" She blinked. "Oh heavens, no." That smile touched her lips again, but he noticed it looked as if it were attached to a millstone. "Why is that relevant? You can't require me to talk about my personal life, can you?"

"Actually, there's a statute that says I can. It's very complicated."

She gave him a dubious look, went and sat down in the driver's seat of her car, slipping those shoes back on, this time without the hose.

Stacie tugged the heel straps over her ankles, crisscrossed and re-buckled them, letting her hair fall forward over her face. He was back to giving her that detached, speculative look. What was she doing, really? What would one moment of fun help? Especially when it could be so easily disrupted by the slightest mention of the life she'd tried to leave behind for one night.

"I think I should tell you, I stole the car."

"What?" That cop look snapped back on his face so fast she wondered if she'd imagined him responding to her brief, pathetic attempt at flirtation. He probably got hit on all the time.

"Well, he was being such an ass. I mean, it's bad enough I'm there as his show pony, but to tell me I can't even laugh when I want to laugh. And his boss does look like a giraffe, I'm sorry."

Jake pinched the bridge of his nose. "So you took off with his car."

"I got his keys out of his coat. It's not like he knows how to drive it anyway. He likes pretty cars and pretty women and has no idea how to handle either one of them."

When she looked up at him, she couldn't keep herself from lingering over the terrain. Or from saying the words that came out of her mouth, which seemed to be disconnected from her brain. "I bet that's not a problem you have, do you? Officer..."

"Chance. Lieutenant Jake Chance."

Jake sighed. He needed to cut this one loose before he did something incredibly stupid. "Let me run the plates, make sure he hasn't reported it."

She nodded, but he wasn't sure she even heard him. Her mind seemed to be elsewhere. Before he went back to the car, he couldn't help himself. He stepped forward, brushed her shoulder, catching his fingers in the strap to tug it back onto her shoulder. Dipping her head, she laid her cheek against the top of his knuckles. Not sexual at all. A simple gesture of gratitude for the kindness. It was intimate, familiar, as if they'd known each other for awhile. When she looked up at him, it was so obvious what she wanted and needed, it left him nowhere to go but in retreat.

It was the honorable fucking thing to do. Damn it. He nodded awkwardly, extricated his hand and moved away.

As he strode back to his car, Stacie closed her door, leaned her head back on the seat and watched him in the rearview mirror. So was that it? An odd moment shared with a stranger, one they'd each recall later, her with some embarrassment, him with some perplexity? Would either of them wonder what would have happened if they'd taken it just a step farther?

It had been a while since she'd had the heart to believe in Fate. She studied the way the dark sleeve of his shirt stretched as he bent his arm to bring the radio to his mouth. Perhaps, even though she hadn't had the courage to give Fate a chance lately, Fate had decided to give her one.

Chance. Jake Chance.

He couldn't make the decisive move. He was a decent guy, she could tell, and he wouldn't disgrace the badge by taking advantage of the authority it gave him. But if she made it clear this wasn't about that, not exactly… That she was willing to cross boundaries if he was and move into a territory where a whole other set of rules applied…

A smile flirted around her lips. She couldn't possibly.

Oh why the hell not?

She twisted the key in the ignition. As the engine came to life, his head snapped around, those gray eyes narrowing, his jaw flexing in a very attractive way.

Lowering the window, she leaned out. "Lieutenant Chance." She hit the gas once, punctuating her call with the response of the Porsche. "Can that muscle car hold its own in a good chase, or does it just look good?"

A series of expressions crossed his face, faster than the car could move, but she was almost sure one of them was arousal at the unmistakable taunt, the purr she put into her voice.

"Don't even think about it." He was trying for that stern look again, the one that got her juices flowing even hotter. "Miss…"

Jesus Christ, what was her name? Jake took a step forward and she goosed the pedal, rolling several feet. "You've managed to get out of a ticket up to this point." He tried for calm, even though that light in her eye made him feel anything but. Fire was licking through his vitals, and the revving of that engine reverberated in his own body. "Don't push your luck."

"Stacie. I don't want to get out of a ticket." Her lips curved, the girl-next-door suddenly the siren of his most prurient dreams. "But tell you what, Lieutenant Chance. If you can catch me, you can try to get me out of these clothes. Though you better have handcuffs, because I fully intend to resist arrest."

He swore. "Dammit, woman—"

She hit the gas. A spray of gravel and dirt peppered the front of the Trans Am as she peeled the back tires deliberately, skidding back onto the asphalt and heading up the deserted highway, the car's flanks flashing in the light of the rising yellow moon.

"Goddamn it." Tossing the radio back in the car, he yanked open the door, sliding behind the wheel. Little idiot probably wasn't wearing her seat belt. Or any underwear. Firing the car, he hit the gas, not bothering with a seat belt either because he wasn't sure he'd get it over the hard-on she'd just brought to full life on him, even though common sense told him he needed something to chafe it back down to a size that would allow him enough blood in his brain to think.

Her boyfriend hadn't reported the car stolen. Probably figured she'd steam it off and come back. No, not her boyfriend. Her escort. He went up to a higher gear, remembering she'd said that. His vixen wasn't attached. Well, that was about to change, at least for tonight. Though for some reason, the idea of taking her home and keeping her was plenty appealing.

Chapter Three

൩

Oh he had good reflexes. She'd only gotten a quarter mile on him when he was closing the gap. She of course was holding back some, not just because she was now a little more cognizant of how fast she was going but also because flat out on an open road a Trans Am wouldn't have a chance in hell against a Porsche. She didn't have any intention of losing him. She grinned at the thought.

However, those refitted cars had some serious power under the hood. She suspected the driver did as well. As she whipped into a turn, she accelerated coming out as if there were an egg under the gas pedal, a slow roll, just the way a fast car liked it. The Porsche leaped forward. As she straightened, she watched that black muscle car take it the same way, coming on low and mean after her.

The tractor road came up suddenly, but she hit the brake, spinning out the back wheels for a fast ninety-degree turn. God, she'd missed this. When her dad had worked the pits of the dirt tracks, he'd taught her how to handle the cars like the young NASCAR wannabes. This car was as responsive as a hard and hungry man. Like the one she felt closing in behind her.

A fork came up and she veered right, shooting over a bump that flew her over a sizeable pothole, the tires almost leaving the ground. She landed as light as a unicorn on the other side of a road that was barely more than a deer track.

Get me out of these clothes. She'd meant it and far more. *Get me out of this life, if just for a night. I'll be everything everyone needs me to be tomorrow. Tonight, let me just belong to myself...and you, Jake Chance.*

*****

She was headed for Cutter's Bridge. He cursed. This road was only used by farm equipment moving between the corn fields that whipped by them, green, gold and silver in the moonlight, the silk tassels waving like race pennants, their movement like the roaring crowd.

Damn, she could drive. But that didn't alleviate the fear in his gut. If anything, it increased it. Because the road was unused by regular traffic, there was no reason to post warning signs that Cutter's Bridge was unsafe. The support beams had rotted out some time ago. She'd approach it at the cool seventy she was doing now on the dirt road and wouldn't notice it until she and that little car were in the middle of it. He'd been an idiot to get carried away by this.

Well, she'd started it—he'd finish it. Get her stopped, get her back to the highway with a pat on her head and a careless grin, try to make her believe nothing real had led to this moment, no undeniable connection that still had him hard thinking about it. He was a cop first and foremost. Human came second. Being horny had to be dead last.

He gunned the car as they took the curve into the straightaway to the bridge. Three hundred yards and no options. There was a slight incline on the right shoulder, a shallow gully on the left side. Her chances were better with the incline. Flooring it, he swung around her in the narrow space and swerved toward her driver's door, wondering if six months of his salary would cover body work to a Porsche.

Be as good a driver as you seem to be, baby. Don't flip it.

Her eyes snapped toward him and she yanked the wheel right, hard. She jumped into a sea of corn, the back end of the car careening as she fought to hold control.

Hold it, honey. Hold onto it.

The car spun, but the corn formed a good break and she straightened, rolled to a halt.

He'd already slammed on his own brakes and was out of the car headed toward her when she came out of the driver's side unhurt, her eyes bright, face flushed with adrenaline. She was barefoot again. The significance of that registered just a moment before she shot him a reckless smile. And took off.

Here he was, having heart failure, and it hadn't even fazed her.

"Catch me if you can," she called out, backpedaling, waiting to see if he'd follow, if he'd play her game. The feverish look was gone. What he saw was careless abandon, a devil-may-care desperation he couldn't help but answer when she had her bare toes gripping the earth, the strap falling back down her shoulder and her hair shiny and disheveled around her pixie face.

Hell with it. He would play her game and show her some rules of his own. He backed up one step, two steps, keeping his attention on her face, watching disappointment gather there, the apprehension that he was about to become an officer of the law, beyond the touch of her charm and desires.

Yeah, right. He didn't think even his sergeant, a guy with forty years on the force and so by the book they joked that it was surgically implanted up his ass, could have resisted the magic of this precocious fairy.

Unlocking the trunk, he put his gun in there, re-locked it. Then he moved back toward his car door. Puzzlement chased its way behind her eyes, those tempting lips forming a luscious pouting shape that made him want to groan. Leaning into the open window of his car, he reached across the passenger seat, came back out with handcuffs.

A flush of heat spread across her cheeks. The game had just shifted, and he could tell she knew it. He'd accepted her gauntlet and his body was tense and ready to deliver on it.

"What's it going to be, baby? You going to come quietly, or am I going to have to get rough?" He waited. While his voice was husky, he wanted to leave her an option. The reality might be more than she'd wanted, since she was obviously seeking a fantasy. But he wanted her with a pounding need that was raw and entirely real. So he would give her a choice only up to a point. "You start this, it may not end here. When I like what I see, I tend to hang on to it for a while."

Stacie swallowed. Those handcuffs winked in the moonlight. She could imagine them holding her wrists, his mouth on her skin, his fingers driving her. With him, she suspected she'd *never* come quietly.

She knew what tomorrow would bring. Because of that, she also knew what she needed now, even though her body trembled at the thought. As his gaze registered it, the heat in his eyes increased.

She tossed back her hair. "Hope you didn't eat too many donuts today, Lieutenant. I don't go down easy."

Jake thought she'd go down on him real easy. Slick as butter. He bolted toward her.

With a squeal and a yelp, a snip of laughter, she took off, that little slip of a dress fluttering up her thighs as she tried to evade him.

She ran the way she drove. Full out, with unexpected nimble twists and turns, keeping an edge on him longer than he expected. But he was wearing sneakers, she was barefoot. He was in top shape and a lot taller. He feinted left with her, and when she spun, he moved right with her, making her retreat from him again. When he was closing the gap, she made the mistake of glancing over her shoulder at him, losing a stride, and that was all he needed. He put on a burst of speed. She made a dash to her left, then startled him by lunging back, knocking into him. When he stumbled around her, she twisted neatly under his arm, obviously intending to double back on him. He fell back, catching her around the waist, and tumbled them both to the ground, landing with an armful of gasping woman and silky fabric.

Damn if the little siren didn't make good on her threat. She was down but not out. She squirmed, she writhed, she threw elbows, but she was laughing so hard she was breathless. He found himself grinning ear to ear himself as he tussled with her across the ground. His hand encountered a thigh, the trim nip of her waist, the silk teasing his fingers. The spaghetti straps had both fallen, giving him tantalizing glimpses of the soft swells of her breasts. She snatched at his handcuffs and he fended her off. In a deft move, he rolled her shrieking to her stomach and caught one wrist above her head, pinning her with the gentle but inexorable pressure of his knee high on her back. When he locked one cuff on the wrist, he realized he had her. Realized what that meant.

She realized it too, for she was suddenly still. She laid her cheek on the ground. Closed her eyes for a moment, making him wonder if he'd gone too far. Then, before he could ease off, her gaze lifted. Looking up at him, she slowly brought the other arm up above her head. Then she looked back down, her lashes sweeping her cheeks.

He swallowed. He liked his women submissive in the bedroom, enjoyed bondage play enough that it was almost a requirement. He guessed he was one of those Dominant personalities the S&M sites talked about. Regularly dealing with the seedy side of people's sexual urges, he wasn't really comfortable calling it that. Even though he knew his desire to bring a woman pleasure while she was restrained was not a criminal act, he never would have guessed such a sweet little thing would ask for that, want it like this. The idea of it was enough to make his cock larger and harder, pressing tight against his jeans. It made every part of him eager to take. But did she really understand what she was giving? *Be careful, Jake.*

"You don't know what you're playing at, little girl," he said roughly. It was as much slack as he could give her, because he wanted her too much to give her an easy out.

When he eased the pressure of his knee, moved it off her, she shifted her head and laid her cheek on it, pressing her lips to his leg. She caught the inseam of the jeans just above the knee with her teeth, a playful tug of the denim before she let it go. It put her head practically in his lap and he bit back a groan.

As she rolled over, she kept her arms stretched above her head, her body open to his, vulnerable. She was shaking, but her lips were parted and moist, her eyes hungry with things he knew she didn't even know she wanted. As his gaze coursed over her breasts, the slope of her stomach, the expanse of her thighs revealed almost to the crotch by the hike of the dress, he could tell she was offering anyway.

Her blue eyes were full of the night's mysteries, drawing him in. "A cop is supposed to be a guardian. A protector," she said softly. "Every woman wants to believe that, Lieutenant Chance. I do. I need to. I need you to take over. I don't want any other options tonight."

This moment could be called many things. The wrong choice, something that either or both of them would call an attack of hormones in the morning. A bad career decision for him most certainly, a weak moment of shame for her. Time played those kinds of tricks on people. He paused, feeling the heated breeze on his face, hearing the rustling of the corn, seeing the low-riding moon out of the corner of his eye. Its light shone on the pale skin and lovely face of the woman on the ground. Everything about this moment felt right. So right it had to be wrong.

Lifting her uncuffed hand, she reached toward his face. When he caught her wrist just before she got to him, she managed to brush her fingertips along his jaw.

"It's all right," she promised. "I won't hurt you either."

Time could make a lie out of that as well, he knew, but he understood what she meant. This moment belonged to them, a magical space of time for something to happen that never could have happened otherwise. Perhaps that was the definition of magic. She was saying they would both try to remember that later, no matter what happened.

Leaning over her, he took her wrist back to the ground over her head. Her lips parted, eyes following him as he stretched over her, cuffed the other wrist. A look of peace—the only way he could describe it—warred with the leap of desire in her eyes.

"I guess you're going to do whatever you want with me now, and I'll have no say in it." Her voice was a whisper.

Did the sweet thing realize her voice was quavering? That she was torn between desire at being at his mercy and fear at being there? Did she realize how that made him feel, how he might come at the look in her eyes alone?

He stared down at her. Stacie wondered if he knew he'd gone stern and unsmiling again, in that way that made her pussy so slippery.

He could have started a variety of ways, but Jake followed instinct. With deliberate roughness, he reached between her legs, pushing up the flimsy barrier of her skirt, and pressed the heel of his hand against her mound. When she arched up like a firecracker detonating, he swore. Fervently. She was soaking wet and wearing just a lacy thong beneath the garter belt. He let his fingers play with the thong's back strap, teasing her buttocks, making them clench.

Hoping what she was wearing wasn't some ridiculously priced scrap of fabric, he did what his gut told him to do. Make it real for her. It sure as hell felt real to him. He took hold of the front of the dress and ripped those straps loose, pulling the front down to her hips to display her to his avid gaze.

A demi-cup bra, just as he'd expected. Strapless so her breasts were barely in it. A flat belly, just a little rounded curve below the navel, with that smooth feel of peach fuzz.

Though he'd touched her first between her legs to underscore his desire for her, he didn't want to rush this. Now he took his time, easing the hem of the dress up her thighs. He watched them tremble as he let his thumb graze her skin, revealing to his gaze what he'd already touched.

He pulled the thong to the side so he saw the lips of her pussy, damp like the tiny patch of silky curls there.

"You're so delicate all over." He stroked her there, watched her fingers flex and then curl into helpless fists as he stimulated her, made her wetter. "Such a pretty little thing. With a sassy mouth."

She smiled a little, too dazed with desire to make it focused, and he loved it. "What are you going to do about that?" she managed to rasp out.

He wanted more. He wanted inside of her.

As he stroked her clit harder, her thigh muscles loosened, her body moving restlessly up toward him. "Let me…" She hesitated, a flush staining her cheeks.

"What, baby?" He kept up his manipulation, slid one finger into her. She whimpered and struggled, trying to take him deeper, her pussy bumping against his knuckles. "What should I let you do?"

"I want…" Stacie thought those two words summed it up. But the things moving inside of her were dark desires, things she'd never thought of wanting with John or any other man, let alone voicing.

"Please, I want…you. In my mouth. Make me…"

Those gray eyes could spark with fire. It rippled over her like flame on her exposed skin. His hand between her legs was stoking an ache that was spiraling high and wild already, igniting a chaos of reaction in her body.

"Suck my cock." He said the words she couldn't, but as he did, her muscles convulsed against him, giving him his answer. He swallowed, that sculpted jaw flexing with the motion. "That's exactly what I'm going to make you do. Stretch that sassy mouth."

"Yes. Please."

Slowly withdrawing his hand, he pinched her clit, making her buck with reaction, a gasp leaving her lips. He brought the fingers to his mouth, tasted her. When she made a soft yearning noise in her throat, he couldn't wait another second.

Standing up, he lifted her to her feet, an effortless move that made Stacie's stomach drop. Almost as much as when he pressed on her shoulder, his face uncompromising, unrelenting, making her do his will as he eased her back down to her knees, controlling her descent. His gaze watched the changes in her face so intently, a way she'd never been looked at by anyone, as if he was registering everything about her life in how she reacted to every new thing.

Jake thought if she wet her lips once more, he was going to explode. "Open my jeans."

Bringing her cuffed hands up, she obeyed, unbuckling the belt and slipping the button to take the zipper down in what felt like slow motion. Suddenly, as if sensing his urgency, she moved much faster, yanking it down and spreading her hands across his pelvis, her fingers curving inside the jeans to dig into his hips as she moved forward on her knees. He stifled a groan, stripping the belt out of the way and dropping it as she mouthed him through the fabric of his underwear, biting him, trying to get it out of her way as well. When he pushed her touch aside, he shoved down the garment so that his cock stretched long and hard out of the opening of his pants. She closed both hands over him and rubbed her cheek along his length in an oddly tender gesture that mixed something else with his hard desire. God, she was the perfect little submissive. Enjoying his control of her while she made him want to beg.

"Put me in your mouth. I'm going to go fucking crazy if you don't."

She took him in without reservation, generously, and he had to close his eyes to keep himself from jetting from the first touch of her soft lips. She probably wore some type of lipstick with a name as innocent as she was. Primrose, or Pink Blush. The fact she'd barely hesitated to take his cock like this didn't make her less innocent. Working on the streets, he'd seen homeless people with it. Sometimes even the younger drug dealers. It was something unblemished in a soul, something that could be beaten down or even destroyed, a loss to the whole world, but it couldn't be changed. She'd be the type of person who would light up in surprise at a bouquet of picked flowers. Stand at a kitchen sink in the morning, watching birds feed from the window feeder.

It wasn't hard to put those two thoughts together and create a bunch more. He could imagine her in one of his T-shirts, playing with the trio of daisies he'd given her from some roadside wild garden. She'd put it in one of his spotted beer mugs. Probably his favorite one, just to tease him. He'd stumble into his kitchen, grumpy and groggy, and she'd be standing at the window at the sink, watching the sun rise along with the birds. The room would smell like the coffee she'd put on. The shirt would show enough of her slender thighs that his fingers would want to find her under that shirt and drive her to climax as he bit her tender nape, waking up in a way that even coffee couldn't match.

Closing his eyes wasn't helping. It'd been too long since he'd had a woman he wanted to keep. Maybe he'd even had a bachelor's tendency to avoid anything as good as what was on her knees before him now. This one could make him change his mind about that, but maybe she only wanted this moment, this fantasy. What was he going to do about that?

Her moves weren't well-practiced. She was being driven by whatever fire was burning inside of her to touch and taste him everywhere she could reach. That raw desire called a response from him he wasn't sure she could handle. He wasn't sure if he could. Then she reached up to caress his stomach and forgot the cuffs were positioned below his cock, pinching tender skin.

He flinched and her gaze snapped up to him. "I'm sorry, I didn't..."

"No." He fisted his hand in her hair, rubbed his thumb along her temple. "I'm sorry. I should have done this first." He didn't want to tell their kids the first time their mother had kissed him, it hadn't been on his lips. Catching her by the shoulders, he lifted her back to her feet and lowered his mouth to hers.

Oh God. Yes. Stacie closed her eyes and let herself be swept away by the firmness of those lips, the wet heat as he invaded her mouth, biting at her before he sealed the pressure there, teasing her, exploring her mouth. With her hands cuffed she could do nothing but be held by him, experience the explosion of sensation. Who knew that having one's lips caressed by a man's tongue could send electrical current through every part of the body? He had one arm banded around her back, the other behind her head. Her arms were bent so her wrists pressed against his chest, pinning her arms. His cock pushed between her thighs, only the thin dress in between. When he lowered that arm, palmed her ass and hitched her up so she straddled it, holding it between her thighs so he could do a slow rub against her clit, any sense of shame fled. She rubbed back, tightening her buttocks under the knowledgeable kneading of his fingers, standing on her toes on top of his shoes, straining for every sensation. As he lifted her off her feet, holding her even more tightly, she whimpered into his mouth.

When he pulled away, her body was looser than it had ever been and radiating like a nuclear core.

"I'm sorry I hurt you," she managed. "I—"

"I want you to want me so bad you don't mind hurting me to get what you want. If you don't," a slow smile spread over his face, "I'm doing something wrong."

Stacie felt her lower body turn to heated wax at that smile. "Same goes," she whispered.

Chapter Four
ஐ

That smile died away as she took hold of his shirt, used it to lower herself back to her knees without his compulsion. Keeping her eyes on his, she covered him with her mouth, taking him in as far as she could. Hot, hard, musky male. His hand came back down to grip her hair, his facial features tightening with his desire. With her hands cuffed she had to hold onto the root of his cock with both hands, the base of her palms pressing into his testicles, still half hidden in his underwear.

She'd never wanted to do this for John. Never felt the slightest desire. But now she was exactly where she wanted to be, her body coiled like a spring, so aroused she couldn't help the noises of hunger she made as she went down on him again and again, sucking, nipping, flicking her tongue. She felt the convulsion of his hand on her head, knew from glancing up that his face was suffused with hard lust, eyes burning with it as he watched her, every muscle taut. She took pleasure in that as well, this time carefully stretching her fingers so that she could tangle them in his pubic hair, put a little dangerous, sensual pressure on the base of his cock with the cuffs as she teased his lower abdomen.

Catching her head in both hands, Jake lifted her mouth roughly away from him, nearly groaned at the sheer pleasure of it when her tongue swiped at his tip, taking the fluid that had collected there and added it to the moist glistening of her lips.

Jesus, he wanted her. But he didn't have any way to... he could use his mouth on her, make her come, but he wanted more out of this than just the two of them going down on each other. This was deeper than that. He knew he was being stupid but...

"I want you inside of me. Please."

He closed his eyes as she spoke the words so fiercely echoing in his own head. He had to make himself shove away the desire to be careless. Guardian and protector. That's what she'd said. He couldn't let her down on that. He'd do his best to sate her desire without relieving his own need to spread her legs, plunge into her, make her his.

"Baby, I'm sorry. I don't have anything to keep you safe."

She didn't care. Stacie stood up on her knees, brought the cuffed hands out from beneath his cock and up to run her palms under the T-shirt and feel how his arousal had made his firm skin damp. Pushing the fabric out of the way, she kissed him across his stomach, flicked her tongue over a hip bone, touched his navel. He caught her hands when they reached his chest and tugged her to her feet. With her hands trapped between them, he cupped her ass, bringing her hard against his cock, rubbing her there again. The sounds of hunger in her throat were increasing, and when he tightened an arm around her waist and pressed his leg between hers, she rode his thigh with ruthless abandon, gasping as he squeezed her buttocks, goading her to an even more frenetic rhythm. The man was standing and holding her on his thigh with one arm. The idea of such strength was delicious.

Though she knew a physically strong man didn't translate into security or being emotionally strong, she could pretend it did, since she hadn't asked for more than this night. But oh, to have a man like this as a part of her life. He would only have to be one half of the fantasy he'd been so far to be enough. Just give her love, gentleness, a sense of safety and passion. Passion like this would keep her warm no matter how old she was when she recalled it.

She supposed it was just like a woman to mix these kinds of thoughts with an unadulterated, lustful moment. He probably wasn't thinking about anything like this.

Jake was thinking she was a generous lover, a beautiful woman with a fragile, pure soul that practically shone through her pale skin. And a mouth that could suck the chrome off a trailer hitch. If that wasn't a man's idea of perfection, he didn't know what was.

Stacie blinked as he drew back to rearrange his clothes, hiding his still turgid length from her and wincing as he worked to tuck it back in. Before she could protest, he caught her under her arms and legs, simply scooping her up in his arms to carry her to the front hood of the Porsche. "We'll do this another way," he growled. "I want to hear you scream."

She wanted to scream now. Why couldn't farmers produce fields of condoms instead of corn? It was such a ridiculous thought it helped loosen the strangling band of frustration in her vitals.

"What, you weren't prepared to take home a band of groupies at the game?" she attempted to tease him.

He smiled, though desire kept his jaw in a tense set she couldn't help but caress with her bound fingers as he set her on the hood. "We don't like to admit it, but firefighters always get the best pussy. We did kick their asses seven to five though."

Her answering smile died as he put one hand on her sternum, his fingers spread over the curves of her breasts in the low-cut bra. Holding the cuffs, he pushed her back slowly, his eyes coursing over her body until she lay all the way on her back. He kept hold of her wrists, resting them on one of her thighs, his fingers touching her there.

"I don't believe that," she murmured. "Not if they had their eyes open."

"If you come to the game, honey, next time I'll bring a full dozen condoms." He gave her a heated look that was contagious, spreading fire on her skin. "You better expect to use the first two or three before we even get out of the parking lot."

"Why, that sounds like a date, Lieutenant."

He let his free hand drift down her quivering stomach, down to her mound. It stayed there, his fingers teasing her as he gathered up the edge of her skirt again, one inch at a time.

"I don't fuck women on back roads. I don't pick them up in bars. I've had two or three adult relationships, some one-night stands. Most of the one-night stands were mistakes."

"Do you think that's what this is?" She wasn't sure if she wanted the answer.

"I don't know. But I will if you show up at the next game."

He eased the crotch of her thong aside again, revealing her pussy to the night air. Cicadas made their rasping songs and frogs warbled, telling her there was water nearby, perhaps a fishing pond. The air was heavy with summer's heat, but the cool touch of the moon gave the night some breathing room, not that she could tell. Because of the look in his eyes, she was having trouble getting oxygen into her lungs.

"Touch your pussy for me, little girl."

"Oh..." She knew it was ridiculous, as forward as she'd been until now, but she'd never done that type of thing in front of a man. Only in her bedroom, alone...

"I wasn't asking. Do it."

Reaction shot through her, leaking out of the area in question, such that his gaze registered it, flared hot. "I'd say just close your eyes and imagine you're in your bedroom, no one else around, but I want you to see how hard my cock is and how much I like watching you play with yourself. Make me suffer, baby."

He guided her resisting fingers across her thigh and up onto her pussy. At the dual touch on her vibrating skin, she couldn't help straining up for more.

"Un-unh." He took his hand away, leaving it all to her. "You don't get anything from me until you play with that pretty wet cunt, show me how much you want my mouth there. Or maybe I should get my nightstick from the car. Maybe you'd prefer something long and hard up inside of you, my lips playing with your clit until you come. You have a gorgeous little ass. I might need a finger or two up there as well." At her startled look, replaced by aroused speculation, he growled his approval. "A virgin in that area. Makes me all the hotter. I want to take you everywhere, so no part of you hasn't had me in it."

All of it sounded wonderful. How could it not? But she wanted his cock inside of her pussy the most, completing her and connecting with her. This yearning in her was more than just physical. As she looked at that lean body, she wasn't just seeing some pin-up in a magazine where the muscle was two-dimensional and glossy. He had a scar on his forearm. His face was handsome but lined, probably from the stress of his job. It occurred to her then how difficult that job must be. He was also probably exposed to outside elements a lot, some combination of all those factors creating a face with character. His T-shirt had a stain on it that looked like salsa or ketchup, maybe from chips or fries enjoyed at the game. He didn't go to a great hair stylist, which was why she guessed he kept it so short, besides the military-style dress code of his job. His short nails weren't entirely clean at the moment, coming from the ball field. He had dirt and grass stains on the knees of his jeans. He'd tried to brush them off. Otherwise she would have noticed it before now.

She wondered what position he played on the team. Who his friends were, what he did when he wasn't working, other than playing baseball. There was one part of her brain interested only in the here and now, another part reaching for something else. But she'd wanted a fantasy. Why was she looking for more? Did she really have the type of life where she could pursue anything after tonight? Why was having him inside her like that so important?

She knew the answer. Even a woman's fantasies had to touch her heart as well as her body. Otherwise they weren't worth having. Or remembering.

"You're thinking too hard, honey." Bending his head, his tongue slid between her fingers, licking along her clit, and then dipped inside of her.

She cried out and bucked. Catching her thighs, he held her as she moved her hands, sought a purchase on him. She ended up with a two-handed grip on his shoulder, digging in and pulling hard on the T-shirt, balling it up in her fists as he continued to eat her pussy. His hands raised her up to him the way he might lift a split coconut, cupping her buttocks in both hands as he sipped, feasted, bit, not minding the juice that got on his mouth and chin. In fact, he seemed to be alternating his forays inside with a liberal rubbing of his mouth on the outside, rousing her with tongue and teeth as she dug her fingers in further and cried out, trying to pull away as the sensation became overwhelming.

He wouldn't let her, making it clear she was not in charge.

When he told her it wasn't a request, all the things she was always responsible for doing had run through her head. The choices she was required to make every day, truly horrible things no one ever thought they'd have to face. All that had been swept away by a tidal wave of relief. He'd made it a hundred percent clear he would take care of this one, vital thing. Her pleasure.

"No...no. Please stop."

He bit her lightly, spoke against her flesh. "Not happening, honey. I'm going to feel you come against my mouth."

"I want to do it with you inside of me. Please. Please." She pulled on the T-shirt with each plea.

He lifted his head, regret crossing his face. "Baby—"

"Glove compartment." She gasped as his five o'clock shadow rasped against her with an incredible friction. "He always keeps some there. I'm sure of it." *God, please let me be right.*

Jake's gaze narrowed. "You said he isn't your boyfriend."

"He's not. He's..." She shook her head, the truth mortifying. "He's the pity date my brother arranges for me. We've had sex a few times. Mostly for him. Mostly because I wanted to feel something. Kept hoping to feel something...like this. Though at first it didn't matter. I just needed...someone." At his expression, her desire curled into a cold defensive ball in her stomach, a lump rising in her throat. "You think I'm cheap." She tried to get up. To struggle away from him. "Some kind of slut. Oh God. Of course you do. Look at me. I don't even know you. I—"

"Hush." He yanked her up by the wrists and covered her mouth with his again. Bringing her to the edge of the car, he made her wrap her legs around his hips, reaching beneath the skirt to take a proprietary grip on her ass.

She tried to pull away. "Let me go. I'm not like—"

"I know that." He gave her a little shake, commanding her attention. "You think guys are the only ones allowed to get lonely and take something empty because it's the only thing available? You think we don't know the difference between that and something more special?"

He wasn't thrilled about envisioning her in this guy's arms, but it did increase his satisfaction quotient to consider taking her on his car hood. A male dog driving a competitor out of the competitor's own territory. Being a woman, she'd probably think that was silly. Wouldn't get it. But John sure as hell would.

When Jake put his firm pressure against her, she rocked despite herself, making him grit his teeth and put both his hands on her ass to hold her still. "Hold on a moment," he said hoarsely. "You've got to give me a moment, darling."

"No. I don't want to wait. I need you inside of me." She pinned him with desperate eyes. "You don't...it's different."

"Sshh. I know that. Stop worrying about it." Jake dipped his head. "Put your hands around my neck."

She linked them there behind his nape and he felt the cold steel of the bracelets. Hitching her up, he lifted her, carried her around to the passenger side where the window was open. Holding one arm around her back to brace her against him, he reached in, popped open the glove compartment, fished around distastefully and came out with a fistful of condoms. Dropping them on the seat, he took one and eyed it critically.

When he looked at her, she was staring at it, moistening her lips. She was still feeling uncertain, he could tell. "Hey." He touched her with the corner of the plastic wrapper, chucking her cheek with it, chasing and teasing her until she was ducking her head away, trying not to smile. Pressing her back against the car frame, he held her there and dipped his head down, nudging hers to the side to kiss her neck, touch his lips to that sensitive pulse point. She shivered, her nipples hardening against his chest. "Ah, sweetheart."

Gripping her head and keeping his hand around her back, he turned her, brought her back to the hood. With her arms around his neck, he had to go down with her a certain amount, putting him on top of her. She played with the hair on his nape while he studied her face inches away, felt her thighs on either side of him as she spread for him, pressed her pussy against his erection. He nuzzled her lips, coaxed some teasing kisses out of her, nipped at her tongue until she was squirming against him, rubbing and mewling with her desire, enough that he knew he'd driven any worries from her mind. Only then did he take her arms from his neck and make her stretch them over her head, laying her out for him. He knew exactly how he wanted her, and that was how he was going to have her.

Stacie's breath caught in her throat as he took her torn dress off her body. Freeing her garter belt, he dropped it so she felt it caress her ankles. He opened the front-closing bra with seeking fingers, brushing the curves before he bent to press a kiss on her sternum. When she started to lift her arms, he shook his head, spoke against her skin. "You're my prisoner, sweetheart. You stay still or I'll go get that nightstick."

She subsided but couldn't help but feel a jolt of reaction at the serious look in his half-lidded eyes. It made her imagine what it would be like to watch him insert it into her, her muscles clutching the inanimate object the way she wanted to clutch his cock, making it slick with her fluids.

Then he took off the thong. She was naked, sprawled on the hood of a Porsche in a gleaming silver, gold and green cornfield on a summer night, the sounds of the night creatures surrounding them. No other people. Nothing but the two of them and two now silent cars. The bridge was a silent silhouette behind them.

"God, you're beautiful."

How many times did a woman get to hear that, knowing a man meant it? In a special unique way he'd never mean in the same way to any other woman? She could almost believe it from the look in his eyes.

"Jake." She spoke his name on trembling lips. "I want you so much. Please..."

"I like you begging." He kissed the curve of her left breast, traced a hand down her belly, dipped into her navel. "It makes me hot. Makes me want to do other things to make you beg."

Unzipping his jeans, he pushed them and his underwear out of the way. While she watched him, he tore open the condom, rolled it on.

"No going back, sweetheart."

In answer, not sure of this wanton creature she'd become, she lifted her legs, spread them wide, displaying herself to him, her hands coming down in the cuffs to finger herself, bring wetness from inside and spread it on the lips, making his eyes go molten hot.

"Please."

He put his big hands on either side of her bare hips and thrust home. A deep, hard penetration with a cock big enough to be a tight fit. It caused her to moan at the brief pain, the stretch, then respond to that tight fit, her cunt rippling along his length.

"Yeess."

"Yes," he agreed, his face intent, mouth held firm. She loved that mouth, loved the way he looked at her as he fucked her wholly naked. As if she was his entirely, his to fuck naked while he stayed clothed. He hadn't even taken off his shoes. She wanted to see that hard body bare. Shower with him, clean off the dirt from the game, maybe kneel and take him in her mouth again. Feel him explode against the back of her throat. Ah God, she was having a fantasy while experiencing a fantasy, and the double shot was sweeter than anything she could imagine.

When she lifted her hips to take him more deeply, he caught her ankles, bringing them up to his shoulders. Holding onto her hips, he rammed into her, increasing his thrusts, shooting her up a roller coaster. The first hill, one click at a time, signaling an approach to the steepest crest where the speed would be a thrilling rush.

All the frustrations and emotional pain, the sense of impending loss weighing upon her soul all the time now, came off her in healthy sweat gleaming on her skin. Purging and purifying her as she immersed herself in this, in the feel of his body taking hers over. Just as she wanted. Was it greedy to want more? To imagine more things she'd like to have?

I tend to hang onto things I like...

If they could just stay in the moment... But knowing she couldn't do that, she let go of everything else. She abruptly levered herself up off the car, brought her legs down and around his hips, and hooked the cuffs over his head again. Clasping his shoulders, she held her body to his, increasing the friction against her clit, the rub of his cock on the densest spot within her.

"Oh God..." She pressed her cheek to his throat. His buttocks clenched under her heels as he drove into her. She could handle anything, knowing she'd had this.

Colors flashed and his cock ripped something deep within her free. Her moan escalated into a guttural cry, into the scream he'd wanted. Clinging to him, she pressed her lips to his neck, tasted the salt of her tears as the force of the orgasm washed all of it from her, overcoming her. She went over that first hill and kept flying.

"Come for me. Please..." She gasped it in his ear. She wanted to feel him come while she was coming.

He gave in to her, pressing her hard against him, thrusting in and out, holding her buttocks in tight hands that would leave bruises on her ass. She didn't mind. She liked the idea of looking in the mirror and seeing them, feeling the soreness of her body. Too soon it would fade into a memory with no landmarks, but as long as it was this vivid in her mind, she suspected she'd remember it for some time to come.

She'd been immersed in death and loss for so long, she'd forgotten that life was more than enduring. When Jake Chance had gotten out of his car tonight, somehow he'd touched her with a magic that had reminded her that life was worth living. That it could always surprise you. That no matter how the pain and sorrow closed in on her, there was always room to cut out a window and see something new. Something like hope.

She had no words for that, so she settled for shattering the night with her cries, holding onto him with every ounce of strength she had, giving him all of herself.

Chapter Five

He supposed it could end here. A few moments of cuddling, nuzzling one another like contented cats. He admitted he liked the kittenish way she was rooting into his neck. Placing soft, moist touches of lip and tongue there, her breath caressing him in a way that made him think he'd never again feel a summer breeze whisper across his skin and not think of this moment in a remote cornfield.

But the moon had barely risen. If she didn't have anywhere to go...

"Do you have anywhere to be?" He took care of the condom, wrapping it up to put it carefully in the pocket of his jeans. When he helped raise her to a sitting position on the edge of the car, she stayed that way, her head tilted. Her innocent pose, the somewhat self-conscious way she had her restrained hands folded in her lap, made him stir to life again.

"Not until dawn." That impish smile crossed her face as she lifted her wrists. "Besides, what would it matter? I'm your prisoner."

"Yes, you are." Deciding, he scooped her up. "We're going to go find a softer spot for what I have in mind next."

"Police brutality? Harassment? Interrogation?"

When he pinched her, she giggled and writhed in his arms. It made him want to be naked too, to feel the drag of her nipples across his flesh the way they were rubbing against his T-shirt. But maybe her fantasy was that he be clothed.

"Behave yourself."

She complied with a tiny smile, those eyes so big and round in her face he wanted to stroke the lashes, coax them closed. Overwhelmed by the intensity he saw in them, he wasn't sure he could handle the way they made him react. Love didn't happen at first sight. Strong attraction did. Lust. Love took time, needed friendship to be real, years of understanding building on experiences shared together. But maybe some levels of attraction made you want to take that leap within a few minutes of meeting someone. Maybe your heart and gut just knew what it took your mind years to fathom.

* * * * *

"You're getting the family bug," Detective Nichols had told him at the last department picnic. Jake had spent most of the afternoon playing with Nichols' two boys and picking at his wife with platonic flirting, letting her mother him. "That bachelor life of yours is losing its appeal, no matter how much you deny it. You want a woman to come home to."

"Men don't have biological clocks." Jake had tried to shrug it off. Nichols shook his head.

"Bullshit. They're just a different type. Mark my words. When you find her, you'll know her. The way your luck runs, she'll fall right in your lap."

* * * * *

Hadn't he thought the same thing only a little while ago? And if they'd been sitting, her cute ass would have been pressed into his lap right now.

Lust. Just lust and attraction. *Keep it easy, Jake. Give her the fantasy.*

But it was difficult to remember that. Especially when she hooked her arms around his neck again and hitched herself up so she could spread her elbows and grip his shoulders like an embrace. Her hair brushed his neck, her face nestled below his ear.

"We're going to stop here a moment, hon." He let her feet down at his car. Freeing his neck from her hold but keeping a steadying hand on her elbow, he opened the driver's door, popped the trunk.

She looked into his back window, studying the personal items he'd been carrying. Baseball gear. A car magazine with a well-endowed blonde in a string bikini stretched out on the hood. She cast him an amused glance.

"It has good articles," he said.

"I'll bet." Her laughter was rusty, unpracticed but honest. Her look altered then, changing his amusement to something else. Backing a step from him, she turned and strolled completely naked except for his cuffs to the front hood of the Trans Am. Giving him a sultry look, she slowly leaned forward, bracing out her legs the same way the models did. Only instead of a tiny strap of bright yellow bikini outlining the plump oblong shape of her pussy, there was nothing covering it at all. She put her elbows on the car's hood, dipped her head to shake her hair over her face and then tossed it back in a lithe move, looking over her shoulder at him. The strands spilled back in a shiny wave that just grazed the top of her shoulders before the breeze caught and caressed her lips with them.

He'd no idea what he'd been intending to do in the trunk. He moved toward her, one step, two steps, just as she touched her tongue to her upper lip, swept her gaze down. She kept her ass tilted up, the natural result of arching her back from tossing her hair in that sexy way.

"Up on your toes, darling, as if you were wearing a pair of really high heels. I want to see those muscles strain."

Hot desire licked through her at the demand. Before Stacie could blink, he'd closed the distance between them, reaching forward to stroke between her legs, his thumb parting her buttocks.

"Oh...I... Oh." She couldn't finish her protest, for he was tracing her rim in a way that made her lose the thought, her hips jerking against him as he played with her clit as well. Her nails dug into the top of the car, her arms straining, unable to help her cries of need. "Jake..."

"What, baby? Tell me what you want."

"You. Please..."

"Please what?" His voice was husky, seductive, drawing the words from her like a bee keeper drawing honey from a hive.

"Please...take me. Again." Her breath left her in a hitching gasp as he continued his slow kneading, drawing her lower body into a taut spring. "I...need you." She couldn't say the rough words. All she knew how to say was what was in her heart. He voiced the primal desire for them both.

"Show me. Lift those hips up and down on my hand. Show me how you'd fuck my cock."

God, his command of her was making her blood run thick and boiling through her vitals. She pumped against his hand, masturbating herself with increasing speed. She'd never been this way. But she didn't want civilized. She was spiraling up toward another climax, faster than she'd imagined was possible, coming so close on the heels of the first. A quick glance at him showed he was also more than ready for her again, and she knew men took longer. Usually. But then, this was her fantasy, wasn't it?

She'd have smiled at the thought if she wasn't suffused with such a knife edge of need.

He tugged open the top button of his jeans, pushed the zipper open again, took hold of her hips and drove into her, keeping such a hard grip on her that her toes barely brushed the ground.

"That's it, sweetie. Put your ass high in the air for me." Jake caught his fingers in her silky hair and held her head up, her neck arched so he could watch the wobble of her breasts as she took him in, took his thrusts. She was drenched, slippery. She'd been holding it in for too long, apparently. And he... Hell, he'd never been so turned on in his life.

"Don't want to hurt you, but..."

"Hard.... Hard as you want." Her eyes were wet, tearing. "I need to know you want me. That you want me like you've never wanted anyone. Even if it's a lie, I want to believe it tonight."

"Ah Jesus." He snaked his arm around her waist and this time he didn't hold back. He slammed hard into her body again and again as she lost her balance and just had to let him hold her, his hand coming up through the circle of her arms to grip her breast, his forearm diagonally across her sternum to keep her up. "My cock's never been this hard for anyone. I'd kill to keep fucking you right now. Anyone who tried to take you away from me. Who looked at you. You're mine. Mine."

It wasn't what she'd asked for, but it came tumbling out of him before he could stop himself. She pressed her temple against his biceps, gasping, her body trembling.

"Let it go. Scream for me."

As she obeyed, her response rippled around his cock and spread outward, tightening her all over so he felt the tension in her buttocks, in her shoulders against his chest. Then the rippling became an excruciating suction of her inner muscles on him, such that he couldn't help but follow her. He groaned, jetting hot, soaking her further as she gyrated wildly on his cock.

His own private pin-up girl, the gentle creature who'd just fulfilled a fantasy he'd had since he picked up his first hot rod mag at twelve years old.

She was wet, drowning him, her cunt so hot, so perfect, so—

Jesus Christ. "Oh, Christ."

As she shuddered to a halt, he pulled out slowly, not wanting to but thinking he had to do what he could to fix what could be an unfixable mistake. How could he be so stupid? "Oh, baby. I'm sorry. I didn't even stop to think. I didn't use anything this time." What was he, some irresponsible teenager?

She pressed her cheek to his arm, brushed him with her lips. "It's okay. There's nothing we can do about it now."

"That's not—"

"I take contraceptives." She tilted her head, looked up at him with serious eyes, lips swollen from his kisses, from the stretch of his cock there just a little while before. "I wanted you to take me this way. And now I'd like to lie in a corn field completely naked with you and watch the stars."

* * * * *

He would have taken the cuffs off as a reminder real life had to step back in at some point, something to keep him from being so stupid twice, but she wouldn't let him.

"I'm yours to do whatever you wish with until dawn," she said quietly. "When the cuffs come off, it's over. I don't want it to be over. Not until it has to be. Which is dawn."

When he led her deeper into the corn, his hand light on her forearm, she shifted so she was gripping his hand in both of her bound ones, like kids holding hands, only she was completely naked and cuffed. And unlike a pair of kids, they probably both knew exactly how rare and amazing this night was. So for a little while they didn't say anything. Just ambled along holding hands like that, looking up at the stars, though he kept sneaking looks at her.

He'd grabbed a blanket and a couple other items from his trunk, wrapping them up in the blanket so she couldn't see them. He held them in one arm as he led her with the other.

He thought one corn row would be just like another, but he knew they'd found their spot when they came upon a sprinkling of star-shaped white wildflowers that had managed to push out of the tilled ground between the rows of stalks.

The angle of the moon touched the flowers with a luminescence that reminded him of the white of angel's wings. So he reluctantly released her to set the items to the side behind a cluster of stalks and shook out the blanket.

Something he didn't expect came tumbling out. Before he could retrieve it she bent, picking up the teddy bear as it rolled to a stop, face down.

Stacie looked at the shiny dark eyes, felt the soft plush of the fur give under her grip. Because she couldn't help it, she brought it to her cheek and lifted her gaze to find Jake watching her, a light smile on his firm mouth.

"You keep these for kids at crime scenes."

He nodded. "You watch your news programs. You can have him if you want. We always get new ones whenever we use one."

She closed her eyes, her lashes sweeping down, fanning her cheeks in a way that made him want to nuzzle them, blow on them to watch them shut more tightly, her full lips purse in a near smile, like she did now.

"You forget how this comforts. Holding one in your hands." She opened her eyes. "If I had a cop like you telling me it was going to be okay, and giving me this to hold, I'd never be afraid again."

"Come here." He drew her to him, pressed the teddy bear between them as he cupped her neck, ran his thumb over the line of her cheek. When she raised her chin, he rubbed his lips lightly over hers. "I'm not sure you're as safe from me as you think."

"Well, Lieutenant, I'm not a little girl." Those lashes that had looked so innocent a moment before now looked anything but as she shot him a sultry look through them. "Maybe the last thing I want is to be safe from you. Maybe you're not safe from me. You haven't even frisked me for weapons."

"You're right about that." Tightening his hold on her nape, he dipped his other hand, cupped her mound, earning a gasp, a darkening of those eyes as he teased her clit, slid two fingers along the opening of her pussy, finding moisture gathering there again. Damn, if she wasn't the most responsive little thing. Her thighs loosened for him, her stance widening, and his cock amazed him by proving he could more than keep up with her.

Her arms were bent at the elbows, so her hands now curled into his T-shirt, tugging. "Please take off all your clothes. I'll do anything if you take them off."

"Oh yeah?" His voice was throaty. "Well, you go lie down on that blanket and spread your legs for me. If you do exactly what I want, I might get naked for you."

Another small smile curved her mouth, so he couldn't help his fingers dipping into her, holding her pinioned. She went to her toes, her lips parting, eyes locked on his as her muscles clamped on him.

Giving in to the desire, he dropped his other hand from her neck and took possession of one nipple, holding her with one set of fingers deep in her cunt and the other tormenting her nipple as she held onto him and writhed, whimpering. She bumped her leg against him, grazing his groin, and the bare amount of friction was enough to make him ready for her again.

But he wanted to do something else first. She'd planted the seed of the idea and he couldn't get it out of his head until he did it.

He slid his fingers from her, turned her toward the blanket and gave her a firm smack on the ass, liking the handprint he left there when she jumped.

Jesus, Jake. Do you want to brand her or something?

Yeah, he did, in a way. He believed in wedding rings and a woman taking his last name, proving she wanted to be his. Proof he'd made an oath to safeguard her happiness, protect her with his name and possessions, his very life—for all of her life.

She'd jumped at the blow, but the gaze she tossed over her shoulder wasn't startled or cowed. In fact, if he wasn't mistaken, it suggested she was thinking of more ways to get him to do it again. Which brought to mind the image of her in his bedroom, her panties at her ankles as he gave her a firm spanking for some trumped-up thing, like erasing his pre-recorded sports show. Her mischievous smile would say she'd done it because she wanted to be spanked. Wanted to pursue a sport far better than anything the NBA or NFL could offer, even on their best day.

He didn't know her, but somehow he knew that was the way it would be. Or maybe her desire to fantasize was contagious.

When she dropped to the ground, he had to stifle a groan as she went to all fours before she turned to her hip and then her back, spreading her legs, laying her wrists over her head without even being told that was how he wanted them. But then she'd said that was what her fantasy was as well, right? To have him keep control over her.

He withdrew the item he'd concealed from her in the corn and saw her eyes widen, a tremor go through her body at the sight of the wooden black T-baton. It wasn't widely in use anymore since the expandable batons had gotten popular, but he'd found it very useful for tangling up the legs of a running suspect. Now that he had another much more pleasurable use planned for it, he was glad he'd kept it around.

About an inch and a quarter thick and quite long, it would impale her, limit her mobility for what else he had in mind. He'd never gone this far, even with women far more adventurous whose limits he knew, because none of them had ever looked at him like this. Begging to be dominated, brought to screaming pleasure so intense they'd never forget it. Trusting him to do so.

Stacie knew that forever after she'd be able to pull this moment out and remember it when her real life threatened to destroy her belief in fantasy. When he frowned, moving two steps toward her to stand tall and forbidding between her spread legs, Stacie's breath caught. The curve of his cock and testicles was prominent in his snug jeans. Her eyes coursed from there over the muscles in his arms that flexed as he held the baton in one hand, tapping the other a moment before the stick dropped, tapped her smartly on the inside of one thigh.

"Wider."

Response trickled from her. When his eyes fired at the sight, she spread herself wider, offered him everything. Being taken over like this, she didn't have to think of anything else. Only what he wanted, while it set her body on fire.

He squatted, showed her the baton. "You want me to fuck you with this?"

"Yes." She managed it in a whisper.

"Why?"

"Because... Next time you use it, I want you to remember it...in my pussy."

"Honey, remembering any of this is not going to be a problem. I may just keep that bear for myself. Make you come by rubbing it on your cunt and then keep it near my pillow ever after so I can smell the lingering odor of your pussy on it."

When she moaned in response, it made his need to take her beyond arousal and straight into mindless insanity even more fierce. Watching every flicker of expression — the parted lips, the desperate eyes, the arch of her throat — already had him there miles ahead of her. Jake slowly lowered the baton, making sure her eyes latched onto it so she'd see it go into her. He spread her slick lips wide with his thumb and forefinger, his thumb pushing up on her clit as he began to insert the baton. She quivered, her nostrils flaring.

"Breathe deep, baby. I'm putting it in deep. Once I've got it seated, you're going to hold onto it with your muscles. I want you to milk it so hard I'll see it twitch when I let it go."

She rocked against him, pulling it in, her head starting to thrash back and forth.

"You keep those hands over your head."

Her hands locked together as if they were around a bedrail, the white flowers tickling the curves of her arms, her pale skin gleaming like pearl.

"Jake…please… Oh God…"

He took it in about eight inches and stopped, letting the weight of it rest on his knee, holding it steady in her as he reached for the other thing.

In the semi-darkness, it looked like a thin black stick with a metal edge that flashed in the moonlight. When he laid the end against the side of her nipple, her eyes opened at the new touch. The moment she did, he tapped the control on it.

The hot stick was set on the lowest setting, a shock capable of a mild current of power but packing a lot of stimulation, if her reaction was any gauge.

She jumped. At the same time the T-baton began to twitch rhythmically, her hips moving in the act of fucking.

"You like that, baby?"

"Oh…God."

He kept it up, erratic charges so she couldn't predict it as he held the T-baton, withdrew it almost all the way and then pushed it back in until she was crying out each time. Still he wouldn't let her come, fascinated with the way her nipples were so hard, erect and large, her pussy so soaked the wood was glistening, the moisture trickling down to his hand and pooling in the crevice between thumb and forefinger.

"Please, please, let me come. Let me come. Oh…"

As he let the hot stick drift down her belly, her eyes were on it again, as they had followed the baton. Showing that she knew where he was headed, what he was going to do, and she wanted it. God, he wanted to fuck her. Her lips parted, breath shallow and fast, and he watched her face, her absorption as he rested the tip on her clit. Gave her a zing.

She bucked up, the baton moving furiously. He hit her with a slightly higher voltage as the first scream broke from her lips, twice more as she kept screaming, milking the baton, her body arched back like the crescent moon above them, her fingers digging into each other, her wrists held by his cuffs. Her ass slapped hard on the ground in a staccato rhythm that became even more erratic as she thrashed.

"Oh...it's too much... Please...stop..."

"You're not stopping until I say stop, baby. Keep going." His voice was harsh as he watched, too choked up for more words as that simple sentence sent her over another peak, her voice getting hoarse as she cried out her desire, long, drawn out notes of pleading. He was immobilized, watching her come all over his baton, her cunt spasming on it, her nipples as erect as his cock.

He stopped the shock, dropped the device to the side and now rocked the baton, keeping her going until he could tell he'd exhausted her. When he eased it out slowly, he was enthralled by the way she shuddered and whimpered with the resulting aftershocks. Laying it to the side, he stood on his knees, straightening to strip off the shirt.

"No." She reared up before he could do it and curled her hands in the fabric. She managed to catch her nails in an apparent weak point, or maybe her adrenaline was making her that strong, because she ripped the fabric away from the collar seam. When she leaned against him, panting, he curled his fingers over hers and helped her finish it, tearing the shirt open to just below his rib cage. He dropped his head on his shoulders as she passed her thumbs over his nipples, threaded her fingers into his chest hair and tugged savagely.

He shoved his jeans down his hips and tossed the shirt away before he wrapped his arms around her, pinning her hands between them and took her to her back, sliding into her as one continuous motion. She was just going to have to wait on having him completely naked because he was going to die if he wasn't inside of her now.

She wrapped her legs around his hips, her heels drumming his ass as he pounded into her, her wet channel gripping him again with sure muscles. He felt like he'd been away from that welcoming, heated home for far too long, though it had been less than thirty minutes. Rimming her with his still wet fingers, he found her anus and slid into her there, making those blue eyes widen further. Her mouth formed an "oh" of startled reaction. Then she went wild. She bucked against him, making him feel the clutch of her ass muscles, the ripple of her pussy that sent him right over the edge.

He cried out his pleasure to the night the way she'd screamed hers, two wild, primal animals under the watching face of the moon.

Nature would forever be a mystery to man, binding together elements in complex and beautiful ways. But as he felt her go over again, Jake thought a man could share that power, at least in this one perfect way.

Chapter Six

When he opened his eyes, he was lying on her and her fingers were making circles on his chest where her hands were pinned. She was still quivering, her buttocks clinging tightly to his fingers, her cunt gripping his cock. The moonlight created slivers of silver in her hair and cast shadows that etched out the line of her cheek, the upper slope of her breast, the cleft in between.

"You're going to have to let me go, baby," he whispered, soft and tender, sliding from her ass. She held on reluctantly, making it torture. "You stay right there. There's something I need to do."

When she looked up at him as he stood, he remembered. Toeing off his shoes, he stripped the jeans and underwear, the socks, and just stood there a moment. Not because he was vain, but because he couldn't move with her gaze traveling over him as if she was memorizing every inch of him in the moonlight.

It made him want to fall to his knees and worship her. But because this was her sexual fantasy, he gave her a slow, thorough perusal instead. It wasn't a hardship, with her body naked and still quivering from her climax. He squatted again and laid his hand high on the inside of her thigh, applied pressure, making her widen their spread. When she resisted somewhat, that shyness coming to the forefront again, he laid his other hand on the opposite one, opening her further to him.

"Let me see your pretty cunt," he murmured in a husky tone, liking the way her cheeks got stained with color. "You've never had a man talk that way to you, have you?"

She shook her head.

"But you like it."

A quick nod and that charming sweep of her lashes.

"You took all of me in well enough."

Stacie couldn't stop looking at him. Tanned, with a few pale places. Her cop didn't go to tanning beds and apparently had a certain amount of personal modesty. He was as perfect as any man she could imagine. A fine pelt of pubic hair. His cock lay against the soft nest of it, the curve of his heavy testicles just below. He was lots of lean thigh and arm muscles, with a well-cut stomach. Broad chest and flat pecs with a light thatch of hair that narrowed to his groin. It wasn't that she hadn't covered the territory before. It was just each time she detailed it she got the same sweet rush through her vitals. Perhaps it was good they wouldn't be together after tonight. The constant need for him might kill her.

As if he wasn't providing her enough sensual eye candy, he gave her a full sugar rush by ordering her to stay on the blanket and turning to walk into the corn. His ass was likewise firm and tasty-looking, his back wide. Some old scars and new scrapes, the latter probably from tonight's ballgame. A man's man, not afraid to play as hard as he worked. She was sure of it.

A moment later he was back. He wasn't self-conscious with her, so she could enjoy the way his cock moved as he moved his body. Forever after she'd know what he looked like naked when he walked, even when he was wearing his work clothes. His gun...

A smile crossed her lips as he knelt by her. She noticed he had a couple packs of crackers and two sodas.

"What?"

"I was just wondering if you had a gun belt. You know, the kind that goes around your hips?"

He picked up on the gleam in her eyes immediately. "Oh no you don't. You bad girl." He tore open a pack of crackers, popped one in her mouth before she could get the suggestion out. "That's where I draw the line. There are just too many cheesy one-liners."

"Like don't make me draw my weapon—"

"Don't talk with your mouth full," he reproved, but he grinned when she tried to bring her hands to her mouth to cover her laugh. Unsuccessfully, because she baptized him with a small spray of crumbs. "Imp. You were looking a bit pale. If we have until dawn, you're going to need some calories. I had these and a cooler in the backseat of the car."

"You have some. You'll need it too." Stacie kept the tone light, even as something caught in her throat. He was feeding her, not allowing her to do it for herself, and it made butterflies in her stomach. The way he took the soda to her lips before taking a drink himself, his eyes on her again as he made her take another cracker from his fingers. The way he watched her lips, his gaze flickering with sparks of fire, telling her he was turned on by it as much as she was.

She'd never shown this side of herself before to any man, perhaps because she'd never known it was there. It was like Jake had had a secret key that unlocked this desire. She'd wanted a man to take her mind away from the reality of her life for just a little bit. Since John couldn't ever give her even a minute of that, perhaps she'd forgotten that there were men who were capable of it. But Jake... He'd sent her spiraling into a whole new plane of perception. Whether it was reaction to the excessive amount of control and discipline she had to have in her own life, or if it was something else, she didn't know. There'd be years to analyze it later. Right now, she just wanted to be experiencing this, taking sustenance from his hand, watching his gray eyes darken and his cock rising again from the stimulation of controlling her completely. Of her willing submission to him.

* * * * *

It was an effort to keep his hands off her, but Jake knew he might only have one night with her. Ironically, that meant he shouldn't rush it. He needed to give her body some time to recuperate, and it probably wouldn't hurt him to give his dick a few minutes to reset launch mode.

"So tell me how you ended up taking care of your dad. Don't you have any other family to help you?"

As he took a couple crackers for himself, Jake noticed what she gave him was cautious, reluctant. Maybe because she didn't want to ruin it. Maybe because she had a Southern woman's tendency to believe that nothing asked of her was too much and she shouldn't complain.

Or maybe she was laconic because she didn't trust him enough to reveal details of her life to him. Why that should bother him, he didn't know. Realistically, they'd just met. But accepting reality didn't seem to have a place here. Not tonight.

She did trust him in ways women who'd known him longer had never done. But maybe that was because she was at the end of her rope, desperately hoping for one night where someone would take care of her. With no hope for anything more than that one night, the limited time span made it easier to trust him that way. His siren had learned to have low expectations. He saw that in far too many women. While he knew he was feeling way too proprietary for his own good, he particularly didn't like seeing that quality in her.

Patiently, he prodded her for more about her parents. From working over sources and suspects, he knew how to persuade. When to push and how to listen for what wasn't being said as much as what was. Reading between the lines, he quickly determined her brothers needed to be pistol-whipped. He had a Glock and a Sig that would fit the bill nicely.

Reaching out, he traced the lingering bruise on her collar bone. "He had a good hold. How'd you break it?"

"We hit the umbrella stand when we rolled off the china cabinet. I was able to grab one and get it between us. Twisted it and broke his grip. Fortunately, when I did that, he regained some sense of his surroundings. I told him he fell, just knocked me down with him." At his disapproving look, Stacie shook her head. "I wasn't going to tell him he tried to hurt me. It would kill him. This isn't a kind disease, and home care with me…it's our only option."

It wasn't a kind disease to anyone, he thought, his brow creasing at her hesitation. Dementia robbed a family of their loved one, often years before the person died. He thought about it, if it was his daughter trying to take care of him. If he found out she'd lied to him so he didn't know he'd abused her, tried to kill her. He was pretty sure he'd decide to self-administer a bullet then and there.

He wanted to order her to do things he had no right to demand, particularly if she had no one to back her up and help her change things. He needed to ease off. No more questions. He already had a pretty good picture of what was going on. She'd drawn her knees up to her chest and was rocking on the point of her buttocks, gazing up at the stars. It was a defensive posture. Her fingers clutched her painted toenails, the silver of the cuffs catching the moonlight against her ankles.

She made a very appealing sight, with her head tilted like that. He followed her gaze so he saw the shooting star at the same moment she did.

"Oh—" She glanced at him. "It belongs to you. You saw it at the same time I did."

"So why should I get it?" He fished a quarter out of the heap of his jeans. "Call it."

"Tails."

"Tails it is."

He saw her fight against a smile. "You didn't even flip it."

"You're right, I didn't. Make your wish."

"It seems selfish to take it for myself. Your dreams may be more important. Maybe you'd wish for the cure for cancer."

"What would you wish for, if you could wish for something just for yourself?" When she didn't respond, he reached out, caught hold of the cuffs, lifted her hands to draw her attention back to him. As he did, his thumb caressed the top of her knee. "What would you wish, Stacie?"

He wondered if it was the moonlight that made him see the brief glint of tears in her eyes. "I should wish for—"

"Stacie—" With a hand behind her head, he hauled her over to him and put his mouth on hers, capturing her lips, tangling with her tongue. He still held the cuffs in his other hand. He'd been sitting cross-legged, so when she fell against him, her fingertips grazed his pubic hair, tangled there, tugging. Stirring his cock to life, particularly since she was lying half over his lap now. "I'm sure you send out prayers and wishes for your parents like raindrops in Seattle. Probably for world peace as well. For the neighbor's husband's colonoscopy, for their dog's neutering surgery." When she ducked her head on a nervous chuckle, he brought her back to him with a firm hand to her chin, making her look at him. "You can have one goddamned wish of your own. What is it?"

They were under a blanket of stars where all wishes could be voiced without censure. Stacie struggled to believe that. But with a ghost of a smile, she said, "That would be cheating. You're not supposed to tell anyone what your wish is."

He gave her an exasperated look. "I've never believed that dreams can be taken away by sharing them." Then his voice softened. "In fact, it may be the best way to make sure they come true."

She swallowed. His eyes were so close, searching hers as if he was looking to find her soul. She'd never been looked at so intently by a man in her life.

"Did he hurt you?" he asked quietly. For some reason, she knew he was referring to John. Or perhaps every man she'd known before the cop next to her.

"No. He just didn't see me. No one has in a long time. But you do." That's what she'd liked about his eyes from the beginning. He'd been looking at and seeing everything about her since the moment he'd stopped her.

"If I could have one wish," she said at last, her voice a shaky whisper, "it would be that this was real. But I'm afraid if it became real, it wouldn't be the same."

He feathered a hand over her brow. "It wouldn't be. It'd be better."

She couldn't tell from his expression if he was serious or just flirting. "That's very romantic," she said at last.

"You're not a romantic?" He raised a brow.

Desperate, she thought. *There's a difference. A difference I can't forget. Or I'll ruin how special this night is.*

Jake noticed she didn't answer him. Just smiled that smile which frustrated the hell out of men. As if women understood the great truth of the universe. That most promises were empty ones.

A man would stubbornly go his own way, like a great white hunter hacking his way through the jungle of his life with a machete, never seeing that what he sought was standing right there with him, with her arms wide open, hoping he'd figure out what mattered the most, the way she had.

Even when his failure to see it broke her heart, a woman like Stacie kept her soul open anyway. A fragile creature who could be fulfilled by something as simple as knowing a man was attempting to love her the best he could. She'd ask for little but need so much it could make a man feel like he was drowning…or that she'd pulled him out of the ocean where he'd been dog paddling for far too long.

"I want you to dance with me," she said. "Dance with me under the stars. Is that romantic enough?"

Leaving behind his disturbing thoughts, he glanced down at himself. "I'm a little underdressed."

Her eyes sparkled. "Me too. I don't mind if you don't."

She offered her hands to him and he lifted her to her feet, her palms sliding onto his chest as he gathered her in and began to sway. Their thighs touched so that he felt the lingering dampness of her skin from their joining. His cock rubbed her as she moved, making her curl her fingers on his chest like a cat kneading. When she pressed closer, capturing his cock with light nips between her legs, her pussy teased him. He circled her waist with an arm and brought her up to her toes, insinuating himself more securely between her legs. Her lips parted, moist.

"You keep that up, honey, I'm going to have you flat on your back again."

She smiled, turned with him, her bare toes stepping on his lightly as they learned to coordinate their movements. "You use a lot of pet names. I like that. Do you do more than slow dance, Lieutenant?"

He grinned and though he was reluctant to let her go, he eased her back into the first round of a shag step, working around the fact her hands were cuffed to guide her and turn her. She didn't know the steps, but he took his time and she followed well, giving him time to enjoy the delight in her eyes.

"Some older stuff..." He took her down the aisle of corn in the camel hobble of the stroll then brought her back with the tango, dovetailing it perfectly into a more intimate Latin step that brought his knee between her legs and allowed him to put his hand down low, cupping her ass with his palm to hold her there. He teased her as he shifted, making those hands of hers clutch on his chest more tightly, with less finesse, telling him she was arousing exponentially to the stimulus. When he guided her hands back over his head to press her bare body against the length of his, his cock pressed against a pussy that had gotten much wetter.

Slowing their pace, he held her close and felt curiously humbled when she laid her cheek on his chest, caressing his nape with her fingers. Though he knew she was aroused enough to go for another round, he followed his intuition and didn't push it. He found he preferred to experience it this time like a sailboat, riding the rhythmic, slow swells of wake. An easy journey toward the ocean of need where their bodies would join together again.

"You're a nice man, Jake."

He laid his jaw on her hair. "How's that?"

"To know a woman's fantasy is as much about this as the rest. To be held." Stacie closed her eyes. *Just held.*

She listened to his voice rumble through his chest, smiling when he said gruffly, "I'm as selfish as the next guy. Just using the excuse of cuddling to rest up."

Stacie tightened her grip on his neck. It was such a perfect meshing of sensations. This sweet quietness. The pleasurable swirling in her lower belly from the memories they'd recently created, so vivid they couldn't help but be rippling through her awareness, keeping her nerve endings sensitized to his every touch on her body. The current sensation of his strong hands on her back, one low on her hip, caressing the top of her buttock. Then there was the promise of more pleasure to come, hardening against her hip.

The past, present and future, all possible with the same man. While she knew the dangers of dwelling on the fantasy of a future, she didn't mind the risk. Some pleasures were worth the pain and this once-in-a-lifetime experience was one of them. Pain would come in life, whether she protected herself from it or not. But this type of moment might never come again.

When they turned, she brushed his instep with her foot so his ankle touched hers. For the first time, she wished for the cuffs to be off so she could touch him freely, but she liked being at his mercy as well, knowing when he was hard enough he'd take her to the ground again, just as he said he would. She'd wrap her legs around his hips, feel his buttocks move, tighten and plunge under her heels, the curve of her calves.

Lifting onto her toes, she brushed her lips against the pocket of his collarbone. Using the tip of her tongue to tease him, she felt his biceps harden against her sides as he increased his grip on her. When she took a nip, she earned an indrawn breath. She remembered what it was like to be on her knees before him, his cock stretching her mouth. She shuddered, more fluid dampening her thighs.

"You're ready for me again, aren't you?" His voice was harsh with needs of his own. She liked it, liked the way he talked to her about his needs and her own in a raw and real way. His cock was now an iron bar against her hip and she ached to have it back inside of her.

Nodding, she lifted her gaze to him, making a soft noise at the desire in his eyes, the promise of what he would do next unmistakable in his expression.

He'd reacted hard and fast to desire each time, driving them up and over as if they were on that zero-to-sixty-mile-per-hour roller coaster, giving her a spiraling, twirling thrill of sensation from which she still felt dizzy. Even in the aftermath she'd felt off balance. Like when she spent a day out on a boat and the memory of the sea's movement kept her body swaying even when she was back on land. An element whose hold was so strong it wouldn't let go.

He didn't take his gaze off her as he took her down to the ground, easing her to her back and laying himself down fully on her, his knees gently insinuating him between her thighs. Because her hands were still hooked around his neck, their bodies were never more than a breath away as they came down to earth together.

Grounded. The word passed through her mind. It could have mundane connotations. It could also be this, this sense of wholeness, of utter contentment. Being joined to his body made her feel as if the connection went far deeper than that, deep into the core where the secrets of Creation were woven into the stratus of the Earth.

"Are you sure you want me this way?" His thumb touched her cheek, traced her lips, making her open her mouth and taste his fingertip with her tongue. "I could go back to the car and get... I know we did it twice without—"

"How do you want me?" She gazed into his gray eyes. "No choices, remember? I'm all yours. How do you want me?"

"Like this. My cock deep in your pussy, nothing between us."

His broad head was at her entrance and she moved, trying to draw him in, but he raised his hips a little, drawing out the anticipation, a light smile on his lips telling her he knew he was teasing her, though she could see the strain in his jaw line. "Ask for me, Stacie."

"Please. I need you." There were so many levels to that statement, she couldn't voice them all. Or, if she did, it would make the thought, the possibility, evaporate away. And that was going to happen soon enough.

From the way his expression stilled, she knew he understood.

The tone had changed. It was too close to dawn. This was it. The last time.

She'd have taken him any way he wanted her because of that. But he'd been her perfect fantasy since the moment he got out of his car. So perfect, she had the disturbing thought that she might wake in her bed in the morning and find the whole thing was a dream. Particularly when he now made it clear he intended to exceed her expectations until the very end.

This time, his hands were gentle, one moving down, the other cradling her face as he guided himself into her. His fingers teased her opening as he slid in, filling her, making her hips rise and undulate to take all of him.

When he rested deep inside of her, his cock in to the hilt, testicles pressed against the base of her ass, he stopped. Looking down at her, he reached over to his discarded jeans, fished out the key and took her hands from around his neck to uncuff her.

"I know you said it would be over when they were off," he murmured. "But I need to feel your hands on me."

How could she resist such a demand, his lips so close, his body joined to hers? Particularly since she could think of nothing she wanted more at the moment than to touch him.

When he removed the cuffs, her fingers touched his palms and he let the bracelets fall to the ground, twining his fingers with hers such that in the first moment his touch held her as much as the restraints had. Lowering his head, he closed his lips over hers. She melted under the power of that kiss, moaning into his mouth as he coupled it with a slow stroke into her body, teasing her clit. His lips and tongue, firm, clever, persuasive, seduced her all over again. As his touch whispered along her wrists, the pulse points fluttered beneath his fingertips, sending frissons of energy down her arms into her chest and lower.

He curled one hand under her neck, his thumb sweeping her jugular, his other hand lowering to her hip, gripping her thigh and lifting her leg higher, rocking her up for a deeper angle of penetration that made her cry out into his mouth. When he answered with a growl, she reached for him, feeling the breadth of his shoulders under her palms for the first time. Bare, warm muscle and bone. The strong line of his throat. Then she touched his jaw, moving her fingers over his lips, his face, into his hair, feeling the short ends as her body bucked in slow waves beneath his thrusts. Savoring every inch of him, inside and out, she glided down the slope of his back, her hands resting on the taut curve of his buttocks. Her body reacted by becoming a spring-loaded coil of erotic tension as she felt those muscles tighten and release under her touch. Curling her legs over the small of his back with a helpful hitch from him, she reveled in his strength. Even more when he changed the angle and took her higher, sinking so deep a grunt of urgent need broke from her throat. Her head tilted toward the night sky, her eyes closing so she could just focus on how he felt, everywhere he was touching her, inside and out.

"God...perfect," she managed, soft, breathy words as her body climbed and climbed, responding to every stroke, getting hotter and hotter. The coil of her body was ready to release, and it would be capable of shattering even a brick wall of control, let alone her simple network of flesh and bone, which was wide open, eager to embrace the impact.

He bent, catching his hand in her hair and tilting her head to give him access to her throat, raking it with his teeth. Even with her hands free he was underscoring he was in charge, commanding her. But his hard body was shuddering, even trembling, injecting her with a searing wave of feminine power. His chest hair rasped across her nipples. When he dipped down, took one into his mouth while increasing the speed and force of his strokes, she lost the ability to think. Everything was tugging, wet-hot sensation. She opened her eyes and found the whole sky was becoming a series of shooting stars, a thousand wishes coming true in the magic of the moment, dreams unrealized or never even voiced until now.

As he suckled her, squeezing her, she writhed, rising to meet him now, wanting the fire to become a conflagration. But he kept to his own pace, making her gasp in his mouth, beg. "Jake...please. I want to come for you. Please..."

"Stay with me, baby. We go when I say we go."

She could come from the sensuous abrasion of his tongue on her nipples alone. It seemed he'd gotten even harder and thicker inside her and then he came to a complete stop, making her feel the impact of that hard thickness filling her from clit to womb.

She knew he wanted to draw it out, make it last. Her body was quivering on the cusp of release, every limb trembling, but Jake was taking his time, moving from one breast to the other with his mouth. Even when he squeezed them together to play in the cleft, making her plead with wordless moans, he only growled his response. He held still within her for endless moments, refusing to move as her hips twitched, her muscles spasming against his cock. She was milking him as hard and fast as she had the baton before. She knew he wanted her because his long lean body had become iron wherever it touched her, all those sexy muscles drawn tight.

"Jake, please..."

"Kiss me." At last, he seized the back of her head and brought her half off the ground, holding her on the strength of one arm as he started pistoning into her, moving them across the ground with the force of it.

Wildfire, sweeping across the forest of her soul, burning it to ash so she had no refuge but his arms. She bowed up even as he held her mouth to his, swallowing her screams. She savored the vibrations of his guttural response as he met her, spasm for spasm, jetting into her, spinning her orgasm to greater heights. She had to let go of his hard backside and cling to his biceps, her head resting fully in his palm like a weak infant. She let him hold her up as he pumped into her and she bucked in response, slamming hard against his body. She wanted to make this last, wanted to keep him so badly she wanted to fight about it and so she did. She took her pleasure and found the strength to pummel against him now, raking his back, trying to take every drop of what he was offering her and more, needing it all.

He gave it to her, took her over peak after peak until she gave up and clung to him in exhaustion, convulsing as if she were in the grasp of a sensual fever.

Only when they began to slow to a rocking motion, so dreamy and rhythmic it was like the pulsing of a heartbeat, did she press her face and lips to his throat. She curled her arms around his back and neck and hid her face. Inhaling him deep, she wished the protective wall of flesh, the close proximity of his heart and soul, the touch of his breath, were all something she could have forever.

I love you, she thought in amazement. *I love you for this moment. For the type of man you are, that you would give me this.*

I'll always love you, always pray for the world to keep you safe and cherish you the way I do. The way I wish I could cherish you forever, if my life was different.

Dawn was beginning to light the sky behind his shoulders. For the first time in her life she took no joy in the rose and blue beauty of a sunrise. She wouldn't let herself grieve, however. She might not be able to keep him, but this night had been every fantasy she could wish to have. It was a gift that most women with much less problematic lives never got. Whatever Divinity was, It had given her this. She had to honor that.

Which meant she had to close the book on the fairy tale and go home.

Chapter Seven

"Well, I certainly feel served *and* protected." She had to keep it light. Told herself that, even as she thought about how good he looked standing there by her car door.

"You drive this thing home under the speed limit," Jake told her.

They'd helped each other dress with a lot of slow kisses and intimate touches that had the enduring sweetness of first love. The night was waning, but strangely the magic wasn't, as if it didn't know that something this wonderful couldn't last.

"And if I don't drive the speed limit?" Stacie managed an impish smile.

Leaning through the window, he captured her lips as his hand eased down the front of the dress she'd repaired with two safety pins from her clutch purse. Finding her breast, he cupped it, rubbed his thumb against her so the nipple hardened, already eager for his touch again. When he drew back, she was breathless.

It's over. I have to go. I have to.

"If you don't," he said, "I'll chase you down, pull you out of that car and give you a bare-assed spanking on the side of the road where everyone can see."

"Why, Lieutenant." She grinned up at him even as she felt a flush course up her neck at the thought. "All those women who will be speeding just to get your attention."

"Brat." But his expression sobered. "You going to be okay? The nurse will stay until the afternoon so you can get some sleep?"

"Sure." She didn't really know if she would, but she had no hold on this man, wouldn't make him feel he had to watch over her. "I'll be all right."

He eyed her. "I'm not going to give you my phone number."

She blinked. Well, that stung a little. "I didn't ask you to."

"No, you didn't." He took hold of her chin. "Which is why I'm not going to ask for yours either. You wanted this to be just a fantasy. Okay. It was a hell of one. I'm privileged to be part of it. But what's better than a fantasy is figuring out how to be with someone you're meant to be with. I know we can't say for sure that's what's going on here, but I think we got a hell of a good start."

She stared at him. "Jake...my life. I just... It wouldn't be fair to you."

"You think it's fair for a woman to be with a cop? Our divorce rate is huge and domestic violence...well, you wouldn't ever have to worry about that with me, but—"

"Were we talking about marriage?"

The way she was looking at him with those wide blue eyes, Jake felt crazy enough to be doing so. Which told him he needed to step back before he scared her to death.

"I come home mean, a lot," he continued doggedly. "I do things that will make you worry. It's not fair. But love isn't about fairness. It's about wanting to be with someone so much none of that matters. You willing to see if we've got that?" He leaned in again, stopped just a hair from her lips. "If you do, come to the ball field next Saturday. If you don't, I won't pursue it further."

Like hell he wouldn't. Still, he kept his gaze on her face, brought his lips to her mouth, the barest of touches. "Bye, baby."

Walking back to his car without looking back was the hardest thing he'd ever done.

*****

And apparently the stupidest. Eight innings. He was playing like shit, and no sign of her at all.

"What's got your dick in a twist?" his sergeant demanded. "If you don't hit the ball this time, I swear I'm going to stick the bat up your ass to give whatever you've got rammed up there company."

"I hit better with a stick up my ass than most of you clowns do on your best days."

"Yeah, yeah." A few more razzing comments from his teammates, thrown punches, and he felt more fortified to go to the plate. He narrowed his gaze at the pitcher who smirked at him. The bat was going to connect with something this time that would knock him on his grinning ass.

Damn it, he had connected with *her*. He could find her. It wouldn't be so hard with all the resources he had at his disposal. He'd persuade her. Nibble on that sensitive spot on her neck and she'd give him anything.

Then he saw her. Just sitting down on the top bleacher in a little cotton dress and sandals, looking as pretty as the summer day. When she saw him looking, she gave him a tentative wave, telling him she wasn't sure of his welcome. Well, fuck that. He handed the bat to the umpire. "I'll be right back."

Vaulting over the four-foot chain link fence like it wasn't even there, he took the bleachers two at a time up to where she was. When he got to her, he didn't give her any preliminaries. She started to speak, but he bent down, caught her by the upper arms and took her mouth in a hard, demanding kiss that told her exactly how much he'd been thinking of her. There were catcalls and whistles from the dugout, laughter from the bleachers and somewhere in there his sergeant's voice.

"Chance, get your ass down here and bat."

All that mattered was how she melted in his arms, the way she curled those slim fingers into his T-shirt and held on, bringing back all sorts of memories. When he lifted his head, her beautiful eyes were soft, aroused. "I wasn't sure if you meant it," she said quietly.

"I don't say what I don't mean." He nipped her chin, lifted her hands and kissed one at a time. "You might need to remember that now."

At her curious look, he smiled. "Remember what I said I'd do if you came to a game?" He leaned down, whispered in her ear. "I've got a solid dozen in my wallet."

Her laughter filled his ears as she wrapped her arms around his neck. He tightened his grip, lifting her briefly off her feet, burying his face in her hair.

"I'm glad you came," he murmured into her ear.

When he let her down, she briefly swept her lashes down in that shy way that stirred his libido, remembering her cuffed and stretched naked across the hood of the Porsche.

"Well, what woman passes up the Chance of a lifetime?" She teased him with his surname, but as she raised her gaze, she became more serious. "I'm not sure if I'm good for you, Jake. This may be a mistake you'll regret but..." Her shoulder lifted. "I want you. So..." She took a deep breath, her fingers flexing nervously on his chest. "I'm here."

Ah hell. Screw it. He swung her up in his arms, delighted to catch her startled expression a moment before he headed back down the bleachers with her in his arms. He shook his head at his teammates, indicating he was out of tonight's game.

There were shadows under her eyes. She needed someone to help out, take care of her. She probably thought she'd come tonight and they'd have a repeat of their night in the corn field. Then he'd let her go home and take care of her other life all by herself.

Well, if he'd gotten her here with the offer of more, he was going to live up to it. They'd have the fantasy, but he'd show her he could be part of her reality too. A part she wouldn't regret having there.

She was his chance of a lifetime as well.

Epilogue

All-night stakeouts had gotten a lot harder to bear. Knowing what was at home, curled up in his bed waiting for him made him want to just shoot the suspected perps and let God sort them out. Jake grinned at himself, ran a hand over his sweaty neck. Well, at least they got a good collar tonight.

Out of habit, he tried the knob on the laundry room door and frowned as it turned easily, letting him in. Damn aggravating woman. Even as he had the thought, the smell of coffee and breakfast curled its way around his senses, trying to distract him from his annoyance. But even though he was a man who lived by his stomach, it couldn't hold a candle to what the sound of her humming in the kitchen did to him.

She hadn't done that at first, but as time had passed and things had gotten better, he'd found it an endearing habit. One he suspected she was rediscovering. Right now she was singing an off-tune version of a Rod Stewart classic. *You're in my Soul.*

In the beginning, he thought it was his job to be the white knight. He'd already plotted it out. A word to his cousin in the New York DMV, and her brothers would have enough traffic violations on their records that every cop in the state would be pulling them over. If they really pushed him, he'd talk to his college buddy who worked with the Bureau. Tom and Carl would believe they'd been put on the FBI's Most Wanted list with scum like bin Laden.

However, in the end, it was Stacie who'd made things better. Not just for her parents but for all of them. Jake included. All she'd needed to know was that she wasn't alone. That she had someone in her corner.

The little spitfire had marched herself up to New York, planted herself in Tom's office, called in Carl and laid it out for them. Their parents deserved quality care. There was an excellent facility within ten minutes of the house and she'd already talked to the administrator about hiring on there part-time, the balance of her hours to be spent in direct care of her parents, in a place where she'd have the resources to give them what they needed. She further informed them if they didn't agree to kick in where insurance wouldn't, she'd stand outside their office with a very large sign stating they'd embezzled funds from one of their major clients.

They'd actually had the brass balls to test her, but the next morning she'd shown up on the sidewalk in front of their snazzy office with a brown bag lunch and a large printed placard in hand. Just like that, the fight was won. They even repaid her the funds she'd pulled from her own meager savings to pay the nurse who'd covered the dayshift for her while she was in New York. Jake had handled the night shift and had learned firsthand in three days what she'd been dealing with for over two years. Enough to make him want to zap their testicles with the hot stick on its highest setting.

He'd been so proud of her though. He'd wanted to go with her, but she'd taken his hands, her eyes shining, chin firm, and said, "You've given me the strength to do this. If you'll take care of my parents while I'm gone...I want you to know them. And them to know you."

Her mother took to him right off. It tore out his heart, how fragile and light her body was when he moved her in and out of the bed, even as she was able to make him laugh with the sassy sense of humor she'd given her daughter. Her dad played a vicious game of checkers, though he and Jake had to start and stop it over a day's time to finish it. By the time Jake helped move some of their things into the long-term care facility, he cared enough that he ached for them, particularly when he saw they wouldn't share a room together. But Stacie had worked out having them on the same hall, despite their differing conditions. Her mom didn't have much time, and her father's lucid moments were decreasing at almost the same rate. But already, when Jake came to the hospital to join Stacie for dinner, he saw a peace in her mother's eyes, the worry she'd been carrying for her daughter and husband now not as sharp.

There was sadness and pain. A lot of tears. But there was also happiness and the discovery of what being in love was all about, in the shadow of two people who had truly lived it, were living it to the very end.

Things had changed so much for both him and Stacie. Love was like that. Magic. Just like all the books said.

He slipped into the kitchen. The shadows had disappeared from beneath her eyes and she'd put on some weight, in all the right places. One of those places was very pleasingly displayed as she bent over, loading the dishwasher. Thank God, she was wearing the white nurse's uniform he liked so much, the one with an above-the-knee skirt. It wasn't immodest, but it hugged her trim figure like an hourglass and had a zipper down the front that gave him no end of fantasies, to her amusement. She hadn't yet donned her ankle socks and comfortable orthopedic shoes, which while good for work, tended to minimize her sexy legs. Of course, he didn't mind that. There were too many male orderlies and doctors at that place she worked as it was. He'd be glad when that diamond on her finger had a second gold ring keeping it company.

She was rearranging the plates he'd tossed in haphazardly yesterday morning. He needed to do better about that. He'd rather conserve her energy for other things.

He eased up behind her and as she straightened, he caught hold of her waist, making her jump, but when she tried to turn, he held her fast, sliding one hand up to claim one breast, easing down the zipper to find curves cradled in a thin lace bra. As a sexy little tremble ran through her, he pressed his attentive cock up against her soft ass.

"You didn't lock your door, little girl. Look what kind of trouble you let into the house."

"Mmm..." A shudder rippled through Stacie as his fingers teased a nipple while his arm held her fast. God, she loved his strength. The way he smelled, the heat of him. The way he made her want to devour him alive one moment and then the next, she wanted just to curl together on the couch, feeling him doze off from a long day, his arm still holding her close. Or the way her knees went weak, every time, when he arrived at Rivershores to have dinner with her and her mother or play checkers with her father. He always cleaned up first, made sure he shaved for her parents. Wore a clean shirt and brought her mother flowers.

She'd found far more than a lover the day she'd been stopped by Jake Chance. She'd found something she'd never realized a man could be. A best friend.

Though friendship wasn't at all what she was thinking about now as he ran his hand down her thigh and started to gather up her skirt in front, reaching under the uniform to find her panties. She smiled as his clever fingers found the lace thong she'd had time to slip on before he arrived.

"You'll have to make it fast," she whispered, laying her head back on his shoulder as he bent his head to her throat, bit. "My fiancé is due home any minute and he's very jealous. He's a cop," she added. "He has a gun." As he pressed harder against her, she smothered a giggle. "A great...big...gun."

His hand came up, collared her throat. "You are going to start locking that door, or I'm going to start spanking you."

She braced her hands on the sink, wiggled her ass against him, at first to tease and then with more serious intent, a rhythmic stroking up and down his length. "That's supposed to discourage me from doing it?"

He groaned. "It will if I really tan your hide." But a moment later he had the zipper to her waist and his hands full of her breasts. Stacie gasped as he fondled her with those far too knowledgeable fingers, making her pussy's reaction trickle down her legs. "How long before that fiancé of yours gets here?"

"Any minute. I think I hear him parking now. You better hurry."

He opened his jeans, pressed her against the kitchen counter with his thighs and bent his knees just enough. "Pull up your skirt for me, baby. Show me that pretty ass of yours that needs a spanking."

As she reached back, Jake growled appreciatively at the way it thrust her breasts out. He felt hard as iron, ready to explode. As soon as she pulled the hem up, revealing her round buttocks provocatively accented by that bit of lace between the cheeks, he caught the crotch of the thong, pulled it aside and thrust home.

She was ready too. She cried out, began to spasm around him almost immediately. She loved it when he played rough with her, his kitten with her own sharp claws. He caught her throat again, held her back up against his chest, her cheek alongside his jaw so her cries caressed his face with her breath even as he pounded into her wet cunt, imagining her wearing this tiny scrap of lace all day long at work, the uniform cloth rubbing against the bare cheeks of her ass.

The image sent him over, as he suspected she knew it would. Whether she'd planned to wear it today or snuck it on just before he pulled in and—damn, which probably meant she'd unlocked the door just to give him a reason to get tough with her—she knew what got him going. She also knew what kept him together. As good as she was at driving him insane and keeping his cock in the begging position, she was just as good at listening. At knowing when he didn't want to talk, needed the feel of her arms around him, snuggling up to him while he nursed his beer and unwound after a tough day. He just liked hearing her move around the house, watching the curve of her delicate cheek in the lamplight, the flicker of her beautiful eyes. The way she got ready for bed. Her cotton sleep shirts, the way she stuffed her feet in bunny slippers and raked her fingers through her hair when she first got up in the morning. Damn if Nichols hadn't been right all along.

He worked her hard against the sink and she gave him just as good back, squeezing him, rubbing her bottom against him so he couldn't resist. Still hard, slick from her juices, he pulled out and put it back inside that tiny rosebud opening, taking her down deep and propelling her finished climax into a whirlpool of aftershocks that had her thrusting back against him again, her breasts quivering. As their breathing slowed, began to synchronize, he ran a hand down her front, a soft caress of her breast, fingers dipping into the dent of her navel, then down to cover her mound, pressing his fingers on her clit so she arched up hard, breath leaving her fast, her ass squeezing his cock like a vise.

"Ah God." He buried his face in her hair. "Missed you." She always made the ugliness go away. He didn't need to tell her about it. She cleaned him with just a touch.

"I can tell." She pressed her lips to his throat, her body still trembling where he was caressing her, up and down. He could have her hot again in no time, wanted to, but damn if breakfast didn't smell good. He grinned at himself then lifted her hand that had the engagement ring on it to his lips.

"I'm going to keep riding you about that door. Did you unlock it right before I came in?"

Her eyes sparkled at the double entendre. "I'll never tell."

"Stacie Marie—"

She put a finger up to his mouth, her eyes soft, lips wet with his kisses. "Some chances are worth taking." Then, at the lingering worry in his eyes, she relented. "Yes. I unlocked it when I heard you pull into the driveway."

He gave her rump a little slap and pulled out reluctantly. He went for the wash cloth, but she beat him to it, wetting it with warm soapy water and then caressing him with it, giving him that shy look below her lashes as she cleaned his cock for him. Breakfast maybe could wait. God, she was going to kill him.

"What you were just talking about...that's what I intend to do."

"Hmm?" She glanced up at him as he put a finger under her chin, tilted her face up. Her hands continued to cosset him, but her fingers were firm, stroking, the light in her eye telling him she was on his wavelength about breakfast.

"Once I marry you. There's one particular chance I intend to take. Over and over and over again. Mrs. Chance."

She rolled her eyes but moved in for the kiss, let him wrap his arms around her and take her under again.

While she'd agreed to marry him, she'd wanted to wait to get married at Christmas, in a candlelight service like her mother had done with her father.

When she told him that, she'd cried. That wasn't the first time she'd cried. Now that she had a shoulder offered, she let the tears wash through her more often, to help her get up and face it every day. He stood at her back every way he could, physically and mentally, and wondered what he'd done to deserve such an angel in his life. His wild angel.

"I don't care what they say," he'd told her once when it had overwhelmed her. "When you love a woman like your dad loves your mom, the way I love you, even if some son of a bitch disease takes your mind, you always remember her in your soul. Deep inside him, he knows. He'll remember her, how she was a part of his life."

"But he won't remember her dying," she said softly. "That's the blessing Mom wants to give him. That's why she'll make it until Christmas. She knows by then he won't be able to remember."

His tender-hearted angel. He'd proposed to her a month after they'd met, and it was her dad who had made it happen.

During one of their checker games, he'd been alerted by a prolonged silence. He glanced up from the board to find her dad had a hundred percent checked in, suddenly a very lucid father, eyeing him closely in that way that would have any man straightening up, feeling a little nervous.

"What do you intend to do about my daughter?"

He had Stacie's eyes, midnight blue. His body still had the hint of the rangy, tall man he'd been. Jake not only saw in his eyes that soul-deep memory he'd talked about but the man who'd taken her to the track, loved her joyous recklessness even as he helped her find her path to adulthood.

"I intend to marry her, sir. Love her with all I've got and take care of her for the rest of her life."

Fate had Stacie walking in at just that moment, so there it was, his proposal out on the table. But Jake had looked at her and known it was how he felt, what he wanted. The soft expression in her eyes gave him the terrifying and exhilarating realization she was going to say yes, agree to be his forever.

"Good. Isn't any good to finish a race alone." Her father jumped two of his reds. "Competition keeps you alive. Letting someone keep you sharp. It's all about taking chances."

Her lips curved in a soft, poignant smile and Jake was lost in the vision of her.

"Yes, sir. You're sure right about that."

A LITTLE LESS CONVERSATION
By Rhyannon Byrd

ଔ

Dedication

This book is dedicated to Deborah Hopkins Smart: travel agent extraordinaire, Capricorn sister, first-class proofer, book signing buddy, and last but not least, one of the most amazing friends a girl could ever have! One fateful trip to Nashville…and now you're stuck with me forever. LOL. Many thanks for always being there for me, for never tiring of our chats and my sometimes bizarre questions, and for always making the perfect suggestions. I don't know what I'd do without ya, Debs! I wish you bagel days in the office and a life overflowing with love and happiness, sweetie, because no one deserves it more than you!!!

Trademarks Acknowledgement

The author acknowledges the trademarked status and trademark owners of the following wordmarks mentioned in this work of fiction:

Cirque du Soleil: The Dream Merchant Company Kft.
Corona: Cerveceria Modelo, S.A. de C.V. Corporation
Diet Pepsi: Pepsico, Inc.
Foster's: Carlton and United Beverages Limited Australian Public Company
Heineken: Heineken Brouwerijen B.V. Private Limited Company
Jose Cuervo: Tequila Cuervo La Rojena, S.A. De C. V. Corporation
Marlboros: Philip Morris Inc.
Porsche Boxster: Dy. Ing. h. c. F. Porsche Aktiengesellschaft
Porsche: Dr. Ing. h. c. f. Porsche Aktiengesellschaft Corporation

Chapter One

It irritated the hell out of Mark Logan that at the age of thirty-six, he'd been reduced to mooning over a pretty face from across a blasted street. But damn if it wasn't true. Each day, for the past six months, the interest had grown like a verdant vine within the otherwise barren, disillusioned landscape of his heart. It'd been planted, and like a fledgling seed showered with the giving life of rain and sunshine, it had thrived.

It was sappy as shit, but there was no denying that he enjoyed the tight, hungry, kinda needy feeling the sight of her face put in the pit of his stomach. The kind of feeling he'd never thought to have there, twisting him into knots, and he was damned if he knew what to do about it. Normally, if there was a woman he wanted, he went after her with his intentions up front and with a brutal honesty. They'd share some mutually satisfying, physically intense, sweaty time between the sheets, and when the need was relieved, she'd be more than welcome to come in and share a beer at his bar, but nothing more. No commitment, no messy emotions…and no pretending that their mutual physical appetites were going to lead them into deeper, unknown territory that he'd never felt the urge to explore.

At first, it had just plain pissed him off that the sight of Melanie Green's smiling face, deep dimples, and sparkling cinnamon-brown eyes had changed all that. He'd struggled against it, like a fish snared by the cold steel of the hook, until he'd finally given in. Now he just hungered…and ached…and god only knew it was pathetic, but he yearned. That empty hollow in his gut twisted with boyish eagerness for each glimpse and casual meeting in the small seaside town of Foggy Bottom Beach, and it wasn't enough.

He needed *more*.

It scared the shit out of him, but Mark strongly suspected he needed a hell of a lot more—as in all of it, all of her, because this woman was different. Different from the women he'd known, and different in the way that she made him feel. When they met up again after a raging night of raw, hot, grinding sex—after wrecking the bed with wild, primitive fucking—Mark wanted to be sharing coffee with her over his breakfast table, not a beer and pretzels over the gleaming oak of his bar.

"Are you mooning over that little Mel again?" his older brother Cain snickered at his back, looking over Mark's broad shoulder to catch a view of the glass fronted travel agency located directly across the street from *Mark's on Main*.

"I'm not mooning over her, you nosy shit."

Cain arched a dark brow at the muttered words, and Mark watched from the corner of his eye as a hard grin spread across the even harder line of Cain's mouth, teasing and intent. "Hey, whatever, bro. But I never pegged you as the miss-goody-two-shoes type."

Mark rolled his head across the tight tension in his shoulders, but didn't take his eyes off the laughing vision Melanie made as she chatted on the phone, slim fingers clicking away at her keyboard with lightning speed. "I'm not any type, you moron."

"Hey, don't let me go ruffling your feathers. Maybe I'm just trying to save you from some humiliating heartbreak. I mean—she's lived here for half a year now, and in all that time, have you ever seen her out in the town with a man?"

"What the hell does that have to do with anything?" he practically growled, thankful that Melanie didn't seem the casual dating type, since he'd have been sorely tempted to break any guy's kneecaps if he so much as laid a finger on her. The only hands he wanted on her were his own, the only body drilling her through her mattress—*his*. Shit, it was like a virus that he couldn't shake, this craving to get as deep into her as he could possibly get. Balls-deep and saturated in heaven, surrounded by Melanie Green, those luminous eyes shocked wide with physical awareness of him, lips swollen and bruised from his kisses, cheeks flushed and soft breasts quivering as he moved within her, cramming in every inch, riding her with all the pent-up hunger he'd carried since setting eyes on her.

One smile, and the need had slammed into him like a freight train. *Whap!* And he hadn't been thinking straight since. If he had, he'd have figured out a way to get around her shy, quiet nervousness with him and have her in his bed, under his hard, hungry body, keeping her there for...

Hell, *forever*, if she'd let him—and that was the problem. If she didn't, he didn't think he'd be able to take it.

"So she doesn't do the whole casual sex thing," he muttered, wiping the gleaming bar down with a towel before setting an ice-cold Heineken out for his brother. "So what? Maybe that's one of the things I like about her."

Cain snickered again as he moved around the far end of the hand-carved bar, then reached for his beer. "Huh. I think she's just one of those women who doesn't like men."

"Maybe she just doesn't like *you*," Mark replied with a silky rasp, knowing Cain was trying to push his buttons.

"Yeah, and maybe she just likes pussy," his brother laughed, settling his tall, powerfully muscled frame atop a swiveling bar stool. "I mean, hell, what's not to like?"

He stopped restocking the wineglasses long enough to cut a piercing look at the man who had practically raised him, though only five years separated their ages. "And did you ever think it might be fun to have something to say to a woman after you're through banging her?"

"Not unless I'm talking in my sleep," Cain drawled, another sly smile curving his wide mouth, which crinkled the cynical corners of his sky blue eyes.

Mark shook his head with brotherly disgust. "You're a pig."

"So my last girlfriend said. You been talking to her?"

"Naw, Becky had the IQ of a cucumber," Mark snorted, fighting a smile of his own before his gaze caught again on the delectable sight of Melanie Green. She was talking to a new client now, and the image had the muscles across the top of his back and neck going tight with more of that telltale tension he'd been trying to shake off. He didn't like the fact that the client was a guy, from the looks of things probably in his late twenties, and had left a sleek little Boxster parked in front of the travel agency where she worked.

Cain waggled his brows, oblivious to the scene that had snagged Mark's attention from across the street. "Yeah, well, you shoulda seen what Becky could do with a cucumber. Who needs conversation when a chick can suck-start a—"

Mark ripped his frustrated gaze away from Melanie and "Mr. Porsche" long enough to glare at his brother. "Why the hell do I even try talking to you?"

"Damned if I know. You'd think after all these years you'd have learned that I can't be reformed." Cain took a long swallow of his beer, then added, "And if you had any balls, you'd be over there trying to talk to her, before someone else snags her. A woman like that isn't going to stay unattached forever, you know."

Mark cut him a suspicious look. "I thought you didn't even like her."

"Naw, it's that spitfire she works with who rubs me the wrong way, but Mel's an angel," Cain explained, pulling out his Marlboros and jerking the pack, before lifting it to his mouth to snag one of the dislodged cigarettes. He lit it and took a long drag, then grinned and said, "She just seems a little innocent for my tastes. Come to think of it, she seems a little too innocent for yours too, Marky boy."

"That's the problem," Mark muttered, "and how many times do I have to remind you that you can't smoke in here?"

Cain looked at the glowing cigarette pinched between his thumb and forefinger with quiet regret, then took another long, satisfying drag before dropping it into the empty beer bottle Mark held out to him. "You know, I figured it was that air of innocence surrounding her that has you grumping around here with your tail between your legs," he laughed, downing another long swallow of his beer. "There's only one thing to do, man."

"Oh Christ," Mark sighed, shaking his dark head while his lips twisted with wry humor at the thought of Cain Logan giving advice on women. The man was a walking, talking relationship disaster zone. "I don't think I want to hear this."

"Yeah you do," Cain drawled with a smile. "Hell, someone has to look out for your ass, and there's only one answer to your problem."

"S'that right?"

"Yep. You're just going to have to corrupt her, bro," Cain announced with a wicked grin worthy of any arrogant, oversexed lothario, his blue eyes shining with devilish humor within the tan, rugged landscape of his face. "Now stop being a puss and get your ass over there before some other stud steals her out from under you, and I'm stuck listening to your moaning for the rest of my life. If I can handle that group of she-men they've got me training down at the station, I think I can handle things around here for you tonight."

Mark turned his head to look once more out the tinted front window of his bar, his narrowed eyes immediately finding Mel, still chatting away with the same suit-slick client. A sick feeling somersaulted in his stomach at the thought that she might even be making plans at that moment, agreeing to go out with the guy, gifting the smug bastard with her sweet smile. Mark wanted to kill him. But more than that, he finally accepted the fact that Cain was right.

"Well, at least half right," he muttered to himself. If he didn't make his move now, some other asshole was going to steal her away, and he'd have no one to blame but himself. God only knew he'd skirted the damn issue long enough, so fucking afraid of putting one foot wrong and screwing himself before he'd even started. But he couldn't just set out to corrupt her, no matter how badly he wanted to. Christ, he wasn't that much of an ass.

No, it wouldn't be easy—hell, it'd probably kill him—but he was just going to have to bite the big one and choke on his lust until she was ready to deal with what one lover had referred to as his "often raw, rough-n-tumble needs in the sack". And with the way he felt about Mel, he could only imagine how difficult it was going to be reining in those needs. To be honest, he wasn't even sure he could do it. Melanie Green released something in him, something primal and dark, and when it was finally set free, he feared it'd be like that first escape of pressure on something bottled up too tight.

Raging. Powerful. Explosive.

If he hoped to make this work between them, he needed to keep his cock under control until he'd figured out a way to convince Melanie that he was for real, that despite his reputation, he was ready for something so much more fulfilling than a raunchy tumble. If he didn't—if he went raging in like a bull and managed to seduce her right off—he knew there wasn't a chance in hell he'd be able to control himself. He'd find himself riding her so hard it would blow both their minds, and end up scaring her off before he'd even had the chance to convince her he was looking for something more.

Damn, he couldn't let himself screw it up like that.

But he *did* need to make his move.

A terrible sexual tension tightened the long length of his body, muscles taut and poised for action, while his jaw hardened and his heart pounded like a son of a bitch. Mark took a slow, deep breath of wood polish and sea-scented air into his lungs, held it, and as he let it out, he said, "Thanks, man," and tossed his register card at a smirking Cain, then headed for the door.

*****

Melanie Green sighed a deep breath of relief when the shifty-eyed, cologne-drenched, overgrown prep boy of a client walked out the front door, and without any conscious thought, her gaze automatically tracked to *Mark's on Main* directly across the street from her office. Instantly, her mouth went dry and her face went hot, a prickly sensation of breathless suspense zinging beneath her skin.

"*Ohmygod*...Kyra," Melanie hissed, trying to catch her best friend's attention as the curvaceous coworker gossiped with her sister on the phone. "Hey, he's looking over here again."

The petite redhead sent her a wide-eyed look, and shot her a grin along with the thumbs-up sign, all without breaking her stride in the nonstop stream of fast-paced conversation as she filled her sister in on the latest jerk she'd dumped.

"That's right," Kyra sighed, glossed lips puckering into a scowl, "he was a total tool. He actually thought I wouldn't mind that he'd been having phone sex with his ex-girlfriend in Michigan. I swear it's guys like that who make me wish I was bi. I mean—every guy I've ever dated has turned out to be a creep. I must have been some kind of sadistic bitch in a past life to deserve this kind of karma crapfest year after year."

In the next moment, Melanie found herself blinking hard, determined she was imagining Mark Logan walking out the front doors of his bar, and heading straight toward her across the cobblestone Main Street that ran down the center of the small town of Foggy Bottom Beach.

"Holy crap, I think he's coming over here! Kyra Marie Morgan," she growled, wheeling her chair back to Kyra's desk as her thundering heart threatened to erupt from the confines of her chest. "Did you hear me?" she repeated, the panic in her voice coming through loud and clear even to her own ears. "I think he's coming over here!"

Kyra sent her a startled "did aliens just land on our roof" look, her smoky green gaze cutting to the front window as she whistled softly under her breath. "Holy mother of Moses. Ang, I gotta go, hon. I'll call you about Mom's birthday tomorrow, 'kay? Later."

"What am I going to do?" Melanie groaned as Kyra hung up the phone. She rapidly fanned her face with one hand, wondering if her nachos from lunch were going to make another appearance as her tummy did this odd little flip and twist, reminding her of something she'd seen at Cirque du Soleil.

"Now, sweetie, don't get your panties in a bunch," Kyra murmured with a soothing smile, completely ruined by the wild jump of excitement in her almond-shaped, sage-colored eyes. "This is the chance you've been waiting for to make some serious headway with that hunk of stud meat. And he's such a doll. Nothing like that pain-in-the-ass brother of his, even if they're both drop-dead gorgeous."

"Kyra, he is *not* a doll...and he is *not* a hunk of stud meat," Mel gritted through her teeth, her cheeks burning and heart rate tripling the way it did every time she came face-to-face with Mark Logan. "He's the man I've been fantasizing about for the past six months...the one who makes me tongue-tied every time he so much as smiles at me! Any of that ring a bell?"

She tracked his progress as he headed around the parked cars lining the sides of the street in slanted, parallel lanes, breathing a short sigh of relief when Roy Baker, the corner coffee shop owner, stopped him for a chat. The late afternoon sun hung low in the sky, illuminating Mark's mouthwatering physique, the long shafts of smoldering gold painting his tall, hard, muscle-ridged body with iridescent beams of heat, showing off the blatantly male strength beneath his faded jeans and soft charcoal gray T-shirt to perfection. He could have been dressed to the nines in tux and tails, and he couldn't have looked anymore delicious than he did at that moment.

Thick, raven black hair tossed in the whipping breeze against the sharp, wholly male angles of his face. His soft green eyes, just a shade darker than Kyra's, shadowed beneath the raven wings of his brows and thick black lashes, narrowed against the sunlight. His cheekbones were cut high, his nose a long, aristocratic affair roughened by a slight bump at its crest, attesting to an earlier break. Every time she ran into him, whether it was at Roy's shop or the local grocery store, she wanted to press her lips against that slight bump, then trail them down the stubble-rough bronze of his cheek, not stopping until she found the corner of that wide, wicked mouth and learned, firsthand, if those rough-silk lips tasted as sinfully delicious as they looked.

A small, dreamy sigh escaped her, and Mel shook her head hard to regain her focus—but it wasn't easy when something that gorgeous stood no more than twenty feet from where she sat. A chill raced down her spine, making her shiver as the heat beneath her tingling skin flared hotter, and Melanie swore she could almost *feel* the physical waves of sharp, raw-edged power pulsing off that magnificent bod and breathtaking face that invaded her dreams each night, like a thief stealing into her psyche.

Mark Logan was six-foot-three of rock-hard male animal, dangerously seductive, and she had a case of the hots so bad she was surprised steam didn't rise from her body when his smoldering green gaze cut from Roy's animated face straight to her again, zeroing in on her through the window of Elite Travel like a hawk spotting its prey. She gulped and tried not to melt into a puddle of lust, while Kyra whistled softly beneath her breath.

"Oh honey," the outrageous redhead sighed, "if that ain't a hunk of stud meat, then I'm a nun."

"You're certifiable, is what you are," she groaned, trying not to panic as he sent her a crooked grin, then turned an impatient look back on Roy. "Honestly, you're supposed to be helping me, not drooling over him."

"It's a conditioned reflex, hon. I see stud, I drool. Something like the moon and the tides. It's an unstoppable force of nature."

"More like a freak of nature."

Kyra sent her a sympathetic smile. "Oh man, he's ditching Roy. Now act cool."

"Cool. Uh...what universe are you from, woman? I'm the dopey geek type, remember? I wouldn't know cool if it slapped me upside the head and called me Mama."

"Mel," Kyra laughed, winking at her as she grabbed up her purse and Diet Pepsi, "he probably just wants you to smack his ass and call *him* Mama."

"You know," she murmured, shaking her head, "you have dated some seriously sick whackos. We're talking freaky deeky."

Kyra snickered under her breath, lifting her sloping red brows. "No sweetie, I just read a lot and have a really kick-ass imagination."

Mel shot her a wry smile. "I pity the fool who finally tames you."

"Yeah, well, he'd have to kill me first. And anyway, I'm swearing off men, so it's now your duty to womankind to go and overload on orgasms for those of us who're deprived."

"Uh...overload? More like lucky to get one," she snorted softly, several brief flashbacks from her two failed semi-serious relationships sticking in her mind like broken records, before she gritted her teeth and forced them down like a bad-tasting medicine.

Her best friend sent her a sharp look that said, "Get your head out of the sand and wake up". "Mel, that man knows his way around a woman. I bet he could make you squeal just by talking to you."

Now there was a visual image sure to fry her brain. "Mmm...can a man really—"

"Hello? Earth to Melanie," Kyra laughed, snapping her fingers. "Did I lose you there in la-la land, hon? Here he comes...and here I go. Good luck. Knock him on his ass, babe, and twist him around your finger. I know you can do it!"

Mel leapt to her feet, ready to grab hold of the smiling redhead and tie her to her blasted chair. "What? You're leaving me?"

"Three's a crowd," Kyra snorted, "unless you're like that jerk Brett that I dated there for a while, before I realized what he was into and tossed his ass out. But we won't get into that right now. Trust me, you don't want me cramping your style when Mr. Dreamy Eyes comes in and asks you out for that date."

"Kyra, for the love of god, he probably just wants to buy a cruise."

"Melanie Green...that is not an 'I wanna take a quick jaunt to Acapulco' look he's sporting. That's an 'I want to spread you naked and taste you from head to toe, lingering on all the good parts in between' look. *Hasta*, sweetie. I'll be in the back if you need me."

"What I need is to beat you silly for abandoning me," she muttered, pushing forward in her chair. When she was once again seated behind her desk, she ran her hands over her curl-crazy hair, trying to tame the wild mass without looking like she was primping. He had just about reached the door when her damn phone went off like a wailing banshee, startling the hell out of her, and she jumped to answer it. In her excitement, she miscalculated and her elbow crashed into the corner of her latest scrapbooking project for her recent travel conferences. The scrapbooks and loose photos scattered over her desk in a mess that screamed *I'm clumsy and a nervous wreck.*

Damn. So much for coming off as cool and sophisticated. No...she might as well sit back and get ready to assume what was her customary role with men—that of "please pour out your woman troubles to me as if I give a damn or could actually help", sisterly, asexual female friend. Lord knew she could play it to perfection. Even her last boyfriend, Craig, had wanted her for little more than his gal pal.

Hell, the man had come to cry on her shoulder when the twenty-year-old he'd been seeing on the side, much to Mel's surprise, had dumped him for a younger guy. And the really sick part was that she'd done it. She'd patted his back, told him everything would be okay, and then taken him out for pizza. They still talked every few weeks, and for the life of her, Melanie couldn't understand why they'd ever thought they should date. Passion with Craig had consisted of a stiff, three-minute session in the sheets to blow off steam, and then a nice long talk about anything from politics to what they should go see at the movies.

But that wasn't what she wanted from Mark Logan. No, with this man, Melanie wanted a little less conversation...and a hell of a lot more body language. Because no one had ever made her heart thrum and her body do the funny little shimmy from her privates to her eyebrows that this guy did. Heck, he even made her toes tingle, and she knew she had it bad.

It'd been that way from the first time they'd been introduced. And the thought of taking on her usual role of confidant, of actually becoming this guy's buddy, rather than his red-hot sex siren, made her want to bawl like a baby.

Melanie hardened her jaw and plastered on a smile, determined not to make such an ass of herself. With her heart in her throat, she watched as he reached the door and grasped the handle. Chimes sounded as he pulled it open, and Mel sent up a fervent prayer for help to any benevolent love goddesses who might be listening.

Chapter Two

Why he hadn't just done this months ago, Mark couldn't say, except that the thought of screwing up and blowing it with this woman put a cold chill in the pit of his stomach. Damn, it scared the holy living hell out of him.

He took a deep breath and walked through the front door of Elite Travel, and found himself alone with a smiling, bright-eyed, phone-holding Melanie Green who looked so jumpy he was surprised she didn't bolt from her chair and make a run for it. But even as he walked forward, careful to keep his movements slow and easy, she took a deep breath and held her ground, making him admire her backbone. It was painfully obvious that he made her skittish, but she was too proud to run and hide, and he wanted to pull her into his arms and kiss her silly for not bailing on him.

Hell, he wanted to pull her into his arms and act out every carnal fantasy he'd ever entertained since the age of puberty, and considering he'd been a horny little shit, that was saying quite a lot. She whispered a hasty goodbye into the phone, hung up the receiver, and smiled up at him as he reached her desk.

"Hi," she all but sighed, and he couldn't miss the breathless edge of her voice in the simple word.

"Hey Mel. I was just wondering if you've got time to talk?" he asked, nodding toward her desk. "I don't want to keep you from work or anything."

"No," she replied in that same husky tone of hers that never failed to make him think of sex-tangled sheets and sweat-slick bodies, "it's okay." She licked her lower lip, and he nearly groaned at the sight of her pink little tongue stroking against the deep rose of her mouth. Using a slender hand adorned with silver rings, she pushed her chin-length, silky-looking honey brown curls behind the dainty shells of her ears and said, "We're getting ready to close up soon, since it's, um, been pretty bagel today."

A wide grin broke across his mouth, and she turned crimson, the dark flush in her cheeks making her look like she'd been burnt to a crisp in the beach-bright sun, obviously realizing what she'd just said.

"Bagel, huh?" he smiled, choking back a rumbling bark of laughter, since the woman looked like she wanted to sink down in her chair and hide under her desk.

"I meant to say slow," she mumbled, though the sexy as hell, lush line of her mouth was curling into a wry, self-deprecating grin. "It's been fairly *slow* today."

"Uh-huh," he murmured, trying not to make it too obvious that he was still trying not to lose it.

"Oh go ahead and laugh," she groaned, shaking her head. "I would too if someone started speaking Martian to me."

Not trusting himself not to just reach out and pull her into his arms, Mark shoved his hands deep into his jeans' pockets and rocked back on his heels. "Let me guess. Some kind of code, right?"

"Uh, yeah." She busied herself with organizing her desk, suddenly refusing to meet his eyes. "Whenever Kyra or I make a comment about the day being nice and slow, we jinx ourselves and all holy hell breaks loose in this place."

"So you say 'bagel' to stop the jinx," he said softly, wishing she'd meet his eyes again and stop hiding from him.

"Yep." She went to work scooping up an overturned paper clip holder while the corner of her mouth twitched with a smile, making him fight his own grin as her eyes lifted to his mouth. "And we've been extra careful this week, since Lara and Tom are out for a conference."

He bent his knees and lowered his head to the side, trying to catch her gaze. "So what other code words do you two have? If a hot guy walks in here, what do you call him? Cream cheese?" he teased, trying to put her at ease.

But it didn't work, and he realized too late that he shouldn't have tried teasing her when she was already so embarrassed. For the brief flash of a moment, he witnessed her turning bright red, and then she suddenly lowered her head to the jumbled surface of her desk and began banging her forehead against what looked like some sort of photo album. Mark smiled down at the crown of her head, enjoying the sight of her honey brown curls spilling over the cluttered surface, and watched as she reached out with her left hand, searching until she found a large, heavy three-ring hole punch. Without lifting her head, she picked up the punch and held it out to him.

"Please do me a favor and just put me out of my misery now," she said in a muffled voice. "A nice, swift bonk on my noggin with this should do the trick quite nicely, if it's not too much trouble."

Mark let go the suffocated laughter he'd been holding in, unable to resist lowering one hand to stroke through those silky, tumbled curls. She stiffened at the touch of his hand on her scalp, then at the side of her face as he gently pushed her hair back, trying to read her expression. "Am I making you nervous, honey?"

He could see her eyes squeeze tightly shut, lips rolling inward before she whispered "Yes", sounding utterly miserable.

"Thank god, because you pretty much terrify the hell out of me," he admitted with all honestly, even though he'd never confessed such a thing to a woman before. But then, he thought with an odd feeling of realization, he'd never actually felt nervous around a woman the way he did around Melanie Green. But it wasn't a bad feeling. No, in fact, he kinda liked it. Liked the way it made him feel alive—jacked up on energy and excitement—like when he was thirteen and Cain had dared him to jump off the end of the pier when a wicked storm was raging all around them.

Of course, his brother had to jump in to save him when a ten-foot swell slammed him into one of the pylons and knocked him unconscious. It was a sobering memory, because Mark suddenly realized that if he screwed up here, with Melanie, there wasn't going to be any cavalry coming to rescue his ass. He'd be done for, and have no one to blame but himself.

"I scare you?" she asked with a heavy dose of disbelief, setting down the hole punch before pressing her palms flat to the desk and pushing her upper body upright, tilting back her heart-shaped face until he was able to snag her with his gaze.

Though his instinctive reaction was to laugh off such a telling statement and retreat behind his customary air of casual indifference, he found himself doing neither. Instead, he stared down at her and gave her the absolute truth, sensing that she would see right through him anyway, even if he tried to coast his way through all nice and easy by keeping his own feelings close to his heart. "Damn right you do. Why do you think it's taken me so long to work up the nerve to come and talk to you?" Then, thinking she might mistake his intentions, he felt the need to add, "For starters," and a lean grin of anticipation kicked up the edge of his mouth.

She blinked up at him in surprise—long, thick lashes casting shadows upon the freckled curve of her cheek, and he could see her reassessing him. He knew the second she came to the understanding that they had some common ground here, both of them nervous and wary, though she wasn't quite sure she believed him yet. Her eyes were wide and watchful, the set of her mouth hopeful, yet questioning. No, the jury was still out on that one.

Trust with this woman wouldn't come easy, and for some bizarre-ass reason, Mark found himself actually looking forward to convincing her that he was for real. That he was looking for more than just a quick screw from her, and wasn't going to be satisfied until he had it all.

She nibbled on the inside curve of her upper lip, then asked, "Why would I make you nervous?"

"Why wouldn't you?" he murmured in a low voice, losing himself for a moment in heated, erotic, gut-twisting visions of what he could be doing to her lush little figure on that desk. There wasn't a whole lot of her, but what there was looked womanly and soft, and he couldn't wait to get her under his hands, naked and warm. He wanted her in his home, laid out on his big bed and spread wide, where he could uncover, explore, and investigate all her sweet little secrets 'til his aching cock threatened to explode, learning everything there was to know about her. Claiming it all for his own. "Why wouldn't you make any guy nervous, Mel? Hell, with that soft, sweet smile and those big, bright eyes? You're like something shiny and real in a sea of—"

"All your other women?" she laughed, shaking her head, and he didn't like the bitter edge lurking there behind her brave show of humor.

"I don't have *women*, Melanie."

"Uh-huh." She pushed her hair back from her face again, and set about straightening her blouse, then went back to trying to restore some kind of order to her desk, and he felt like he'd been dismissed.

He didn't care for the feeling.

"I haven't dated anyone for a while now," he heard himself explaining without any conscious direction from his mind, his tone more aggressive than he would have liked, but there was no help for it right then. She was setting off all those animal, primitive hungers inside him, and he found himself wanting to drag her over that damn desk and bury his tongue down her throat, putting his scent and taste on her for every other male to recognize. Marking her as someone who belonged solely to him.

She flushed a bit more at his biting tone, and the thought flashed through his mind that he'd love to see those freckle-sprinkled cheeks flushed like damp, pink silk while he crammed his dick hard and deep and fast into her pretty, pinker cunt—where she'd be even hotter, wetter...silkier. Her skin was so soft and creamy, he knew her little sweet spot nestled between her thighs would be like satin, so tender and swollen, a bruised rose and slippery with juices if he could just get her under the aching need of his body. His balls tightened and a knot thickened in the root of his shaft, but he choked down his lust with every ounce of willpower he possessed and struggled not to go hard.

But it wasn't easy. She quite simply fascinated him. There was no other word for the strange feeling of euphoria pumping through his system, as if he'd done too many shots of *Jose Cuervo* on an empty stomach.

To distract himself, Mark let his gaze wander across her desk, and the sight of a photo poking out from the edge of a bright blue folder caught his attention. Well, actually it was the shapely, naked leg that snagged his interest, and he reached out and snatched it up before she could stop him.

"Damn," he muttered when he got a full view of the picture, feeling like he'd just been socked in the gut.

"Hey," she gasped, "give me that!"

She reached out to grab the picture, but he stepped back out of her reach, lifting it high as he took another nice, long, lingering look at the photo pinched between his thumb and forefinger. "Hell, Mel, where was this taken?"

A groaning sound of frustration broke from her throat, and she plopped back in her seat with an exaggerated sigh of impatience, crossing her arms as a mutinous expression settled between her softly arched brows. "Since I don't know which one you're looking at, how am I supposed to know where it was taken?" she grated out, clearly piqued with him.

Mark ripped his heat-filled gaze away from the photograph just long enough to send her a suggestive smile. "You on a beach, half-dressed in some kind of dark blue bikini and wraparound skirt thing." He paused to look back at the photo, adding, "Shells around your ankles and one wrist, with a big, pink flower in your hair."

"Tahiti," she grumbled, holding out her slim hand. "Please give it back, Mark."

The sound of her saying his name sent a warm curl of satisfaction through his body, matching the wave of pulsing heat the sight of her sexy bod on a beach in Tahiti had delivered to his cock, and he found himself shaking his head, pushing the photograph into the back pocket of his jeans. "I don't think so, Mel."

Her eyes dropped to where his now empty hand rested against his thigh, thumb hooked into his front pocket. "What are you doing?"

"Keeping it."

"You can't," she sputtered, leaning forward in her chair. "You can't just *keep* it!"

"Why not?" he challenged, enjoying the flash of fire — of need — of keen, blazing desire in her eyes, the way her pulse hammered in the base of her throat, her eyes round and wild, skin warm with heat. He wanted to run his tongue over that sensitive female flesh and watch it burn brighter beneath his hungry exploration. Wanted to sip from her until her taste replaced that of every other woman he'd ever known. Wanted to consume the sweet promises of her body and her heart.

Man, he had it so bad, he was becoming poetic, and he hadn't even kissed her yet. It was pathetic.

"You can't keep it because we're strangers, that's why," he heard her explaining, and he struggled to pull his mind up from his cock head and back into the head on his shoulders, where it belonged. "And strangers don't let strangers confiscate pictures of them in bikinis."

"If they don't, then they sure as hell should," he shot back with a hard smile, knowing his narrowed eyes glittered with excitement that he was having a hell of a time trying to hide. "And we don't feel like strangers, Melanie Green. I say 'Hi' to you every morning at the coffee shop, and you blush at me. I stare at you every second I have during the day, and you sit here pretending not to notice. Hell, we have more interaction than half the couples I know."

She arched a suspicious brow, cheeks going crimson again at his words. "You know couples?"

"A few."

"Hmm..." she murmured, narrowing her cinnamon-colored eyes as she studied him.

"What's that supposed to mean?" he asked, arching his brow at the assessing way she was looking at him.

She sucked the plump pad of her lower lip through her teeth, and this time Mark actually felt his cock pulse in response to the action, his damn eyes nearly crossing as something hot and hungry seemed to uncurl inside him, stretching its claws, the knot of his tightly leashed control unraveling more with every second that passed by.

"It's just that you don't look like the type to hang out with guys chained down by domestic bliss."

His shoulders shook with silent laughter. "Well, now, that all depends on how one's using the chains, sweetheart."

And just like that, her blush bloomed deeper, like spreading wildfire across her creamy skin, and he could have sworn she went pink from head to toe. A bright, blushing rose that flared down the slim, pale column of her throat, slipping across the enticing expanse of her lightly freckled chest before dipping into the modestly cut neckline of her pale pink silk blouse. It made him want to kiss her all over, tasting that rosy glow on the eager pad of his tongue as he worked his way up from her cute little toes, not stopping until he reached the lush pink promise of her wide, giving mouth.

"Have dinner with me tonight. Right now," he suddenly rumbled into the heavy quiet of the office, the only sound that of their breathing and the gentle hum of a fax machine as it worked softly in the corner. His words weren't a request, so much as a statement of intent. It was already after five, and no way in hell did he think he could turn around and walk away from her before taking things a step farther. Before somehow discovering a way to stake his claim.

"What?" She blinked up at him as if he'd asked her to explain the theory of relativity while patting her head and rubbing her tummy.

"If it's the 'strangers' bit making you nervous around me, have dinner with me, and then we won't be strangers," he explained with a casual shrug of his shoulders, trying not to sound pushy, when he longed to demand a yes from her. "Though, if you ask me, I don't see how two people who've known each other for six months can still be considered strangers to begin with."

She licked her lower lip again with the tip of her tongue, and Mark actually wondered if he was going to end up with the imprint of his zipper permanently embossed on his dick as he struggled to keep the damn thing from going hard as a spike.

"I doubt I could eat anything," she finally laughed out on a ragged sigh. "To be honest, I think you'd only make me more nervous at dinner."

"Then we'll sip on a few beers to get you relaxed and just talk before we order any food."

She went perfectly still, not even blinking. "Talk?" she whispered with an odd look in her eyes, repeating the word as if he'd said something dirty.

Huh—and here all those women's magazines complained that men were pigs for never conversing enough. No wonder his sex had such a hell of a time figuring out what women wanted. Even they didn't know what it was!

"Yeah, talk, as in conversation. Man and woman and beer and beach." *And I can try to keep my damn hands off you, instead of dragging you to the sand, pulling you beneath me, and digging in as deep as I can get.* Clearing his throat, he prayed she wouldn't notice the growing bulge behind his fly before he got his traitorous body part under control.

"It'll be great. Come on," he coaxed, trying not to sound like he was pleading, searching for his most charming smile, when all he really wanted was to toss her over his shoulder and get her ass home, in his bed, before he exploded from lust. He rubbed one hand across the tense muscles at the back of his neck, and said, "I'm not taking no for an answer, Mel."

Talk...talk...talk, Melanie thought with a bitter, foul-tasting surge of disappointment. He wasn't after hot, wild, romping sex after all, despite the wonderful way he'd been flirting with her since walking through the front door. But she should have known. Hadn't she learned enough from past mistakes with gorgeous guys like Mark Logan? They flirted with women—with *all* women—because that was just the way they were. They enjoyed making women feel good about themselves. They didn't do it to be jerks or to shatter hearts, even though they often left a field of heartbroken casualties in their wake. If she was going to survive this date intact, she'd have to remember that no matter how outrageously he acted with her, the most logical scenario here was that he really did just want some friendly female companionship. A smiling face to "talk" to, and god only knew, that was her.

Not that she would ever turn down the chance to spend time with him—even if all he wanted was to talk—but there was a fire of determination burning in her belly that said she should at least *try* to make him want more than conversation from her. What the hell could it hurt, since she was already seriously in deep with her feelings for this man? Problem was, she wasn't even at her best right now. She was a mess.

Melanie looked down at her rumpled silk shirt and wrinkled skirt, her mouth twisting with heartfelt regret, knowing she probably wouldn't ever get a chance like this again. By tomorrow or the next day, some gorgeous beach vixen would grab his attention, and he would forget all about wanting to sit and "talk" with boring little Melanie Green.

"I'd like that, Mark, but I'm not really dressed to go out anywhere," she replied, wishing she'd known this moment was coming so she could have been better prepared. "I'm pretty much a wreck after working in the back all day. We had stacks of unopened brochure stock to put away, and the printers in the tech room were either jammed or out of toner."

"You look perfect," he said with a wicked twist of his lips that she supposed could pass for a smile, if it didn't look so damn carnal and sexy. The burning look of intensity in those soft green eyes almost convinced her of his honesty. But then she reminded herself that he was a natural born flirt. Yeah, that had to be it. Why else would the guy have confiscated her picture?

"Hey, there's no pressure here. Really. We can just grab some Mexican food over on *Cazadora's* patio, drink some Coronas, and then we can take a walk out on the beach and watch the sunset."

"Um, okay, then," she gave in with a grin, unable to resist that gentle urging in his warm green gaze, no matter how breathless she was with anticipation. And it was that air of expectation that had her worried, knowing she was getting worked up over something that was so *not* going to be an issue. He wanted to talk, for god's sake, not ride her silly. And yeah, it might sound crude, damn it, but she wanted the ride. She wanted it all. Good conversation and heart-stopping sex, all wrapped up in the heady emotions of unquestionable trust and undying love.

Hey, it's not like I'm asking for much, she snickered silently to herself, wondering when she'd become so deranged. It wasn't like she was a knockout who had men dragging their tongues around after her, and here she'd set her sights and emotions on the most undeniably sexy, funny, interesting hunk of stud meat that she'd ever laid eyes on.

"Oh god," she groaned under her breath, "I'm starting to think like Kyra."

"What'd you say, honey?"

"Um, just give me two seconds to change into my flats." She reached down and slipped out of her heels, then grabbed her favorite pair of leather sandals from where she kept them stashed in her bottom desk drawer for walking to and from work, since her cute, new little beachfront apartment was just a few blocks away. Then she stood and came around the desk, throwing her purse over her shoulder.

When she stood just a foot or so away in her sandals, it became terribly obvious how he towered over her five-four frame. Hell, she barely came to his collarbone. He looked down at her, those sexy green eyes shining with humor, and tipped the edge of her chin up with his fist.

"I never really realized how petite you are," he said in a low, intimate voice that seemed to curl around her shoulders like a lover's hands, skimming over her fluttering pulse in the base of her throat, trailing up the tender side of her neck, "since we've never stood this close together before."

She shook her head and tried to refocus. "You mean short," she laughed, swallowing a knot of fierce, unleashed emotion at that smoldering look in his eyes. Man, this guy was good. He damn near had her buying the whole "you're a sex goddess" look burning there in his glittering green gaze.

"Cute?" he ventured with that boyish twist of his lips that melted her deep down inside, where it counted.

"You're not helping yourself." Melanie shook her head slowly from side to side, while a warm glow burned in her chest, radiating out in an exhilarating wash of breathless anticipation that tingled in her fingertips and toes.

"Then I'll have to try harder and just admit that..."

His voice suddenly trailed off, leaving those last words unsaid as he continued to stare down at her, those carnal lips parted for the slow soughing of his breath.

"That what?" she prompted, feeling her own breath come more rapidly, heart beating out a heavy cadence of excitement. When he looked at her like that, she could almost believe that maybe he *was* looking for more than just a gal pal to talk to. Could almost imagine that she made him nervous—that he wanted to shatter that infuriating air of innocence hanging over her head and teach her a lesson in corruption that she'd been craving since setting eyes on him.

"What were you going to say, Mark?"

Staring up at him, Melanie knew she'd failed at disguising the longing in her voice, when his jaw tightened and his nostrils flared just that barest bit, like a predator scenting its mate. *Oh man, I wish!* she silently groaned. A warm rush of wet, slippery heat washed through her sex, and she struggled not to take the few steps forward that would bring her into burning contact with all that hard, hot, rippling muscle.

He twisted his mouth with resignation. "If I tell you the truth, I might scare you away before we've even cleared the door."

"Oh, I doubt that," she said with total honesty, tilting her face to the side as she studied him, wishing she could see inside his mind. "You might make me nervous, Mark, but you don't scare me."

He stepped closer, and the pulse in the base of her throat jumped. "In that case, I was going to say that I think I'm going to love the way you fit against me."

"Oh," she breathed out on a small laugh. Forget good. When it came to making a woman feel like she mattered, this man deserved a freaking medal. "And you thought that would scare me off?"

That green gaze narrowed at her expression, as if he'd like the chance to get inside her mind, too. "Trust me, I'm trying so hard to be good here, Mel, but it isn't easy."

"I don't think you could actually be bad," she drawled as a slow smile spread across her mouth.

A rough, male sound jerked in his throat. "Sweetheart, you have no idea."

She pressed her tongue against her lower lip the way she did when she was nervous, and his eyes narrowed, following the action with such heat that she swore she could feel it spiraling down into her core, setting the secrets of her body to a low, molten burn of sharp, sizzling desire. She started to speak, but before she could respond to that leading statement, he cut her off, saying, "Let's get the hell out of here before I make an ass of myself and prove just how bad I can be."

He wanted to prove his outrageous claims? Man, now there was something she would love to see. With her tummy doing that funny little spiral thing again, she swallowed — all nerves and excitement. Twice. And then a third time. When she finally thought she could form a coherent sentence, Melanie murmured, "Just let me say bye to Kyra. She's in the back."

Chapter Three

A few minutes later, after a fast recount of what had just happened between her and Mark Logan, followed by some hilarious innuendos, eye-opening advice, and wishes for good luck from Kyra, Melanie finally joined Mark at the front door. She was still unable to believe that she was heading out on a date with the most gorgeous, virile, sinfully sexy man she'd ever known...and he wanted to "talk" to her instead of jumping her bones.

Gaack.

Plastering on her smile, she supposed she could only hope for the best and pray he'd be hit by an uncontrollable bolt of lust before the night was over.

"Kyra's going to lock up for me. Oh, and she asked if you wouldn't mind telling Cain to shove his smart-ass head into the beer cooler next time you see him."

He rumbled with laughter, holding the door for her as she stepped out into the heavy heat of the late afternoon sun, and then moved to her side, one hand at the small of her back, guiding her through a tangle of tourists as they headed down the street to *Caza's*.

The heat of his palm against her lower back was delicious, and Melanie almost moaned with regret when he pulled it away after they cleared the crowd. Seeking a subject to pull her horny thoughts away from the stud at her side, she asked, "Who's watching your bar?"

"None other than my smart-ass brother," he grinned. "What's up with those two anyway?"

She rolled her eyes. "Cain and Kyra? I'm almost afraid to even hazard a guess."

"I get the impression that they don't get along."

"Yeah, it's kinda hard to miss, isn't it?" she said with a wry laugh, catching at her flying hair to hook it behind her ears as the gusty wind whipped it around her face, the light silk of her skirt flapping frantically at her legs. "But I don't know all the details. I'll have to ask her. I didn't even know they really knew each other."

"Honey, in a town this size, everyone knows everyone."

She shot him a grinning look. "Are we back to that 'not being strangers' thing?"

"I just hope that you don't, you know, believe everything you might have heard about me," he murmured in that deep, whiskey-rich voice that always made her blood race with sinful sensation. "I've lived in Foggy Bottom my entire life, so the gossips have had years to make meals out of me."

Twin bright spots of color seemed to burn across the sexy arc of his cheekbones as she peeked at him from the corner of her eye, and she couldn't stop the playful smile from teasing at her lips. "You mean...things specifically about *you*? Such as your, um, reputation?"

"Oh hell, I don't even want to know what you've heard," he muttered. His pale green eyes cut a sharp look at her, dark brows drawn together in a scowl. "Just don't buy into any of it."

"Hmm...so you think the rumors are, um, exaggerated?" she mused thoughtfully, striving for an angelic look. "I did have my doubts. I mean, when little ol' Mrs. McGilley at the flower shop started going on about your incredible technique, and how long and strong and solid your—"

"She what?" he choked, stopping in the middle of the sidewalk with a stunned look of disbelief stamped across his rugged features. "*Mrs. McGilley?*"

"*Oak bar* is, I couldn't believe that you'd actually carved the entire thing by hand," she drawled with absolute innocence, turning back to him with a blank expression, though she was pretty damn sure her eyes were glittering with mischief.

"You little minx," he growled playfully, shaking his dark head as he caught up to her. His green gaze narrowed, burning with a physical threat of retribution. "You did that on purpose."

Melanie scrunched her nose at him, loving that mischievous grin curving the hard beauty of his mouth, more than ready to accept any form of so-called punishment he might decide to dole out, so long as it was centered around her pleasure. "Well, how could you blame me? It was too tempting to resist."

"I'll get you back, you know. And it's only fair, since I haven't been treated to any juicy gossip about you."

Melanie rolled her eyes. "Oh, gee, thanks. Is that a polite way of saying that I'm an old stick-in-the-mud?"

A gruff sound of humor rumbled up from his chest. "No, that would be my way of saying that you've apparently been much better at being circumspect in your private life than I have."

"Ah…and what on Earth am I supposed to say to that? If I try to defend myself, then I come off sounding like someone seeking the attention of the town busybodies. And if I don't, then you'll think I really *am* boring. It's a catch-22 of the worst sort."

"Melanie, honey, I don't know how anyone could ever think you're boring. You've made me laugh more in the past fifteen minutes than I have in the last fifteen years."

She sent him a pained look as they neared the fresco-covered front of the restaurant, the patio already bustling with several large groups sipping frosty margaritas and soaking down ice-cold Coronas in the nearly stifling heat.

"I hate to have to be the one to enlighten you, Mark, but making a man laugh is only a compliment if you've purposefully set out to do so. Embarrassment doesn't count," she laughed, as he reached around her to push open the iron scrollwork gate that separated *Caza's* patio from the sidewalk. His heat, so close to her body, was breathtaking, but before she could truly enjoy the heady sensation, a strong gust of wind threatened to blow up the back of her skirt and expose her panty-covered bum. Mel shrieked, twisting as she tried to catch the diaphanous length of flying material, only to have the gate slam shut, whacking her on the rear, and slamming her into the front of Mark's hard, hot, impossibly yummy bod. For the span of a second, her lungs froze in shock, then sensation slowly began creeping back into her system and she realized two things at once. Mark Logan had an erection, and the palm of her hand was plastered against the heavy seam of his fly...his even heavier cock resting thickly behind the faded denim.

How it had happened, she wasn't sure. One minute she'd been catching at her skirt, and the next thing she knew the gate had sent her reeling into him. Her hand must have turned to brace her fall...and *wham*, she found herself copping a feel of the most impressive hard-on she'd ever encountered. Not that she'd *encountered* all that many, dang it...but this one had to be legendary by any standard. And growing more remarkable by the moment.

Nibbling on the corner of her lip, she took a deep, Mark-filled breath, taking that intoxicating scent of male heat into her body, and slowly raised her eyes to his. The playful glint in his thick-lashed gaze instantly flared into a harsh, feral look of sexual promise, every long, muscled inch of his powerful body going utterly still at the accidental contact, and neither of them moved to pull away. He stared down at her, those light green eyes smoldering and mysterious, as if lit from within with a burning, brilliant flame. His nostrils flared, black brows brought together in a fierce look of...intent? The beautiful shape of his mouth compressed into a hard, uncompromising line while his chest moved with the rough cadence of his slow breathing. Her mind screamed for her hand to move, but her body refused to obey the command. Instead, her fingers formed an open fist, cradling him, and the fire in his gaze went impossibly brighter, even as his lids lowered and a deep, husky sound of hunger vibrated up from the depths of his chest.

With their gazes locked, her hand sandwiched between the erotically charged press of their bodies, Melanie felt him slowly push forward, increasing the heady pressure, and the bulge behind that worn denim pulsed within her palm. It felt so delicious it made her mouth water, and she moaned a low, provocative sound of want, flexing her fingers against his fascinating shape.

"Ah shit," Mark growled down at her, suddenly catching her around the waist and pulling her into a small hallway that led to the restaurant's restrooms. "What about this, Mel? Does this count?" he demanded in a ragged voice, pulling her trembling length into the animal heat of his body, as he rubbed his wicked mouth against her tingling lips with one slow, teasing pass, followed immediately by another.

Holy hell. Melanie gasped, reeling from the chaotic, breathtaking sweep of sensations, thinking she'd die from the pleasure, right there, pressed against the Spanish-tiled wall between brightly painted doors reading *Caballeros* and *Damas*. She experienced an utter, complete, devastating sensual meltdown as the rough-silk texture of his lips rubbed over her mouth, his warm, enticing masculine flavor flooding her system. She made a sharp, hungry sound in the back of her throat, and went in for a deeper kiss, clasping the bronzed curve of his cheeks within the damp heat of her palms as she fitted her mouth against his, their lips and teeth smashing together. Riding the sharp edge of passion, she pressed her tongue into the dark heat of his mouth, and he growled into her, taking control of the kiss and thrusting his tongue past her lips to seek out the textures hidden within. He stroked over the smooth enamel of her teeth, the sensitive pad of her tongue, and Mel could have sworn she heard herself whimper in frantic, sexual urgency.

They were both breathless, panting, forcing harsh, laboring breaths into each other as their mouths battled for dominance in a kiss that was quickly raging out of control. She pressed against him...hard...and was rewarded by the even harder feel of all those long, strong muscles and the hot, male intensity of his big body as he gripped her upper arms and lifted her against the wall. She hung suspended, one sandal sliding off a dangling foot, and then he slammed into her softness, pushing, trapping her against the colorfully tiled wall, the mouthwatering bulge of his swollen cock locked against the warm, silk-covered vee of her thighs, where she was growing slippery and wet.

Melanie jolted from the sensory overload of stimulation, silent and still for the single beat of a second, before she heard herself make another needy sound, this one like a shivering purr. Something dark and dangerous-sounding rumbled up from him in response, vibrating against the swell of her breasts where they were mashed against that solid wall of his muscled chest, his hard, impossibly long, brutally thick erection digging into her fluttering stomach. He was so solid and hot, searing her front, and she breathed in huge, addictive lungfuls of his musky, sun-kissed scent, clutching at the powerful, roped muscles of his forearms as he gripped her tighter.

"Mark," she moaned, her body feverish and full with a twisting, voluptuous need that seemed to take up all of her, fill her completely from the bottom to the top, until she was heavy and aching, needing the physical promise of pleasure only he could deliver. She knew, because no other man had ever come close to making her feel so much mind-shattering passion, and all he'd done was kiss her. She gasped for breath as he thrust his imposing jeans-covered cock into the giving softness of her belly and bit at her lower lip, the action utterly provocative and male—and then suddenly he stopped, not even breathing, and a terrible tension gripped the warm river of hope washing through her blood.

She went cold, shivering, and carefully released his arms, dangling there in midair against the wall, her toes not even touching the floor.

"Don't...move," he gritted in her ear, forcing the words through his clenched teeth, deep voice dark and tortured, burying his face in her neck as he slowly, in careful degrees of movement, pulled his heavily aroused body back from hers, until at least an inch separated them. He breathed roughly against the sensitive skin beneath her ear, and she trembled, unable to stop the telltale action.

"Why'd you stop?" she whispered, a little shocked by her question, when it seemed rather obvious. They were in a public place, and anyone could have looked into the little hallway and witnessed them going at one another with so much blatant hunger. *That would definitely have the gossips gabbing about her*, she thought with a hysterical inner laugh. But she didn't care, because all that mattered in that moment was that Mark Logan had kissed her like she was the last woman on Earth—like he wanted to consume her—and then he'd stopped, as if shocked by what he'd done.

And suddenly Melanie realized that he'd simply reacted out of instinct. After all, she'd had her hand on the poor guy's crotch, copping a feel of his jeans-covered penis. Sheesh, no wonder he'd kissed her! God, she was hopeless. Here she'd just experienced the most insanely sexy kiss she'd ever had in her entire thirty-one years, and all because she'd accidentally felt a guy up. If it wasn't so damn heartbreaking, she knew she'd have been laughing her ass off.

"I'm...sorry," he finally muttered, lowering her to her feet and moving completely away, until he stood with his back against the opposite wall, his expression shuttered, mouth bruised and wet from her kisses.

"Don't worry about it," she croaked out of a dry throat, trying to ignore the sudden, tearing little rip of pain his words caused, even though she'd been expecting them.

"Christ," he said on a deep, ragged breath, still not meeting her eyes as his jaw worked with frustration and his hands clenched and unclenched at his sides. "I swear that's not what I was looking for when I asked you out tonight, Melanie."

"No, of course it wasn't," she said in a soft, faraway voice, wanting to laugh at herself almost as much as she wanted to cry. Damn her stupid, idiotic fantasies and traitorous sex drive. Maybe she should just become a nun. Well, first she'd have to take care of the whole Catholic requirement, but *then* she was becoming a nun, damn it. She might as well. She sure as hell wasn't having much luck getting laid. Too bad there was only one man she wanted for the job, because he definitely didn't seem too keen on the idea. No, if Mark Logan's reaction to kissing her was anything to go by, the idea of sleeping with her didn't rank very high on his list.

Obviously *that* wasn't what he was looking for, despite the outrageous flirting he'd done back in her office, stealing the picture of her in the bikini and making up all that nonsense about being nervous around her just to make her feel better.

She took a quick peek at his hard face, and wasn't sure who was more upset. Feeling the need to soothe, when all she really wanted to do was grab hold of him and never let go, she forced a grin and said, "Let's just forget about it and grab a table, okay?" The bright smile she plastered on her face felt so brittle, she was amazed she didn't crack, and from the look on his face, she wasn't too sure he was buying it. Before he could open his mouth and crush her even more, she took off around the corner, thankful when she heard him moving behind her, following her to the corner table she chose that bordered the soft sand of the beach. The raging breeze played savagely over the rolling dunes of the golden, Pacific Coast shoreline, washing away the evidence of countless footsteps over its giving surface, erasing their existence as if they'd never been — and Melanie wished the same could be done to the tender, passion-starved landscape of her heart.

* * * * *

Seconds later, Mark found himself taking a chair across from Melanie, and he met her guarded gaze squarely, determined not to hide from her anger. But instead of looking irritated or disgusted with him for all but mauling her back there in that cozy hallway, she looked…disappointed. His gut clenched at the expression on her precious, freckled face. Damn, maybe she was disappointed with him—with the fact that he had the control of a cockroach when it came to her, but what the hell did she expect? She was gorgeous and giving, gentle and soft, and everything about her just made him want to fall all over her, plundering that innocent aura with the brutal intensity and pent-up frustration of his need for her.

Not to mention the fact that she'd practically had his cock in her hand.

In fact, she hadn't appeared put off by his aggression when he'd all but nailed her to the wall. No—she'd dove right in and tangled tongues with him as if she were starving for his taste, and he found himself suddenly off balance again. He, a man who *always* knew how to handle a woman. Yet this shy little travel agent had him twisted up in so many knots, he didn't know what the hell was going on. All he knew for certain was that he wanted her.

Two frosted Coronas with lime were brought to their table moments after he signaled Carlos, one of *Caza's* longtime fixtures. He sent her an easy grin and tipped his bottle against hers, retreating to safer ground. "So, at the risk of sounding totally lame, why don't you tell me all about yourself, Melanie Green?"

She slanted him a dry look. "I thought you wanted to have a good time, Mark, not listen to me bore you to tears. Why don't we talk about you instead?"

He leaned back in his chair and sent her a genuine smile, in spite of the raw ache throbbing behind the fly of his jeans. "Uh-uh. I want to hear about you." Lowering his voice to an intimate, seductive pitch, he murmured, "I want to learn all the dirty little secrets about Melanie Green that no one else in Foggy Bottom Beach knows."

"Then I'm afraid this is going to be the world's shortest conversation," she drawled, a small crease forming between her fine brows as the corners of her mouth tipped into a wry frown. "And you're going to be sadly disappointed."

"Not gonna happen, sweetheart, so you might as well start at the beginning."

She laughed softly, and he wanted to press his lips against that small furrow between her brows to reassure her.

Oh hell, who was he kidding? He wanted to toss her up on the wooden table, rip that damn sexy skirt away, and shove his face in her pretty little pussy until she was screaming and clawing, coming all over him, begging him to fuck her hard and deep...and forever. For several torturous seconds, Mark lost himself in thoughts of what color her nipples would be, the silky lips of her sex, and the drenched, satin folds hidden within. Pale and pink, blushing crimson, or flushed with the deep, bruised rose of her lush, plump mouth?

Damn, he swore beneath his breath, feeling a trickle of sweat trail down his spine, the meandering bead all but steaming against the feral heat of his skin.

She'd tasted delicious, like innocence and sin, all honeyed and sweet, and he couldn't wait to taste the warm spill of her juices as they slipped from her tender little cunt. Couldn't wait to feel the velvety texture of her nipples against his tongue as he pounded his way to heaven, cramming himself deep inside her. Deeper than he'd ever been inside a woman, until she surrounded him and was all that he knew. Until he was wrapped up tight in her soft, sweet scents and tastes, held within the clutching grasp of her legs and her arms, and her rippling pussy.

She was so slight and small...and he knew the tight, silky grip of her body as he fucked her, the gentle cushion of her full breasts and soft thighs pressed against the carnal heat of his flesh while he moved within her, would be more than enough to blow his mind. To rip his legendary control completely from his grasp, and leave him at the mercy of everything she made him feel.

Christ, this woman really did it to him, and he made a mental note to go easy on the beer or he'd lose his head altogether. He was already flying on a dangerous natural high. God only knew he didn't need any additional stimulants to add to the heavy, heady sensations.

He blinked against the bright orange flame of the setting sun on the distant horizon, its vibrant fire turning the gray-blue waters of the Pacific to a roiling, molten gold, and suddenly realized that she'd been talking to him while he'd been lost in thoughts of taking her.

Of controlling her pleasure. Of claiming her for his own.

Damn, was he a glutton for punishment or what?

Clearing his throat, Mark took a long swallow of beer, and said, "What was that, honey?"

Carlos set their hot tortilla chips on the table with a side of freshly made salsa, and Melanie took a salty chip as she gave her best effort at a grin and said, "Just remember you asked for this."

"I sure did," he drawled with a slow, meaningful smile that had her blinking at him, her cheeks flushing with another wave of heat. *And I'll be asking for a hell of a lot more, when you're finally ready,* he silently groaned, wanting to ask for everything right then, at that very moment. Instead, he sat back and listened as she began telling hilarious stories about the places she'd traveled, Kyra's possessed computer in the office, and how much she enjoyed living on the coast. Within no time at all, they were laughing and eating and drinking their beers, enjoying themselves too much to worry about being nervous or shy or horny. Well, he was still horny as hell, but Mark suspected that would be a condition that he'd always suffer in her presence, and damn, but if he didn't look forward to it.

They finished their meals, eating off one another's plates with the intimacy of longtime lovers, as the restaurant became crowded and the noise level around them grew, while strings of tiny dazzling lights sparkled overhead, swaying in the breeze. There was a brief scuffle over the check, as he steadfastly refused to let her pay and she called him a chauvinistic bully, only relenting when he threatened to buy her a serenade from the smiling trio roaming among the tables. Then, with the sun preparing for its breathtaking finale on the horizon, they took off their shoes and headed for the cool, crisp, golden sand.

Chapter Four

Side by side, they walked in the surf, with the cold Pacific frothing around their ankles while the sun-warmed breeze tossed their hair, and Mark found himself telling Melanie Green things that he'd never told anyone else. Certainly not any of the women he'd known, no matter how intimately. They talked of his childhood, growing up with his dad and Cain, his mom having bailed out when he was only four and Cain was nine. He told her about his Dad's attempts to keep him and Cain on the straight and narrow, and how he spent a nightmare summer at a boy's disciplinary camp after borrowing his Dad's car for a joyride at fourteen, nearly killing himself, but thankfully not harming anyone when he wrapped the car around a tree.

Melanie listened with genuine interest, as if she honestly cared, never judging when he was honest about mistakes he'd made as a hotheaded know-it-all in his younger years, and yet not making excuses either. She was steady and real and warm at his side, and it took some prodding, but she finally opened up to tell him more about growing up in a small town in Northern California, with a close-knit family that still got together for holidays. He asked about school, and before long she was recounting more hilarious tales of mishaps during the two years she'd spent at community college, before finally settling on her career and getting her degree in Hospitality and Tourism, because of her love for travel.

And with those gentle openings, Mark felt himself falling farther into another person than he'd ever thought possible. Deeper and deeper, until feelings that had been wrapped up in lust and hunger and keening physical awareness began churning with more emotional want, as if everything inside him was bleeding together, and the raw-edged power of absolute need for this woman became sharper. More defined. More alive. Something he could all but taste on the air, sense through the coursing of his blood. Emotions and desire became tangled into intricate, spellbinding knots, so that it was difficult to determine one from the other, and he marveled at the strange closeness pulling them together. Closer...and then closer, until finally her side was pressed to his, his arm looping around her lower back, securing her against him as they walked through the lapping surf beneath the glittering stars and rising moon, her sandals hanging loosely from one hand.

Mark had known from the start that what he felt for this woman was special, but now he understood its permanence upon his soul, and the fear of screwing it up became a tangible thing.

When the sun finally fell and the breeze blew cool off the vast expanse of the endless Pacific, he steered them back up Main Street, the old-fashioned, newly restored gas lamps lighting their way, setting the shadows of the night alight with a flickering, golden glow. As they neared the open windows of his bar, they could hear the live blues band that played every Friday night, accompanied by voices and laughter, flowing into the cool breeze that surrounded them.

With a sly smile, he took Melanie's hand and pulled her over to the open window that looked into the bustling workspace behind the bar. Nodding his head toward the long, gleaming length of hand-carved wood, its opposite side packed with locals and tourists sipping on everything from wine to beer, many even dining on the tasty fare he offered from his kitchen, Mark lowered his mouth to the dainty shell of her ear and whispered, "What do you think of my handiwork, Miss Green? Does it live up to its reputation?"

A teasing glint danced in the burnished depths of her eyes, and he found himself looking forward to her response with a warm, vivid rush of anticipation.

And she didn't disappoint him.

"You know," she said thoughtfully, pursing her lips, "I'm tempted to say that when you've seen one, you've seen them all."

"Ooh, you're brutal, sweetheart." He winced dramatically, though the effect was ruined since he couldn't stop the choked laughter rumbling up from his chest.

"Although, to be fair," she mused, head tilting slightly to the side as she put on a show of studying the gleaming bar, "I should point out the rather obvious fact that yours *does* seem significantly larger than others that I've...er...examined."

Mark raised his brows, the corners of his mouth kicking up in a purely wicked grin of satisfaction, refusing to make a comment on *that* one, certain he'd find himself issuing her an offer guaranteed to get him into a shitload of trouble. Especially in light of the fact that he was determined to be on his best behavior with her tonight.

"Of course, from its size," she drawled, her expression one of pure innocence, even though her eyes were shining with mischievous delight, "I can only gather that you must be exceptionally good with your hands. And it looks so well cared for. Honestly, I wouldn't be surprised to learn that you...um, stroke it down a good ten to fifteen times a day."

"Oh shit." This time he couldn't keep the deep rumble of laughter inside, shaking his head at her outrageousness. "You win that round, you little minx."

"Well, you started it," she grinned, fluttering her lashes at him. "What is it they say about, 'If you can't stand the heat'?"

"But I'm already going up in flames," he murmured so softly, he wasn't entirely certain that she'd heard him, until she ducked her head, a small smile playing at the edge of her mouth. A heavy, charged silence pulsed between them for the span of a single second...then two, three, four...until Cain finally finished filling an order of cosmos for a group of locals. Mark snagged his attention when he looked in their direction, thankful for the distraction. "Two Heinekens, old man," he called out with a shit-eating grin.

Cain mouthed a "fuck you" at him, and then sent his killer smile at Mel, the one that made most women go all gooey inside, and she smiled back, sending a strange shaft of possession through Mark's blood that he'd never felt with another woman. Damn, and he'd sure as hell never been jealous of his brother before, but this was pushing it close. Too close. He captured her hand again and squeezed her fingers in a gentle hold, pulling her closer to his side while Cain grabbed their drinks, a knowing look in the bastard's deep blue eyes that made Mark want to clobber him.

But then there was Mel kind of melting against his hip, and the sudden flare of jealousy was lost beneath a savage surge of satisfaction, even when Cain started walking toward them and she was still sending the handsome ass that sweet smile that never failed to make Mark want to fuck her. Hell, who was he kidding? All she had to do was breathe and he was aching and ready to take her to the first available surface for a long, hard, mind-shattering ride.

"Hey Mel," Cain called out, his voice booming and loud to be heard over the pulsing beat of the smoky music as he neared the window. "What do I have to do to convince you to ditch my baby brother and run away with a real man, beautiful?"

Mark sent a warning look at Cain, but Melanie just laughed, squeezing the arm he had secured around her waist as she tilted her face up to his, her smile reaching her eyes with a luminous shimmer of warm, heart-melting humor. "What do you think, Mark? Should I ditch you for an older man?"

Cain smiled, saluting her with a bottle before setting them on the window ledge. "Men are like wine, sweetheart. We only improve with age."

A slow grin curved her mouth as she reached for her beer. "If only women were so lucky," she murmured dryly, then gave his brother an appraising gaze, much like the one she had used on his bar, and in a husky purr that had both men blinking in sensual surprise, she said, "Your offer does sound interesting, though. Especially seeing as how Mark has decided to save his amorous affections for all the other lucky gals in Foggy Bottom Beach."

Her tone had been teasing, and yet, Mark had noted a sharper edge to the words that gave him pause. Had Melanie totally misread him earlier, when he broke off that mind-drugging kiss in the hallway at *Caza's*? *Shit*. He'd only been trying to prove that he was looking for more than a meaningless fling with her. Trying to make it clear that he wasn't just looking to work his way into her pants—even though he wanted in there so damn badly it was making him crazed, like he had some kind of wicked jungle fever that he couldn't shake. But she sounded as if she didn't believe he was interested in her at all. *Fuck*.

Cain sent him a questioning look, but there didn't seem to be a damn thing he could say at the moment, especially with his older brother watching him like a shark. A flare of male disgust flashed through Cain's sky blue gaze, and he snorted, cutting his baby blues back to Melanie. "I was always smarter than this little runt, anyway, sweetheart. And I can promise you that interesting is only the beginning," he drawled with more charm than Mark had ever seen the conniving wolf use on a woman. "Just think of the vast *experience* I have on Marky boy here."

Her eyebrows arched, cheeks going pink at the all-too-carnal look glittering in Cain's eyes, and yet she didn't cower or try to rush off, and Mark realized that she was more than comfortable holding her own with his brother. Obviously she was at ease talking to men, and her awkward shyness only came with him, which made him want to crawl inside her mind to find out why. Did it mean that she wanted something more from him? That she might actually be interested in wanting a whole hell of a lot with him? Damn, he wished like hell that he knew what was going on inside that beautiful little head of hers. And the irony of the situation didn't escape him. He was used to being able to read a woman's needs without effort—it was second nature to him—but trying to read Melanie was like attempting to translate a foreign language that he didn't speak. She was a mystery, multifaceted and brilliant, her tender innocence and provocative allure combining to create a devastating blow to his system.

"How...*tempting*," she replied, the word rolling off her tongue in a tone that perfectly matched Cain's teasing one. With an impish grin, she added, "No wonder all the ladies taking classes down at the station are in love with you. All that *experience* must make you a wonderful instructor."

Cain threw back his head and roared with laughter, while Mark found himself muttering, "Over my dead body."

Melanie sent him a questioning look, while Cain braced his hands on the ledge and leaned forward. "Don't let him scare you off, honey," he said huskily, smiling as he sent her a devilish wink. "He's just still sore over the cheerleader I snagged away from him back in his college days. I took pity on the runt, in the end, though, and shared some of the evil genius of my wicked ways with him. Thanks to me, he's not a total lost cause when it comes to pleasing a woman."

One slim golden brow arched in humor. "And that's going to help me how?" she laughed. "Last time I checked, friends didn't let friends..." Her voice trailed off, leaving the rest unsaid.

"Well, if they don't, they sure as hell should," Cain laughed. "And if Marky boy here doesn't measure up, you know where to find me, sweetheart."

"Enough," Mark gritted out. "Stop poaching on my date, damn it."

"She said you were just friends," Cain answered defensively, the look in eyes daring him to disagree.

"Cain," he said in a low, warning rasp, "shove it."

A Little Less Conversation

The irreverent ass grabbed her hand and pressed a slow kiss to the inside of her wrist, precisely over the point of her pulse, and Mark choked on a growl when he saw her slender fingers curl into her palm from the sensation. Then the smug bastard winked at her as she laughed, and he found himself grinding his back teeth.

"I'll be back later to help you close up," he practically snarled, all but dragging a laughing Melanie away as Cain snickered knowingly behind them, heading back to the customers at the bar.

"Your brother's a riot," she said into the quiet stillness of the night, as the music faded behind them. The flickering glow of the gas lamps softly punctuated the thickening darkness, while the distant surf churned softly, the sea-salty tang of the ocean washing over them in the gentle, sultry breeze.

"He is that, all right," he agreed with a wry twist to his lips. "Not to mention a royal pain in the ass."

"I think he just likes picking on you. Kyra does the same to me."

"Yeah? Then maybe we should get the two of them together."

"God, they'd kill each other," she laughed. "And anyway, you know he loves you," she said with a smile, still holding his hand, and he tried not to grin like a loon over that simple action. Tried not to lose it at the sweet touch of her fragile, feminine flesh against his own. All the intimate details of her, the little things he'd taken for granted with other women he'd known, worked to undo him, making him feel shaky and pumped up on the steady surge of adrenaline spiking through his system. His heart pounded, pulse racing, from nothing more than the sheer delicacy and tender strength of her lithe female body moving in step beside his tall frame. It was a maddening thing, the way he wanted to ravage and shelter her all at once, making his head feel thick—his cock feel thicker.

Trying to distract himself, Mark focused on her words. "Yeah, I suppose he does love me, in his own warped way."

A soft, thrumming tension trembled through her as she said, "Mark, may I ask you a question?"

He steered them down a side street, knowing it led toward the little walkway behind her apartment, nowhere near ready to relinquish her company, and yet, not sure how much longer he could trust himself to be close to her tonight. "Sure. Shoot."

She looked around, seeming to lose her train of thought as she noted their surroundings. "Are you walking me home?"

"Uh, yeah. I better get back to the bar and help out or it'll be a nightmare when Miller opens tomorrow."

"He's the new bartender you hired, isn't he?" she asked, taking a sip of the Heineken she still clutched in her free hand. "The big scary-looking guy?"

"Yeah, though I don't think he's all that scary," he said with a low laugh, "so much as intense."

"I accidentally ran into him on my way out of Roy's the other morning, and he looked pretty scary to me."

He sought her eyes in the mellow darkness of the night. "Was he rude to you?"

"No, he just didn't look overly friendly. But maybe you're right," she said with a small shrug. "It was probably just that whole intense look he has going. He's got the dark brooding thing down to a T."

"He's a hell of a worker though. I was up to my ass in that place until he came on to help me out. And Cain still pitches in from time to time, like tonight."

"You should be really proud, Mark. You've done amazing things with the bar. It's popular with both the locals and the tourist trade. I don't think Kyra and I have ever been in when it wasn't busy."

His chest swelled with ridiculous pride at her praise, and he squeezed her hand, reluctant to leave her...and knowing that if he didn't, he was going to end up taking her to bed. Christ, if he thought there was a chance in hell he wouldn't ruin things by doing it, he'd already be in her pants, without a second thought. He wanted it—god, did he want it—but he couldn't shake the feeling that if he followed through on the need, he'd be screwing his chance for more than a casual relationship. And he needed more. Hell, he needed all of it. He took another long swallow of his beer, enjoying the sharp chill against his dry throat, and finally said, "You'll have to come in more. I'd like to see you in my place."

"Yeah?" Her head tilted as she shot him a questioning look.

"Yeah." *As in all the time.* He had a vivid vision of her laid out over his bar, his face buried between her splayed thighs as he licked and sucked up her drugging, delicate juices, and wondered how in hell's name he was going to survive this waiting. "Why don't you come in tomorrow and I'll take some time for lunch?" he suggested, trying to sound casual. "We can kick back and talk, and I'll show you around."

And maybe...if I can work into it slowly and manage not to blow it with my damn cock, I'll be able to convince you to take a chance on a guy like me for something serious. Something that'll last.

They neared the quaint seaside building that housed her upstairs apartment, pausing at the slim stairway that hugged the side wall, leading up to her own little private balcony. She turned to him, the expression in her shuttered gaze difficult to read in the pale moonlight, the mellow glow of her outside light not quite reaching her feminine features, leaving her face in soft shadow. "Have you had a good time tonight?"

"You know I have," he answered in a low voice, struggling not to grab her and pull her against the hungry urgency of his body. His dick restlessly disagreed with his response, and he silently snarled for the damn thing to shut the hell up—then wondered when he'd started having conversations with a prominent body part.

One growing more prominent by the second, he realized, thinking of her apartment so very near. Her bedroom...and a bed that would smell of Melanie. Of the wicked, wonderfully intimate things he could do to her in that bed.

Desperate to distract himself, he searched for something safe to say. "You're very easy to talk to," he murmured, but the second the words left his mouth, he knew they weren't the ones she'd wanted to hear. And the temptation to tell her what he really wanted burned so fiercely in his gut, he felt twisted with pain.

"Hey, what'd I do?" he rasped, when she looked away, pulling her face back toward him with the gentle clasp of his callused fingers against her chin. "I'm trying not to screw this up, but I keep getting the feeling that I'm saying the wrong things here, Mel."

She sucked her lower lip through her teeth. "Do you...do you want to come up for some coffee?"

I'd sure as hell like to come, but without the coffee. Better yet, I'd like to take you upstairs, lay you out over the first available surface, and shove myself so far inside you, you can feel me pumping against the pounding beat of your heart.

Mark shook his head at the dangerous thoughts, ready to strangle his damn libido, if he could only get his hands on it. "You know, I'm not sure that would be a good idea, Mel."

"Why not?" There was an off note of frustration in those two little words, but with her expression in shadow and his head fuzzy with lust, in was difficult to determine the problem. Did she think he was ditching her? Or was it something more than that?

"I...uh, really should probably head back to the bar now to help get the kitchen closed down before Cain makes a wreck of it."

And before I totally lose it and fall all over you like a rabid dog.

It was a lame excuse, and they both knew it—but he didn't have a hell of a lot to work with here. His hard-on had sucked all the blood out of his damn brain.

Her downstairs neighbor turned on an indoor light, the golden glow of a lamp sneaking out like a thief from the edges of their vertical blinds, gently illuminating her face. She studied him through eyes that suddenly looked far older than her years. They were too disillusioned. Disappointed. "Why won't you come upstairs, Mark? I...I'd like to know the truth," she said quietly. "It's Friday night, and I know you keep the kitchen open later than usual."

"I think you know why," he grated out in a low rumble of words, silently cursing, and he knew she understood when her breath caught. "I had a great time tonight, though," he added lamely, inwardly wincing over the banal comment. "The conversation was...er...great."

He watched as her eyes closed, the long curl of her lashes casting shadows against the creamy perfection of her freckled cheeks. When she looked back up at him, there was no mistaking the thick wave of desire roiling through her cinnamon gaze. It nearly took him to his knees then and there, and he felt a flash of anger at everything—fate, her, himself— for the temptation he was forced to fight. It was a tight, aching throb of pain in his gut, making him sweat...making his jaw grind as he struggled not to take her to the ground and cram himself inside her in a frenzy that was all about slaking that burning, raw ache of lust. He didn't trust himself, because he knew there'd be no controlling it. She was probably daydreaming about slow and easy, smooth and gentle, when he knew there wouldn't be a goddamn thing easy about the way he'd take her. He felt like a man hanging by his nails, the crumbling ledge of a rocky mountainside his last lifeline...and any second now he was going to go crashing over the edge.

He took two deep, hard breaths, grasping for a hold on the slippery surface of his control, and tipped his beer up to his mouth to distract himself from his carnal fantasies, when she floored him by slowly licking the sexy curve of her upper lip with her pink little tongue in an act that screamed seduction. A mutinous expression washed over her features, and she said, "Yeah, talking. Conversation. That's my specialty." Her voice was breathless, her tone throaty and low. "I've always been so bloody easy to talk to. But would I be easy to have sex with, too, Mark?"

He choked on his swallow of ice-cold beer and could have sworn that the chilled liquid nearly shot out his nose. "*What?*"

She climbed the bottom stair, bringing her closer to his height, and turned to him, the fierce color in her face evident now in the glowing arc of moonlight, painting her fey features in an ethereal, otherworldly glow, glinting off the soft honey of her hair.

"You're right about this being a small town and people talking. I'd be lying if I said I hadn't heard rumors of your legendary reputation with women. Mark Logan never, *ever* takes a woman out without giving her mind-blowing orgasms at the end of the night. So despite what you said about not looking for that when you kissed me earlier, I'm wondering if you're going to—"

"If I'm going to what?" he asked, not sure whether he was more shocked or angry or disappointed, and unable to sort his way through the tangle of conflicting emotions suddenly crashing down on him. He should have thought this was heaven, Melanie Green looking up at him with raw hunger smoldering in those big brown eyes, apparently asking to come, but now he felt strangely like a fool. And a cheap fool at that. She made it sound like she'd singled him out for stud service, and here he'd had stars in his eyes the entire damn time they'd been together.

For the first time in his life, he'd actually enjoyed getting into a woman's head before he made his way into her pants—only to find that it'd meant nothing to her. The companionship and shared secrets. Holding hands and laughing with one another. Hell, he sounded like some kind of wimped-out, maudlin fool, but there was no help for it. She'd worked a major one on his head, all right—and despite the one-night-stand reputation he knew he was famous for, it made him sick to think of sinking into Melanie Green, becoming an intimate part of her, penetrating her with his body...and then just walking away. He'd fallen too hard for the entire package, instead of just her sweet little body, to be able to do it.

But then, maybe she wasn't really who he'd thought she was. No, he'd had his head up his ass and let himself get taken along for a ride. It was like some kind of cosmic payback for the women he'd so casually taken to bed without a second thought. In a move he'd perfected like a pro, Melanie would screw him tonight and forget him tomorrow, getting from him exactly what she thought he was good for.

She licked her lower lip, took a deep breath, and when she spoke, a husky tremor of physical hunger shivered through her words. "I'm not asking you up to talk, Mark."

"S'that right?" he asked softly, while a hard, cynical smile twisted his mouth. Disgust and disappointment for the whole gut-twisting situation filled him, but shouldn't he have known he had this coming? Why in hell had he ever thought a woman like Melanie Green would seek anything worth more than a fast, furious fling with him? How fucking stupid could he get? "You're just wondering when you're going to get the fuck, aren't you?" he asked, angry with himself for sounding so damn surprised by the situation.

She opened her mouth to respond, but nothing came out.

"Yeah, that's it, isn't it?" he said with a slow nod, studying her through narrowed, piercing eyes that he wished could peel away the layers of soft, sweet innocence surrounding her, one by one, until he could get down deep and see what really made her tick. Discover what she was really after here, despite those soft eyes...and even softer mouth. "You agreed to go out with me tonight so you could get some hard cock and a couple of creamy orgasms, didn't you, Mel?"

Instead of answering his question, she shook her head at the new ugliness of his tone...at the suddenly hard set of his face and asked one of her own. "Why do you sound so...upset, Mark? Are you actually *angry* at me for asking you upstairs?"

"Oh, I'm not angry, angel," he drawled with a slow, mean smile, lying through his teeth as a cold, brutal fury burned through his veins, all of it centered on himself for being such a damn fool. "Tell me, is this why you've been staring at me across the street every goddamn day, whenever you didn't think I was looking? Were you just wondering when I'd finally come sniffing around and you'd get the chance to take a ride of your own? Check out my reputation firsthand?"

A strange expression washed over the delicate features of her face at his taunting words, and she seemed to harden, all that beautiful softness dulled by disappointment. "Would it come as such a shock?" she asked softly. "Is it so ridiculous? You said that's not what you were looking for from me, but then you've spent the entire evening flirting with me. All those slow, wicked looks and brushes of your body against mine."

"Just what did you have in mind, sweetheart? A go at it upside the wall? Should I take you right here on the stairs? It might be a little rough, but then you might like it like that," he rasped in a smoky tone that rumbled like thunder, moving closer, crowding her with his size. "Honestly, baby, you should have explained this to me at the beginning of the night and then I wouldn't have wasted my time trying to figure out how to get inside your pants without scaring you off. But I guess those innocent little looks are just that, aren't they?" he asked, tilting his head as he studied her, his free hand reaching out to tuck one honeyed curl behind the delicate shell of her ear. "No, they don't do justice to the hot, hungry little wanton living inside. Just tell me what you were looking for, Mel. Never let it be said that I didn't live up to my fucking reputation," he drawled with a cold, taunting smile. "Or should that be my *reputation for fucking*, sweetheart?"

Chapter Five

Melanie met Mark's taunting stare with a twisting, sinking sensation in the pit of her stomach. She hadn't meant to come right out and blurt her frustrations in his face, but everything had suddenly built up like a pressure cap inside her and she couldn't control it. One second he'd been telling her what a "great" time he'd had, and in the next, she was exploding all over the place like an emotional rocket.

Oh god. She swallowed hard, struggling to keep herself together, but there was a pain in her heart that hurt like all get out. He'd been ready to leave her at her damn doorstep with a smile and maybe, if she was lucky, a platonic kiss on the cheek, when every other woman got the full, mind-blowing treatment of incredible sex. And there was no way in hell she was settling for less.

The whole thing hurt so much more than a mere sexual rejection, because she honestly cared for this man. If she hadn't already believed herself in love with him before tonight, she would now, after having spent the evening with him, laughing and smiling—and of all things...talking. And yet, *talking* with Mark had been like its own kind of foreplay. Their conversation had been vivid, taking on a life of its own, instead of the self-absorbed drivel that men usually poured out to her. Each word had been like a seduction, the string of sentences like an invisible line drawing them closer together, leading up to the ultimate moment where he'd actually admit that he *did* want her for more than talk, more than mere conversation.

But she'd been wrong—blinded by lust or love or who knew what—only to realize now that her initial conclusions had been right all along.

Maybe it was like a sickness. Even the most virile of men who came into contact with her became sensitive souls looking for nothing more than warm companionship and a great gal to talk to—saving all those savage urges for the women who made them burn. The frustration of it made her want to pound her fists upon that solid, mouthwatering chest, the details of which she could so easily make out beneath the thin cotton covering of his soft T-shirt.

And damn it, she wasn't going to stand for it. She wanted to toss him to the ground and show him just how *wrong* he was about her. If she could only have him for a friend, then by god, she at least wanted one night of knowing what it felt like to be *taken*. She deserved it! Mark Logan was every bit as fun and entertaining as she'd known he'd be, and she knew she was already in far too deep for emotional safety. When you threw in the heart-tripping sexual attraction, hunger so sharp it cut, it was enough to make her want to lay him out on her bed and ride his bad boy ass until neither one of them could move.

A single night. Just once. Was that really so much to ask?

He stared down at her, the dark heat of his gaze sending a shiver through her watery limbs, and took her still half-full beer bottle from her trembling fingers, setting it on the end of the step behind her, along with his own. Then his hands lifted to the sides of her face, long fingers sliding up through her hair until he held her head between the controlling pressure of his palms.

"What are you doing?" she gasped, as he tilted her head back at an angle that had her looking up into the hard lines of his ruggedly chiseled face, and for the first time ever, she realized how dangerous he could be. Not that she was afraid of him. No, she knew, no matter how angry he might become, that he'd never physically harm her. But there was a danger about him all the same. An electric, sizzling force that rode the powerful lines of his long body, thrumming beneath her fingertips as she pressed her hands to the hard muscles of his broad shoulders.

"I'm getting ready to give you a taste of my reputation, sweetheart. Isn't that what you wanted tonight?"

She swallowed, struggling to sort out the tangled, hazy mess of her thoughts. "What's wrong with you?"

"Now why would you think anything's wrong? I just wasn't reading your signals right, Mel. If you wanna come, you gotta open up and let a guy know before he gets blinded by those big brown eyes of yours and is afraid of going too far. If you'd told me up-front what you were looking for, I could've saved you the trouble of dinner and dealt with this hours ago."

"Mark," she said carefully, blinking up at him. "I don't think you understand."

"On the contrary, honey," he disagreed in a silky, seductive drawl, "I think I'm finally figuring it all out. Now either tell me to get my hands off you and walk away, or shut up and put that mouth to better use."

The look in those brilliant, smoky green eyes was almost frightening, smoldering with the sharp, dangerous edge of anger, shimmering and wild, like…like the predatory eyes of a leopard gleaming out from between wet green leaves after a violent summer rain in the jungle. There was something very wrong here, but the second his mouth touched hers, she couldn't grasp onto anything long enough to put a name to it. He didn't gentle her into a kiss, but took her with a full-fledged, consuming hunger that wiped her brain clean and sent her body tumbling into a frantic, sexual urgency that had her kissing him back in ways she didn't even know she was capable of. Her lips moved against the rough-silk of his delicious mouth, his masculine, devastatingly male flavor drugging her mind with erotic images of that powerful body moving over her, within her, holding her down and making her scream out her release over and over and over again.

He broke the kiss to trail his mouth over her cheek, the sensitive column of her throat, and there was something so wonderfully erotic about the feel of his lips moving against the damp heat of her skin, while one calloused hand suddenly gripped her ass through the thin fabric of her skirt. His touch was hard and possessive, fingers bold and greedy, rubbing through the sensitive crease of her cheeks. Back and forth they stroked, making her gasp into the brutal, vicious heat of another kiss as his mouth slashed across hers and his hand moved lower. His fingers dipped, stroking over the cloth-covered heat of her sex, and she nearly died. Nearly came from the stroke alone. From the sheer sensation of having Mark Logan touch her body.

A sharp, husky cry broke free from her throat and he swallowed the sound with a stifled snarl, fitting his mouth more tightly over hers, sealing in the sounds of their lust as it broke out of them in raging, ragged bursts of sound. Strong hands lifted her hips, turning and pressing her against the smooth wall of her apartment building, the weathered wood feeling startlingly cold against the warm flames of fire he'd sent licking across her fevered skin, teasing her, urging her on. Her legs trembled as her feet touched the grainy surface of the concrete, and then those strong, rough hands moved to her thighs, pushing them apart as he pushed up her skirt. She swallowed a soft, sibilant sound of surprise, and then he was touching her flesh to flesh, those long fingers digging into the giving cushion of her thighs, his rough calluses dragging over her tender skin in a blatantly male touch that made her inner muscles clench. Her sex felt heavy and swollen between her legs, hungry for whatever mind-blowing, sexually powerful things Mark Logan could do to her.

"I take it you're ready for that fuck now," he said so coldly she actually winced. But she didn't push him away. She couldn't. She simply straightened her shoulders and stared up at him in the heavy darkness, aware that his body trembled against her own.

"Mark?" Suddenly, Mel didn't know what she had been thinking, or where exactly things had gone wrong. What was happening between them? Why had the fact that she wanted him sent everything careening so madly out of control?

"Are you wet for me, Melanie?"

His dark, roughly spoken words rasped temptingly against the pulse in the base of her throat. He lowered his mouth to her skin, and her head moved restlessly against the wall, neck arched to give him better access, while her passion-dazed brain struggled to comprehend his mood.

"Answer me, Mel. Are you *wet?*" he demanded in a husky, provocative rumble, even though she knew he already held the answer. His deft fingers rubbed against the thin, soaked panel of her panties, swirling confidently through the drenched evidence of her arousal. "Are you juicy and hot just thinking about what I'm going to do to you?"

"Yes," she whispered shakily, her mind thick with the powerful pulse of need surging through her veins, intoxicating her. Making her feel drunk with want for this man. For whatever she could have from him. "God yes," she breathed out on a low, frantic moan. "Mark...please."

"Please what, Melanie?" he asked with a hard smile as he lifted his head to look down at her.

A part of her heart broke at the lack of tenderness in his shuttered, guarded stare, but she swallowed against the hurt and focused on the burn of physical hunger she could see smoldering in those smoky green eyes. "Please, Mark. God, just touch me. Put your hands on me. *Please.*"

The sound of his name on her lips, of her begging for his touch, was nearly his undoing. "Don't worry, Mel. I won't leave you wanting tonight," he growled against the moist heat of her mouth. He lost himself in the drugging flavor of her lips, in the lush taste of the warm, sweet well that lay deeper within. The sleek, tender textures of her eager, sweetly unskilled kiss sent his head spinning. "There's not a force in heaven or hell that could stop me from touching you now."

With a rough groan, he shoved his hand into the front of her panties and cupped the wet, damp heat of her pussy in his palm. Oh Christ, it nearly killed him. Soft, slick, slippery and smooth. He wanted to drool. Wanted to howl and bury himself inside her more than he wanted to breathe. She jolted in his arms, and he gave her a moment to get used to his touch, rasping her delicate folds with the scrape of his calluses, feeling her melt against him, all warm and deliciously wet. There was no doubt that she wanted him. No, she was creamy and hot, all but dripping, and the pain in his cock took on a new dimension. A raw, pumping knot of need that seemed to beat in time with the powerful thumping of his heart.

He learned her by touch, letting his fingertips slide through her folds, separating her, opening her, and she shivered between the press of his warm, aching body and the cool wall. His lips found the sweet heat of her scalp, and spoke his words into the fragrant silk of her hair.

"So soft and sweet, Mel. Did this hungry little pussy go all warm and slippery when I had you against that wall at *Caza's*, letting you feel how hard you'd made me? Has it been this way ever since? I swear you're so ready, I think you could spill against my hand any second now."

"*Oh shit*," she moaned, eyes closing as her head fell back to bang against the wall, rolling from side to side, and a low laugh rumbled up from his chest at the sound of a cuss word leaving her lips.

Bracing himself on one forearm beside her head, Mark cupped the slick heat of her mound, his jaw hardening at the feel of it, like smooth silk, so warm and ready. Her unique, feminine scent floated on the air with the gentle stirring of the breeze, and she quivered as he drew a deep, satisfying breath into his lungs, knowing he could get high on this woman's scent. It was that powerful, that erotically intoxicating, and he wondered what her taste in those intimate places would do to him. If he'd be able to survive it, or if it would leave him pitifully addicted.

"So tight," he groaned, his voice strained as he stroked the swollen ridge of her vulva, dipping the thick tip of his index finger carefully inside, testing her. "How long's it been since you had a hard cock shoved up this tiny opening? How long since you had this sweet little cunt crammed full of dick and fucked 'til you screamed yourself hoarse?"

"Mark?" she panted, her own voice coming ragged and breathless, while her shivering body shook in his arms.

"Months? A year?" he demanded, grunting from the incredible feel of her as she clenched around him while he pressed deeper within, penetrating her, stroking the rough tip against those slippery inner tissues. The strong muscles resisted, struggling against his invasion as he forced himself into her. He cursed softly under his breath when the narrow walls trembled, fluttering around him, milking his finger better than any woman he'd ever taken with his body.

"T-t-two years," she stammered, holding onto him as if she expected him to save her, to keep her safe, to offer her some kind of tenderness, when deep down he now knew the ugly truth. Those misty, big brown eyes might burn with warmth and promises, but there was only a basic need hiding beneath. Just a hungry urge to use him and lose him. Yeah, that kind of urge he knew all too well, having gone through more women than he could remember, making use of them to ease his own physical needs. With his reputation, the women he'd known had looked to him for a rough-and-tumble, intensely satisfying ride, which had always suited him just fine, since he was ready to move on the next day anyway. Hell, he was usually ready to move on after a few hours, once he'd screwed them through the mattress and spent himself dry. What was the point in staying after that? His own bed was bigger, less crowded, and a hell of a lot more comfortable than waking up with someone he didn't have two words to say to.

No, the women he'd known knew better than to look to him for the long term, and he didn't look past what he could get out of them. All in all, it'd been an even exchange, all parties satisfied, no unexpected or unpleasant emotions weighing the whole thing down, muddying the water...until Melanie Green moved her sweet little ass to town. Until then, he hadn't realized what he was missing—hadn't understood until he'd found it. Until he'd found *her*.

Before meeting Melanie, he'd considered himself lucky that women understood him for what he was and didn't nag him for more than he could give.

But the fact that she looked at him the same way made him sick.

Hell, it probably wasn't any less than he deserved, but why did it have to be Melanie? Why the *one* woman who'd ever managed to slip her way into his heart, so smooth and easy, he hadn't even been able to mount a proper defense?

Why did she have to be so sweet? Why did she have to feel so fucking right in his arms? It wasn't fair. It was hell.

Shit, it was a goddamn nightmare.

With the softness of a butterfly's wings, she reached down and pressed the warm heat of her palm against the painful, heavy ridge of his cock, then turned her hand to stroke the thick shaft with the backs of her fingers. "I-I didn't really believe all those rumors," she whispered, "but they were true."

Raw lust rolled through his system, thick and sticky, and all he could think was, *Fuckin-A, this woman is dangerous*.

"Is that why you picked me for your ride tonight, Mel?" he gritted through the clenched line of his teeth as sweat beaded his brow. He added a second finger to the first, moving them deeper into her with a knowing, twisting motion, her tender pussy so wet it was making soft, liquid sounds as he thrust into her, forcing his thick fingers hard and deep in an evocative rhythm that matched the needs of his cock. "Were you looking to end your long dry spell with a man who could really make you cream, honey? I wonder which rumor it was that snagged me as the lucky guy. My size? My kinks? The fact that I like my sex a little rough and a whole lot sweaty, wild and out of control? Or was it the fact that I can go all night when I'm in a mood, hungry for it until I can't move and a woman can't walk straight? Which one, Mel? Come on, we're *friends*, aren't we?" he taunted, dragging his teeth down the taut tendon between her neck and shoulder while she writhed on his fingers. Her hips arched against him, pushing him even deeper, while a raw sound of need, desperate and low, caught in her throat. "Come on...you can tell me."

"No," she mumbled, shaking her head as if to clear it from a haze. "I-I don't think you really consider me your friend. Do you, Mark? I wish you'd just talk to me — that you'd just explain why you're suddenly acting like this."

He stared into those misty eyes, wishing like hell he could hate her at that moment, when all he really wanted was to lose himself in her. "Why?" he echoed in a hard, controlled tone. "How about because I don't like feeling used, Mel. It's an ugly fucking feeling, and one I'm not looking forward to repeating. But there's no reason not to take advantage of it while in the moment, now is there, beautiful? God forbid we get hung up on *feelings* here."

Then, before she could respond to that telling remark, he had her about the waist, carrying her up the stairs until they'd reached her small landing and her purse was slipping from its snagged perch at her elbow to thud dully against the wooden planks beneath his feet. Mark took a quick look at his surroundings, then lowered her to the painted wooden bench beside her door, his deep breaths pulling at the thick air, its scent heavy and warm with the smells of potted flowers and lush, green plants that seemed to overflow from every corner. His slightly shaking, impossibly eager hands slipped off her panties, and then found her knees, forcing them apart as he knelt between her thighs. His long fingers fisted into the fragile fabric of her skirt and ripped it to the side, leaving her open and vulnerable. And that's exactly how he wanted her. Wide open, without defense, the same goddamn way that he felt.

A niggling little voice in the back of his head muttered something about dumb-ass male ego and idiotic conclusions, but his pride raged and obliterated whatever small voice of reason might have managed to help him calm down and think the events of the last ten minutes through more clearly.

No, a man's pride was a savage, fickle beast, and Mark couldn't outrun its jeering.

It was too much, and he felt that whipping, whapping crack of his control snap like a sharp, sizzling sound that jerked through his body. "Never let it be said that I left a woman wanting," he said thickly.

He was angry, but he was hurt too, and that pissed him off more than anything. But he was going to enjoy it. If this was all he get could get, damn it, he was going to invade and stroke and consume every sweet little inch of her, before she sent him packing.

"What are you doing?" she gasped, planting her hands against the whitewashed wood at her sides, trying to seek leverage as he pushed her thighs wider apart, making room for the broad width of his shoulders.

"What am I doing? Getting ready to go down on you," he muttered, the words husky and raw. He brought both thumbs up the heavy seam of her slit, using them to part the shy, swollen lips, uncovering the tender, hidden secrets within. "Getting ready to take a slow, deep taste—to eat out Melanie Green's drenched little cunt." The soft glow from her porch light spilled over her shoulders, illuminating the curly riot of her hair like a golden halo, her eyes like twin sparks of light as she gazed down at him with a look of stunned fascination.

Holding her drowsy, heavy-lidded stare, Mark ran his thumbs softly over the slick, sensitive folds, pushing them into the hood until he trapped the ripe bud of her tender clit and pumped it within his grasp. Her swollen lips parted as a low, animal sound purred in her throat, hungry and wanting, and he knew in that moment that he was going to want this woman for the rest of his life. Knew, beyond a shadow of a doubt, that he'd fallen in love with her—and all she wanted from him was sex. An ugly, wrenching knot of angry pain twisted deeper inside him, and he ripped his gaze from that dangerous landscape of her expression, only to find himself focusing on one that tore at him just as deeply.

Despite the pale light from above, her sex remained shadowed in mystery, the glistening flesh only just visible in the flickering light. He used his thumbs to hook her outer labia and pulled them wide, leaving her open and at his mercy.

"Do I need to be more specific?" he groaned roughly. "I can, honey. I can tell you all about how I'm getting ready to suck and lick this hot little cunt that you offered up tonight, Mel. How I'm going to keep you spread wide open, just like this, and fuck this tender little hole with my tongue, shoving it as deep into you as I can get. Give this hot little thing whatever it wants, until you're ready to give me whatever *I* want."

He waited the space of two seconds to see if she would tell him no, and when no outraged denials came flinging back in his face, he pushed her knees up, sending her off balance so that she tilted back against the outside wall of her apartment, her backside nearly sliding off the bench, and pressed his face into the humid warmth of her sex.

Aw, hell. The perfection of the moment nearly killed him.

Driven by need, he pressed closer, opening his mouth over the lush heat of her silken folds, exploring with the deft, greedy stroke of his tongue through the parted pads of her labia. With his pulse roaring in his ears, he licked a long, hungry line from the puffy rim of her vulva, up to the swollen, thrumming nub of her clit, knowing he'd never enjoyed a woman more. Knowing that none would ever compare. Her clitoris pulsed against his tongue like a tiny heartbeat, so eager for ecstasy and release, and he closed his lips around the delicate knot with a soft, succulent suckle, then nipped gently with his teeth, before suckling at the tender peak once again. She was wildly delicious. Mouthwatering. So good, he wanted to keep his mouth on her forever, or at least whenever she wasn't crammed full of his cock.

Mel's back arched, and from beneath the thick fringe of his lowered lashes, Mark watched her press her fist to her open mouth to keep from screaming out her pleasure as the first orgasm hit her hard and sharp, while he milked it from her with ruthless skill. Like a flower unfurling beneath the warm sun, her cunt bloomed, lush and earthy in its desire, exquisitely primal in its quest to lure him in. With a harsh, rumbling growl, he angled his face to the side and pressed deeper, closer, licking and laving with the sensual scrape of his tongue until he reached her shuddering slit and pierced it with a lusty thrust that damn near brought her ass off the bench.

"Oh hell, that's sweet. Sweetest fucking thing I've ever tasted," he all but snarled in a low, smoky rasp, wishing he could detest her for being so damn delicate and delicious. For being everything that he'd ever wanted.

"God, not again," she moaned hoarsely, twisting beneath his mouth as her body tightened once more. "I can't...can't do it again."

"You can. If I wanted to, I could make you ripple and cream all night long, Melanie. Give me another one," he said in a coaxing, husky drawl. "Let me feel this sweet little pussy suck on my tongue. Right now. And I want it *hard*. I want it to feel like you're trying to suck me right up inside you." He tongued her vulva, then pressed into the warm, slick heat of her pussy, using one thumb to press down on the sensitive bud of her clit, while her scent and taste captured him, locking him in its vise—and just like that, she came again. It was a powerful, rising wave of ecstasy that he felt roll through her like a storm-ravaged gust, and a fresh, delicious wash of juices filled his mouth, drugging him with her lush, voluptuous taste, making him want to come so damn badly his dick jerked within the confines of his jeans, the fat, broad head wet and angry and swollen.

Not yet. Goddamn it, he wasn't ready to let her go.

Mark took another long, intimate taste of her tender folds, then raised his head to find her looking at him in the moonlight, big brown eyes so wide, they reflected the hanging pearl of the moon behind him. He imagined that he could witness his own harsh reflection trapped there in those luminous depths, the sharp angles of his face tight with self-disgust for wanting things he couldn't have.

She pulled her lower lip through her teeth and leaned forward, her slim fingers once again moving over the long, distended ridge of his cock as it struggled for release. He tried but couldn't stop the rough growl that broke through his clenched teeth as she stroked him, squeezing him through the soft denim, her sweet rhythm telling him that she didn't know a whole hell of a lot about touching a man, but was more than ready to learn. God, but it tempted him to take her. Just rip his fly open and sink into that fist-tight, velvety heat, giving her exactly what she'd asked for.

He could have her. Right now. It'd be so outrageously fucking easy — but he couldn't do it.

"No," he muttered, stumbling back to his feet, feeling his expression pull tight with tension and myriad unnamed emotions that he couldn't put a face to. "Not like this, damn it."

"*Mark.*" His name slipped from her lips on the ragged edges of a moan, her chest rising and falling with the rapid pace of her breath as her hands struggled to right her skirt and cover the glistening, exposed folds of her pussy, while her eyes blinked up at him, wide and questioning. "Please talk to me," she panted in a throaty plea, and the sound of her voice twisted him up, his own lungs burning with the harshness of his breathing. "I don't understand why — I mean, was what I asked for so wrong? Why are you so angry?"

"If I am, what's it matter to you?" he grated out of a rough throat growing dryer by the second, while her sweet, sexy taste still filled his mouth, tripling the pain in his dick. "I may not be willing to fuck you, but you got what you wanted. You needed to come, and you did," he grunted, wiping his mouth with his shoulder, then ripping the fingers of his left hand through his windblown hair so roughly that it stung. "Harder than you ever have before, I'd be willing to bet. In fact, you were easy, Mel. Even easier than what I'm used to, and that's really saying something, sweetheart."

She jerked as if he'd physically struck her. "Damn it, Mark! Why are you being so ugly?"

"Ugly?" He gave a short laugh, the dull sound completely without humor, and shook his head at her obvious naïveté. "You wanted to get down and dirty and come, and I came through for you. But if you know what's good for you, you'll stay the hell away from me, Melanie, because next time I won't be able to stop myself from giving you *exactly* what you're asking for. And unless you're a hell of a lot wilder than you look, I don't think you'd care for the experience."

* * * * *

Reality was slow to return as Melanie slumped there, propped against the chilly wall at her back, the salty air cool and calming as it caressed the naked heat of her still flushed, mostly exposed skin. With sluggish movements, she forced her muscles to work, pushing the hem of her skirt farther down, until it covered her knees. God only knew what had happened to her panties. Mel sure as hell didn't.

Jaysus, she thought, that man should come with a warning label. *Hazard: sexual overload may fry your brain cells.* Thankfully, she still possessed a few capable of triggering thought, and it was only moments later that she fully realized she'd just let him walk away from her after issuing that infuriating setdown.

Allowing him to have the last word, and a rude one at that!

Damn it, she wasn't going to stand for it. Her ego might take some serious bruising, but she was tough. Tougher than people gave her credit for, at least. Whatever sheepish pride she possessed could afford a few dents, if it meant rectifying whatever bizarre misconceptions he'd taken with him when he'd walked away from her.

With a deep breath, she got to her feet, only to smack her palm against the wall when her legs wobbled, muscles quivering like jelly. Holy moly. He'd turned her body into a trembling limp noodle and he hadn't even slept with her—not that what he'd given her hadn't been breathtakingly wonderful, if you excluded the dickhead attitude that came along with it. Using her free hand to tuck the tangled mass of her hair behind her ears, she gave her head a little shake, trying to clear it of the lingering effects of those whopping orgasms, and squinted against the soft dark of night to find him.

Seconds later, she picked out his tall outline walking down the moonlit stretch of sand, the ocean a dark, endless mystery roiling in frothing laps against the coastline. She bent to remove her sandals, only to realize that she wasn't wearing those either, idly wondering if they'd gone the way of her panties. But she didn't have time to look for them now. Mel sped down her stairs, across the gritty asphalt of the parking spaces she shared with the other tenants, and took off across the giving sand of the beach, the cool, damp grains squishing between her toes as she raced after the tall, imposing figure of Mark Logan. He sensed her as she closed in and turned, just in time to say, "What the he—" before she launched herself at him, tackling his big, hard body to the ground in a move that would have made any professional linebacker smile with pride.

"Who the hell," she panted, lungs laboring from exertion and mounting anger, "do you think you are?"

He stared at her as if she'd suddenly become something to be wary of, the way a hiker might eye a coiled rattlesnake blocking his path. "What the fuck are you doing, Melanie?"

She thumped the ungiving surface of his chest with her palms, emotions tangling inside her until she didn't know what to think, what to feel. All she knew was that she wasn't going to let him treat her like crap and then walk away, blaming her for it.

"I just wanted to make sure that you understood one thing, since you sure as hell don't seem to understand anything else that's going on here."

He held his arms bent, hands up by his head in a look of surrender, staring at her curiously along the sharp line of his nose. "And what's that?"

"I won't let you treat me like dirt." With a hollow feeling in the pit of her stomach, she asked, "Was what I wanted really so wrong, Mark?"

"I told you I don't care for feeling used. Especially for my dick."

"How the hell could you feel used?" she all but shouted in his face, filled with confusion. Was this all some kind of sick game to him? She wanted to understand, but felt like he was deliberately screwing with her. "I don't get it. Was it so bad for me to want sex with the man I've wanted for freaking ever? The man I've fa—"

At the last moment that pride she'd been so certain could take a bruising surged to its defense, and she choked back the words as quickly as they'd broken free. His eyes narrowed, his expression coldly remote even though his gaze fixed on her with a predatory alertness. Beneath her, his body went hard with tension, as if every muscle had been strung to its maximum limit.

"The man you've what?" he demanded in a rough rasp, his voice all gravel and command.

"Nothing," she whispered, shaking her head.

"Damn it, Melanie," he thundered beneath her, shaking her. "What were you going to say?"

"You're an idiot and an asshole," she said huskily, climbing off him, then backing away across the sand as he sat up and watched her retreat, the brutal intensity of his gaze making the green of his eyes burn in the pale moonlight. She shook her head again with quiet regret, and absolutely refused to allow the hot, stinging wash of tears burning at the backs of her eyes the freedom to fall. Not here. Not in front of him. No, she'd die before giving him that kind of sick satisfaction.

"Please don't ever come near me again," she said, surprised by the even, level tone of her voice, when everything inside seemed to be tumbling within, crashing into the empty void that churned in the pit of her stomach, as if she'd simply cave in on herself. Then she turned and ran...never once looking back.

* * * * *

Mark stood outside the entrance to his bar with his body hard and battle-ready, feeling a need for violence clawing at his back, savage and tauntingly intense. He wanted to fight — wanted to plow his fist through something until the pain blotted out the ugly scene he'd just enacted with Melanie. But more than that, he wanted to rewind the clock and start this entire damn day over again. Wanted to obliterate the bittersweet memory of the last few hours.

He stood unmoving, his lungs hurting and hands clenching at his sides. There was a warm, lingering dampness on the fingers of his right hand, and it made him groan, the rumbling sound snarled in the back of his throat, full of vicious frustration and raw, aching hunger. Knowing he was seven kinds of a fool, Mark closed his eyes and relived the intense moments that he'd had his face pressed to the moist folds of Melanie's sex, her salty-sweet flavor spilling into his mouth as she'd quivered beneath his lips.

Christ, he needed *more* of that sweet perfection. He wanted to go back and drag her little ass home to his bed, force those silky thighs as wide as they'd go, and eat his way to some sort of peace right there in the drenched heat of her pussy. He wanted it open and helpless, his to explore and lick and look at for as long as he liked. For as long as he could take it, before he had to get his cock in her. And he didn't want it just once. He wanted it *forever*, just like he'd known he would—and after this bizarre night, he knew this was a hell he'd be carrying with him for the rest of his life.

Cursing long and viciously under his breath, he finally walked through the door, shoving his Melanie-flavored hands deep into his front pockets.

"How'd it go?" Cain called out from behind the bar, a cigarette dangling precariously between his lips as he cleared off the closing rounds, only a few customers lingering as the last members of the band finished collecting their gear. The room fell strangely silent, as if everyone sensed the tension riding thick and heavy on the air. "Are there wedding bells in the air, bro?" Cain teased, picking up an empty Foster's bottle.

Mark looked at his brother's expectant face, and wanted to shove his fist into the smiling bastard's jaw with such angry intent that it almost scared him.

"Do me a favor and shove that damn thing up your ass."

"Hey, what'd you do to blow it, man?" Cain demanded, narrowing his eyes with cool speculation. "Things were looking pretty damn tight between you two when you strolled by here. They couldn't have gone sour that fast. Not even you are that much of a fuck-up."

"No, things were just peachy," he sneered sarcastically, curling his lip with self-disgust, "until she made it clear that she was only out looking for a fast fuck." She might not have come right out and said it, but then, she sure as hell hadn't denied it.

"Huh?" Cain muttered, sending him a dubious look, the dark slash of his brows arched with disbelief. "Melanie?"

"Yeah, Melanie." He ground his jaw at the infuriating disappointment he could hear in his voice. "Sweet, shy, innocent little Melanie Green."

His brother jerked his dark, stubble-covered chin at him. "Then what's the problem, Mark? I thought you *wanted* to fuck her."

"I do want to fuck her, you blind shit." Cold fury tremored through the tight tension of his muscles, and he fisted his hands in his pockets, a cold sweat breaking out across the hot surface of his skin. "But I wanted a hell of a lot more from her than just some raunchy sex up against some goddamn wall!"

"I'm not buying it," Cain muttered, flicking the glowing tip of his cigarette against the mouth of the beer bottle. "Are you sure you read her right?"

"I may not have your vast, ageless experience," he sneered, cutting a sharp glare at his frowning brother from the corner of his eye, "but I know my way around women."

"No, you know your way around those brainless breasts with heads who we normally play 'fondle, fuck, and forget 'em' with. You don't understand jack shit about a classy babe like Melanie Green."

"And you do?" he snorted, the strange twist not lost on him, considering they'd been having this similar conversation from opposite sides of the bar only hours before.

"More than you, apparently," Cain snorted, wiping down the cleared surface of the counter, then tossing the damp white towel over his left shoulder. "And I'm telling you, you need to rip your head out of your ass before you blow it with this woman."

It wasn't so much the words, as it was the cruel knowledge that he'd *already* blown it with Melanie that had Mark picking up the nearest empty beer bottle, then hurling the tempered green glass into the wide mirror behind Cain's shoulder with a violent, raging shout of fury—all the while wishing he could do the same destruction to his dumb-ass heart.

Chapter Six

It had been a bitch of a morning. Not surprising, considering what the past seven days had been like. As far as weeks went, this had been the shittiest. Seven long days and nights since she'd told Mark Logan to go to hell...and the craving for him had failed to lessen in all that time.

She was beginning to worry that maybe he really *was* addictive, because if anything, she only wanted him more, and the brief glimpses she'd managed to steal during the week through the front window of his bar had been nothing short of torture. True, she wanted to smack him for behaving like such an ass there at the end, but the moments leading up to that point had been too good to ignore—or forget. They had...connected, and in a way Melanie had never thought to connect with another person—especially a man.

God, she was going out of her mind thinking about him.

A thousand times she'd thought of going over to his bar and trying to talk to him—to put to use all those stellar communication skills she supposedly possessed, but her pride had refused to budge on the issue that he had jerked her around, and not vice versa. Whatever had been going through his head, all that talk of being used and whatever, still wasn't clicking. No matter how she tried to get her brain around it, the pieces didn't fit.

"Give it up, Mel. Maybe he just didn't want you. Maybe he's just conflicted, off his rocker, and a brick shy of a building up in his head."

Damn it, something had to be the problem. Because she'd added the figures up again and again, and she still wasn't getting a balance.

"And now look at you," she muttered with disgust focused entirely on herself. "A week later and you're still twisted up about him. So much so that all you really want to do is go slipping into work on a Saturday, just so you can try to catch another glimpse of him. Pathetic, woman, with a capital P."

Oh yeah, the week had sucked, and her morning wasn't feeling any better. She'd tried a steady stream of coffee, but it hadn't helped to relieve the heavy weight of unhappiness that seemed to have curled around her, trapping her within its vising grip. Not even her early morning talk with Kyra had lifted it, though her friend had continued to be full of support and furious scorn for the man who'd all but ground her heart beneath the heel of his boots.

Knowing she couldn't just sit on her sofa, staring off into space all day, Mel decided to at least drag her miserable body down to the beach and spend her day baking beneath the California sun, maybe even lose herself in a good book. God, anything would be better than sitting here replaying that night through her tired brain, over and over, watching the individual frames of memory unfold like some kind of warped romantic comedy. Only, Mel knew this was real life, and there wasn't going to be any clever ending for her and Mark. The guy obviously thought she was—hell, who knew what he thought of her—and she thought he was a jerk. Hardly a good beginning for a romance, even one that centered on sex.

She was just reaching for the handle of her front door, when a loud knock rattled the thin structure within its frame, making her jump. Shaking her head at her jittery nerves, wondering if she'd gone past her legal caffeine limit, Mel flipped the lock, turned the handle and came face-to-face with a stern-looking Cain Logan.

"I need to talk to you," he muttered as he pushed his way past her, stepping into her apartment with just enough arrogance to irritate her, bringing the rich scents of coffee, tobacco and warm male animal with him. Wild and untamed.

"Sure, come on in," she drawled, her voice dripping with sarcasm while her mind wondered what on Earth he was doing there. "Really, just make yourself at home."

He turned in the middle of the room, making it seem significantly smaller, and shot her a questioning look, as if he didn't get what had peeved her. Bracing his dark, utterly male hands on his hips, his deep blue eyes pinned her in place. "I came to talk to you about Mark," he muttered, his sexy mouth hardened into a grim line of determination.

"Why do I get the feeling this is really something you'd rather not be doing?" she asked suspiciously. "Did he send you here?"

"Hell, no. He'd probably try to kick my ass if he knew what I was doing, but there'll be no living with him if this thing between the two of you goes to shit."

"How poetic," she softly snorted, crossing her arms.

"Look, Mark isn't like other men," he said, ignoring her comment. "Hell, he isn't even like me. When he decides on something, he sticks. The only reason he hasn't been grounded into a solid relationship before now is because he hadn't met a woman he really wanted. I mean, one that he wanted for...uh," he broke off, jerking his wide shoulders, and she almost smiled at the sudden look of unease on his handsome face as he muttered, "you know, for more than sex. But you—there's no doubt that he wants *you*, Mel. I've never seen him like this. These past seven days have been like a war zone around him. He's gotten into three fights at the bar, fired Miller because the guy told him he was being an asshole, and insulted one woman who was coming on to him so rudely that she threw her martini in his face. And it's all over you, honey. So you had better decide just what it is you want from him, because he's fallen hard. I'm talking seriously nose-dived."

She swallowed a sudden, brilliant burst of surprise, shocked clear down to her toes at the sight of this gorgeous, intimidatingly sexy man coming to plead a case for his baby brother. "As...uh, sweet as this is of you, Cain, I don't think you really understand what your brother wants. Things really didn't go all that well last weekend," she murmured, knowing her words were the understatement of the year. Not that the mind-numbing orgasms hadn't been incredible. No, it was everything else that had claimed top prize as the crappiest moment of her life.

"Yeah," he replied with a wry smile, "I know." One black brow arched in arrogant humor. "Who do you think cleaned up the beer bottle he smashed against one of those framed mirrors he has all over the place when he finally made it back to the bar that night?"

"He threw a bottle?" she gasped.

Cain nodded his head, a dark lock of ink-black silk falling over his golden brow. "I've never seen anything like it, Mel. Mark is always so cool and levelheaded. Man, nothing ever sets him off, and sure as hell not a woman. He's been through more than his fair share, honey, but not a one of them ever made him actually *feel* anything. But this has been eating him up all week."

"What has?" she asked huskily, his words spinning deliciously through her head as she tried to make sense out of them.

He cocked his head to the side as he studied her, those sexy baby blues crinkling at the corners. "I don't know what came down between you two, but he's got some wild hair up his ass about you only wanting him for some fast, mindless sex. Some kind of one-night stand and nothing more."

Despite her best intentions to be sophisticated about this highly unusual conversation, Melanie felt her face go hot. She knew she was blushing clear to her roots. "Er...he told you that?"

A slow, teasing smile played charmingly at the corner of his sexy mouth, so like Mark's, and yet harder, as if he didn't smile often enough. "More or less. So it's up to you, Mel. If he's wrong, which I'd be willing to bet my di—er, my life on," he laughed with a slow smile, "then you're gonna have to let him know what you want out of this thing. But I can tell you that if you want more, it's there for the taking."

"I can't—" she stammered uncomfortably, struggling for the words to explain how she felt. "I just— I wish you were right, Cain, but I don't know. It all got really messed up somehow and now it's just...it's, um, all kinda confusing. Make that *impossibly* confusing."

He took a step closer to her, the mischief-made grin playing over his mouth making him look younger, less cynical than she had ever seen him before. "It doesn't have to be, Mel. Take my word on it and take a chance on him. Let him know how you really feel about him, because I know Mark, honey, and he's serious as shit about this. Hell," he laughed, "if you won't do it for yourself, do it for me. He's been driving me crazy these past six months, lovesick over you—and that was nothing compared to what this week has been like. If you don't put him out of his misery, I'll have to shoot him just to preserve my sanity."

"Yeah, right," she smiled, shaking her head. "You, Cain Logan, are all bluster. No matter what you say, I know you love your little brother."

A mock look of panic fell over his face. "Well shit, Mel, don't go telling him. I'll never live it down."

Laughter bubbled up out of her, but she was afraid to look too closely at the small burst of hope beginning to rise in her chest, making her feel lighter...freer...and unbearably excited. She smiled again, and said, "Thanks for being so sweet."

"Sweet?" he scowled, his look saying she'd clearly just insulted him. "Shit, I'm outta here before you completely trash my bad-ass reputation, you little witch."

Her smile widened. Oh man, it was just too much fun baiting the bad-ass hunk, and she couldn't help but get a kick out of his obvious discomfort with her praise. "You know, I never would have believed it, but deep down inside you're just a big ol' softie, aren't you?"

"Not hardly," he snorted, giving her a suspicious look, as if she'd lost her mind.

Trying to keep a straight face, Mel said, "I can't wait to tell Kyra."

Cain's head jerked up as if he'd been clipped on the chin, the look on his face so comical, she couldn't help but laugh out loud. "Do that, Melanie Green," he growled, pointing one long finger at her, "and I'll have your devious little ass hauled in for disturbing the peace."

"You wouldn't dare," she grinned, not the least bit intimidated by his ferocious scowl.

"Just try me," he muttered. "That woman is a menace."

Hmm…maybe it was time to test her suspicions. "Kyra? Really? And here she thinks you're so cute."

"Huh?" he grunted, looking like he'd been smacked with a tree trunk between those sky-blue eyes. "She told you she thinks I'm hot?"

Melanie had to bite the side of her tongue to keep from chuckling. "Um, I believe I just used the word cute."

"Kyra thinks I'm hot?" he repeated, still wearing that poleaxed expression that made her snicker under her breath.

"When we first met you, she said cute…but I'm sure hot qualifies if it makes you feel better. Actually, she's said quite a few other things over the last few months, but I can't in good conscience repeat them."

"Damn," he rumbled, rubbing one hand against the scratchy stubble on his chin, still lost in thought. "I figured she hated me, with the way she's always ripping into me."

"Well," Mel said softly, "I suspect that's just because she thinks *you* can't stand her."

"S'that right?" he murmured, his mind obviously on a certain sexy little redhead with smoky green eyes. Kyra might kill her for it, but she couldn't help but wonder if all the animosity between those two wasn't just misdirected sexual energy and emotion.

He opened his mouth, about to say something else, when the police pager on his belt let out a high-pitched beep that damn near scared her out of her skin. Cain looked down at the number in the display window, then muttered another, "Damn." He was already walking to her door, pausing only long enough to reach down and press a quick kiss to her temple, sending her a sexy wink, when he said, "I gotta go, sugar, but just think about what I said."

As if I'll be thinking about anything else, she thought. "Thanks for coming by," she called after him, watching as he flew down the narrow staircase, his long frame looking as out of place there as Mark's had last week, on that infamous night. They were both so big and broad and full of life, they seemed to take up all the space, no matter where they were. She struggled to find the right word to describe them, finally settling on dynamic, though things like addictive and mouthwatering came in as close seconds. As Kyra would say, the Logan brothers looked like they were born from sin and twice as thrilling.

Lost in reflection, Melanie shut her front door and leaned back on the hard surface, studying the claret-colored polish on her toenails as her mind whirred a mile a minute, emotions and feelings tumbling over themselves so quickly they all too soon became a jumbled, exhilarated mess. She tried to temper her excitement, but Cain's words kept playing through her mind, tempting and sweet. If what he said was true, what exactly had gone wrong that night? Why had everything that started out so right, gone so off-kilter? And what the hell was she going to do about it? Sit here and make herself dizzy spinning it around and around in her thick skull, or go after Mark Logan's bad boy ass and set him straight about what she wanted once and for all?

With a tight knot of anticipation in her tummy, she turned and wrenched open the door, and came face-to-fist with a hammering hand as it nearly connected with her forehead. Stumbling backward to avoid the blow meant for her door, she swiped at the wayward curls that had tumbled into her line of vision, and blinked against the sight of Mark filling her doorway, his wide shoulders blocking the bright glare of the sun that shone like a spark of flame behind him. He cursed under his breath at the near miss, at the same time her eyes went even wider when they landed on his still damp, stain-splattered T-shirt.

"What happened to you?" she blurted out, followed quickly by a demanding, "What are you doing here?"

"Trying to knock on your damn door," he muttered, ignoring the first question in favor of the second, before stepping past her the same way that Cain had done not fifteen minutes earlier. "Don't you know you should never open a door until you've looked to see who's there?"

Mel studied him from beneath her lashes, trying to figure out his mood. The long, wholly masculine lines of his big, hard body were taut with tension, the wide, sensual line of his mouth compressed into a fierce expression of...she couldn't exactly say. He didn't look necessarily angry, so much as on the verge of something explosive.

Shrugging her shoulders, Mel closed the door. "I didn't think anyone was there."

"Yeah, well, *I* was there."

She made a snarling sound of frustration, blowing another wayward curl from her eyes. "But you hadn't even knocked yet," she pointed out.

"I was getting ready to," he shot back, "and that door is pathetic. Hell, I could have busted through it without even breaking a sweat."

Melanie took a deep breath, then slowly let it out. "Mark, before this turns into a lecture on my home security or a ridiculous shouting match, was there something you actually wanted?"

He jerked to attention, the feral gleam in his eyes stealing her breath. "Yeah, there is."

She nibbled on the corner of her lip, feeling her heart jolt into her throat at the provocative intent coursing through his expression. "Why are you here?"

He took a single step toward her, crowding into her space with his long, strong frame that looked mouthwateringly good in a pair of dark blue running shorts and stained white T-shirt, his silky black hair windblown, the tang of the sea on his sweat-heated skin. He reached out and rubbed the callused pad of his thumb over her right cheekbone, stroking her skin, and in a gravel-filled voice, he rasped, "I'm here to say what I should have said before."

She swallowed against her nerves, barely resisting the urge to turn her face and press her lips against the damp heat of his palm. "Do I...uh, really want to hear this?"

A small smile played at the corner of his beautiful mouth, green eyes moving over the flushed features of her face like the urgent press of a lover's lips, leaving the warm thrum of hope in their wake. "I want more, Melanie."

She blinked against the dark, danger-edged flare of hunger that burned there in those seductive green depths, the thick rim of his ink-black lashes casting shadows against the golden brown of his skin. It seemed impossibly warm in her apartment, despite the cool chill of her air conditioner.

"More what?" she asked, unable to draw enough air into her lungs. She watched his lips part, a rumbling, ragged pattern of breaths breaking from his chest.

"Of you." His voice was deep and dark, an evocative assault on her senses that made her melt inside, going wet and thick like rich, succulent syrup, all gooey and warm.

"Um, after last Friday," she whispered, "I think you've already had more than you deserve, Mark."

"Not like that," he muttered, shaking his dark head as he stepped even closer, the hot, muscled slabs of his chest touching the tips of her shirt-covered breasts, making them pull tight with a tingling, clenching sensation. "I want more than that sweet little pussy between your legs, though god knows I'm all but dying for it. And I don't *just* want it, Melanie. *I need it*. And I haven't...I mean I haven't ever..." he verbally stumbled with frustration. "Jesus, I want to make you understand what this means—how different it is for me—but I don't know how to say it. I'm fumbling here like some kid with raging hormones," he muttered, breaking off with a disgusted scowl.

"No, keep going. This is finally getting good," she said with a dazed smile.

"Look, we screwed up. No, scratch that—*I* screwed up. I was trying to go easy on you, because I didn't want to scare you away from me. I never—*never* didn't want you, Mel, and I'm sorry as hell you...uh, might have got that impression. All I can say is that I handled it wrong from the beginning, but then I didn't know how the hell to handle it, all of this, in the first place." He made a harsh sound of irritation, lowering his head as he ran the long fingers of his left hand through the damp midnight strands of his hair, the musky, delectable scent of hot male coming from his skin in warm, pulsing waves, as if in perfect rhythm with his heartbeat.

"What was I supposed to think, Mark? All you wanted to do was *talk* to me!"

Her words seemed to jar his memory, because his head snapped up and he suddenly gripped her chin with his thumb and forefinger, a fierce scowl pulling the dark lines of his brows together. "Damn it, Melanie. Why the hell didn't you explain things to me that night, instead of letting me make an idiot of myself by assuming you were just looking for a quick screw?"

Mel nervously nibbled on the corner of her lip, fully aware that her heart had just launched itself into her throat. "Exactly what 'things' are you talking about, Mark?"

* * * * *

It was amazing the difference a week of hell, not to mention one pissed off woman and a cup of tea thrown at you, could make to a man's point of view, but damned if that wasn't the case. When he'd finally crawled out of bed this morning, Mark had tried to jog off his mounting frustration with a long beach run, even though he'd known it wouldn't work. Still, he'd needed the grind of the physical activity to keep him from pacing a hole through his floorboards, so he'd pushed himself hard for three miles, and finally found himself sweating in line at Roy's behind a certain smart-mouthed, feisty redhead.

Thank god for tough-ass best friends, he'd muttered as he'd run up the narrow staircase leading to Melanie's second-story apartment only moments before, or he'd still be moping around like some pathetic idiot, instead of going after the woman he wanted.

Now, stroking the lush curve of Melanie's lower lip with the calloused pad of his thumb, he still couldn't believe what a mess they'd made out of everything, both of them keeping their true feelings too close to their hearts. "Guess who I just ran into down at Miracles?"

"I haven't the foggiest," she answered through lips suddenly tight with tension, her normally glowing face pale with an unease that he longed to wipe away, replacing it with something so much brighter and more vital.

"Kyra."

Her eyes widened, and he could tell she tried to sound casual as she said, "And just what did Kyra have to say?"

He raised his gaze from the bruised rose of her beautiful mouth to snag her glittering glare. "Stop going all prickly on me and just answer the question. Why the hell didn't you just explain what you really wanted from me?"

"I tried," she argued, shrugging her shoulders as she tried to jerk her chin free of his grasp. "But you took it all wrong!"

Damn it, she had him there. "Well," he muttered, "you could have tried explaining to me about your past."

"My past?" she repeated in a quiet voice, her brown eyes narrowing suspiciously. "What difference would *that* have made?"

"Knowing how you felt about me, and what you thought I wanted from you—or what you thought I *didn't* want from you?" He snorted, shaking his head in frustration. "Fuck, it would have made things a hell of a lot easier to understand where you were coming from last Friday, I'll tell you that much. And I sure as hell wouldn't have jumped to my own dumbass conclusions when you started talking about my pain-in-the-ass reputation."

A sudden spark of recognition flared in her gaze, hot and bright and angry. "Kyra had no right to tell you anything. Just what exactly did she blab about?"

"You mean after she threw her chai tea in my face and told me along with the rest of Roy's customers what a first-class bastard she thinks I am for breaking your heart?" He sent her a wry smile, holding his hands out at his sides so she could see the full extent of the damage Kyra had inflicted upon his once white shirt.

"Yes...after that," she muttered, though there was an unholy gleam of humor in her eyes when she looked at his tea-splattered clothing.

"Enough for me to understand that the men you've known have been complete idiots." He kept his voice gentle, wanting to show her tenderness, though it was hard when the need to nail her sweet little ass to the nearest wall was driving him so hard. Hell, the need to ride her hard and make her come stayed with him twenty-four hours a day.

"Oh my god," she groaned, covering her face with her hands. "I'm going to strangle her!"

"Why?" he laughed softly, stroking her curls back from her face before trailing his hand down the side of her neck, making her shiver with awareness despite her embarrassment. "Because she's your friend and she cares about you? Because she thinks you deserve some happiness? Because she was willing to make a spectacle of herself to get me to realize what an ass I've been?"

"Some things are meant to be private," she argued, obviously sensitive about the details of her past experiences with the opposite sex, which in Mark's opinion was ridiculous. It wasn't her fault they'd been too blind to realize what they'd let slip through their fingers.

"It's supposed to be some big secret that you've known nothing but a string of idiots who weren't man enough to realize what an incredible, fascinating, sexy-as-hell woman you are?" he grunted. "Tight-assed, snot-nosed little runts in the mud, like that last jerk, Craig?"

Shock jerked her gaze back to his as she peeked at him from between her fingers. "That's it," she growled. "Kyra deserves to have her tongue cut out!"

Mark grasped her wrists and pulled her hands from her pink face, wondering if she was always going to blush in front of him...and almost hoping so, he found it so adorable. "Hey, don't go getting all pissed about it, angel. If she hadn't explained things, I'd still be thinking you were only after my–"

She immediately cut him off. "*Don't* say it," she groaned, her husky voice stifled, thick with emotion. "I did *not* just want you for sex, Mark Logan, but it was humiliating when I realized that you didn't even *want* to go to bed with me!"

"What?"

She thrust out her precious little chin and glared up at him. "You heard me."

"Wait a minute. You mean to tell me you *honestly* didn't think I wanted to fuck you that night?" he asked, dumbfounded by the truth burning there in that brilliant cinnamon-brown gaze. "Shit, Kyra said as much, but I guess I still wasn't really buying it. Not even when she told me—"

"I don't care what Kyra said to make you change your mind about me," she muttered. The mutinous look in her eyes said she was more than ready to do battle with him on the subject. "I do *not* want pity sex from you!"

"What?" he grunted this time.

She huffed and jerked her wrists free, crossing her arms over the gentle swell of her breasts. The soft mounds looked suspiciously free beneath the soft cotton of her T-shirt, making his mouth water. "You heard me."

"Will you stop repeating yourself?" he growled, moving even closer against her.

She answered with a step back. "Then stop saying 'What?'."

Mark took a deep breath, held it, then blew it out slowly, resting his hands on his hips to keep them out of trouble. "Okay, let's start at the beginning. What the hell made you think I didn't want to get your sweet little ass in bed? I've wanted to sink my dick into you, lady, from the first time I set eyes on you, and I've wanted it more every goddamn day. But I've never wanted it as much as I did after spending the evening with you, getting to know you...realizing that I'd—"

She cut him off, muttering, "You were surprised when I asked."

"Only because I'd been trying so *hard* to control myself that my damn hard-on was ready to explode," he gritted through his teeth, feeling the vein in his temple tick with his temper. "I didn't want to fall all over you like some sex-starved maniac and scare your sweet little ass away."

"You got angry!" Melanie argued, refusing to be intimidated by his attitude.

He made a sarcastic snorting sound that was utterly male. "Because I felt stupid as shit. When you blurted out that crap about my reputation, I thought you only agreed to go out with me because you wanted a one-nighter. I thought you didn't care a goddamn thing about me—that you just wanted my body."

"Well, I do want it," she huffed, fluttering her hand at him, before crossing her arms back over her chest. "But I'd like everything else that goes along with it."

"Yeah, well, that's good then, sweetheart, because you've got it. All of it. In fact," he rumbled in a low growl, narrowing his green eyes on her with a primal, savage intensity that made her want to pinch herself to see if this was really happening, "I'd be willing to bet my *life* on the fact that this body isn't ever going to want anyone but *you*, not ever again. And that's not just some line I'm throwing at you. It's the honest-to-god truth."

A deep breath staggered in her lungs, a shivering spike of excitement racing beneath the surface of her skin. He cupped her cheek, staring down at her with so much tenderness, she didn't know how she kept from simply melting at his feet. "Honestly, Mel, I don't know how you could think any man wouldn't give his soul for the chance to be with you," he rasped in a smoky, black magic voice.

"It wasn't just you." At his puzzled expression, she struggled to explain. "Kyra told you the truth. That's what guys have *always* wanted from me—conversation. It's like I'm nothing but a set of ears. Normally it doesn't bother me so much, but with you...*aargh*," she growled, trembling as she struggled to explain. "I couldn't take it from you, too. I wanted to talk to you and get inside your head and learn everything, every single intriguing little detail about you, Mark. But I wanted...I needed..."

"It's okay," he murmured, gentling her with the warm press of his rough-silk lips against her temple as he pulled her close, the animal heat of his body making her jerk with shock, as if she'd pressed her wet fingers to a live wire. "I get it now," he breathed against her hair, his strong arms wrapping around her in a possessive hold, while her hands clutched at his powerful biceps and her nose pressed into his chest, the sinful scent of his skin making her feel drunk with pleasure.

"I was an ass, baby, but not anymore. You wanted this too, didn't you, sweetheart?" he asked in a whiskey-rich voice, moving his hot palms down to her shorts-covered backside and lifting her into the hard evidence of his arousal, his cock an impossibly long, breathtakingly thick ridge within the thin confines of his running shorts. "Unlike those other jerk-offs you've known, you wanted me to rip off your conservative little clothes and fuck your beautiful brains out. Wanted me to cover you with my hungry body and shove my thick, heavy cock hard into you, *inside you*, didn't you, angel? It's okay, you can talk to me," he coaxed with a deliciously wicked grin as he trailed his hands up the sensitive line of her spine, long fingers sifting through her hair as he cupped them around her skull. Using his possessive grip on her curls, he pulled her head back, demanding she hold his stare. "Tell me everything, all of it. There's nothing going on inside you that I don't wanna know about, Melanie. Whatever you want, I can promise you that I want it more."

"*Damn,*" she moaned thickly, knowing her dazed expression mirrored every fascinating reaction zinging through her body, from her scalp down to her toes. Hot and thick, the love and lust pulsed through her system. She could feel it in her eyelids and the fierce heat of her earlobes, down to the tight, aching tips of her breasts...and lower, where it all centered deep inside, her inner muscles clenching with want while her needy flesh went slick with hot, violent desire. "*Oh god.*"

"Just call me Mark, sweetheart," he drawled with a teasing smile, using his hands on her backside to rub her over the hard mass of his cock, making her breath catch at the mouthwatering, head-spinning sensation, even while she laughed at his comeback. Then his smile faded, replaced by a smoldering, serious look in those soft green eyes. "I'm going to be honest with you and tell you what I should have told you that night. I want more with you, Melanie Green, and…uh…I should've made that clear from the very beginning, honey. I want a woman I can talk to and share my life with, who makes me ache to take her with a long, rough ride from nothing more than a smile, and that's you. You turn me inside out, twisting me up inside, and I'm…I…shit, this isn't easy," he muttered, "and I'm making an absolute ass of myself, but I've never done this before."

She smiled up at him, deliciously lost in the moment. Lost in him. "Done what?"

"Mel, I want you. In my life. Permanently. Not just for sex, though the sex is an absolute given. Uh, actually, if I don't get the sex soon, there's every chance I might actually start begging here, but—"

"Yeah?" she sighed, pulling his head down so that she could press a kiss to the hot, silky skin of his cheek, trailing her lips along the hard angle of his jaw.

"I want it all," he growled. "I want you to move in with me. Live with you, be a part of your life every damn day. Have you be the most important thing in mine. For…hell, forever, Melanie. Which…uh, means that someday, when you're ready, I'm going to want my ring on your finger and my name after yours."

Shock nearly made it impossible to speak, but she managed to gasp the words out of a tight throat. "You think you'll want to marry me someday?"

"Not think, honey. *Know*. But I won't rush you into anything, I promise. We've got plenty of time." His arms pulled her tighter into the heat of his body, wrapping around her until she felt wonderfully crushed...needed. "I'm in love with you, Melanie Green, and if there's any chance at all that someday you'll feel the same way about me, then I'm—hell, I'll do anything, Mel. Just tell me what I have to do."

"But...you..." she mumbled into his chest, "all those other—"

It seemed he knew what she was going to say before she even said it. "Forget my dumb-ass reputation. I know I can't change it, but it doesn't mean anything, sweetheart. I don't know how to make you understand what you've done to me, but I've changed," he struggled to explain, a dull wash of color burning across the sharp angles of his cheekbones as she peeked up at him. "That's not who I am now, and I...uh, you gotta believe me when I tell you that, because it's true." He stared down at her, the look in his mesmerizing green gaze begging her to believe in him. "I thought I was content with the way things were, and then I met you and it damn near knocked me on my ass. Hell, it was like being hit upside the head with an I-beam. I want you, Mel, and it just isn't going to be enough until I've got you. That one taste last Friday damn near drove me outta my mind. I've done nothing but think about it...but live it over and over in my head until it's driving me crazy."

"I can't believe that you'd want me," she thought, surprised when she realized she'd said the words out loud, watching as his beautiful mouth twisted with emotion.

"I don't know how you could doubt it, Melanie. You've haunted me, woman. Your taste, your scent," he whispered, his beautiful voice rough with want. "The way you feel in my arms...the way you shatter when I make you come. God, Mel, it's been all I could do to stay away from you. To stay away and not come begging you to want me for more than just a one-shot deal. To want me forever, because the only woman I'll ever want again is you. I knew it all along, baby. I just didn't know what the hell to do about it."

"I...oh god," she breathed out again on a shaky breath, words simply failing her at the burning honesty she could see written upon the rugged beauty of his face, hear within his husky words. "So you really— I mean, you *honestly* want more from me than just some good conversation?"

A sharp laugh jerked out of his throat, but he choked it back when he saw the bruised expression on her face. "God, Mel, how could you even think such a thing? As much as I love talking to you, nothing can compare to having you in my arms." His voice lowered once more, rough and raw as he added, "To having you under me, surrounding me while I sink deep inside you."

"But you haven't even done that...yet, Mark. How do you know it'll be enough?" *How do you know I'll be enough?*

The look in his eyes was so wicked and warm, she felt as if he'd read her mind. "Just because I haven't had my dick in you yet, sweetheart, doesn't mean I haven't been inside you."

She blushed so bright she felt sunburned, and he laughed, a low, wicked chuckle that melted down her spine, making her weak and strong at the same time. "You feel so soft inside, baby. As soft and sweet as you look on the outside, and I *know* it's gonna burn me alive when I finally get in you."

"If you fit," she murmured wryly, shifting back to glance down at the stiff, thick evidence of his massive cock pressing against the thin material of his shorts.

"I'll fit. I'll make sure you're so ready that I'll sink right in. It'll be a tight squeeze, but nothing will ever be more perfect."

Melanie cocked her head to the side as she studied the determined, intent lines of his expression. "You seem really sure of yourself."

"I am. Your sweet little pussy was made to take me...all the way to the hilt, Mel," he growled, the sexy sound making her shiver with excitement.

"But I...I'm, well, I mean, I don't have nearly your kind of experience when it comes to this, um, kind of stuff," she mumbled. "I hate to say it, or even think it, but there's probably a really good chance that you'll get bored with me, Mark."

The green of his eyes was feverishly bright as he stared at her through the thick fringe of his lashes, the pattern of his breathing coming harder, as if he was as turned on as she felt. It was a heady, electrifying thought that nearly had her moaning aloud.

"You're gonna have to trust me, Mel," he said huskily, "when I tell you that there's not a chance in hell that could ever happen. Damn, just talking to you makes me hard. I'm almost afraid to think of what fucking you is going to do."

Her lips trembled into a soft grin. "Conversational foreplay, huh?"

"You can laugh, but do you have any idea what you did to me that night?" he asked with a wry smile. "I was hard under that little table the entire damn time we were at *Caza's*, Mel, from nothing more than the sexy, sinful sound of your voice. When you told me about your last trip to Milan, I got so turned on that I ached. Watching the way your eyes sparkled when you described Paris damn near turned my dick inside out. If we hadn't been in a restaurant full of surfers who were all sneaking looks at you, I'd have thrown the table out of my goddamn way, pulled up your skirt and shoved my face in your perfect little cunt right there, eating your hot little juices for dessert, while you just kept talking about the Seine and the Louvre and that little café with the *pain au chocolat* and *café au lait*. The entire night was like some deviously designed torture session to see how far you could push me, 'til I lost it and ended up scaring your sweet little ass away. So don't ever, *ever* doubt my desire, sweetheart. I want to sink inside you every time I set eyes on you. Every time I think about you. And *only* you, Mel."

She frowned as a sudden thought occurred to her. "I don't want a man who's faithful simply because he thinks it's right, like it's some kind of noble sacrifice."

"It isn't like that. I'll be faithful because you're all I want," he said with far more tenderness than she would have ever thought an utterly alpha male like him could show or feel. "That's a fact that isn't ever going to change. So you had better fucking accept it."

"Oh," she sighed dreamily, wondering if she looked as love-struck as she felt.

"And?" Mark prompted, the hard, yet ridiculously sexy line of his mouth twitching with humor.

"And what?"

"I'd like to hear the same from you," he said with a stifled growl. "Forget like. I *have* to hear it, Mel. I need to know, damn it."

Melanie blinked in fascination. "From me?"

He stared at her so intently, she felt as if he was trying to sneak into her mind. "Don't sound so damn surprised. I want to know that you're mine — and *only* mine — woman."

"Mmm…" she moaned, melting from the evocative heat in his darkening gaze.

He shook his head with exasperation, another wry smile playing at the corner of his lips. "You gonna give me an answer?"

Warm satisfaction curled heavily within her, drowsy and replete. She wanted to bask in the glorious heat of his expression, but sexual urgency pulsed too fiercely beneath her skin, setting her to a fine tremble, and all she could do was grin in return.

"Tell me you want me, Mel," he said, his voice shaking in a low rumble. "I'm hanging by a thread here, and every second I spend without you hurts like a son of a bitch. Tell me you're mine. Tell me that no other bastard is ever setting his fucking hands on you."

"You know," she teased, shaken by the depth of emotion in his words, "you and your talented brother have practically taken cursing to an art form. It's amazing."

"I don't want to talk about Cain," he growled against the sensitive skin beneath her ear, nipping the tender lobe. The hungry urgency in his voice told her that he'd reached the limit of his control. "I want to talk about *us*. I want you to tell me what you want."

There was only one answer, simple and perfect and pure. "You, Mark. I want you."

Chapter Seven

ೞ

"Aw, thank god," Mark groaned, and before she could blink, he had Melanie plastered against the feral heat of his body. His hands clutched at the lush softness of her backside, grinding her against the raging ache in his cock, her soft breasts flattened against his chest. "This first time won't be easy, Mel." He'd tried to soften the vicious thread of hunger in his tone, but knew he'd failed when she trembled against him. "I've waited too long for you. Hell, this first *month* might not be easy, but after that, I...uh, promise I'll be able to give it to you however you want it. You name it, honey. But right now I have to be *in* you."

"Any way you want it, Mark," she said breathlessly, pressing the damp heat of her mouth to his, and the stroke of her eager tongue past his lips damn near turned his cock inside out. "Just so long as I've got you, I'm good. Great. Freaking spectacular."

With a low growl, he broke the kiss to preserve what little of his sanity he still held, and his eyes tracked over the grace of her flushed face, absorbing all the beautiful, purely unique details of her. Lingering over the individual features that made her glow — made her so perfectly special to him. All of it, each soft curve and shape, affected him in the same way as an artist might feel when standing in awe beneath the majesty of Michaelangelo's frescoes adorning the Sistine Chapel ceiling. The dainty, dark freckles that decorated her nose and cheekbones. The gentle sweep of her brows and the feminine line of her nose. The angle of her jaw and the soft curve of her chin.

"You're so beautiful," he whispered achingly as he carried her the few feet it took to reach her dining nook. With uncharacteristically trembling hands, he pushed her back against the gleaming surface of her small table. She trembled, too, beneath the press of his eyes, shivering as he trailed one callused palm down the center of her shirt-covered chest, over the smooth plane of her stomach, the feminine flare of her hips. Then he turned inward, burrowing into the humid warmth of her cloth-covered sex, parting her knees with his thighs.

He leaned over her, and Mel's hands clutched at his shoulders, fisting handfuls of his shirt, struggling to pull it off. A low laugh rumbled in his chest and he straightened, watching her desire-filled expression as he ripped the stained T-shirt off over his head, his cock jerking in his shorts at the drugged look of pleasure that fell over her face. Her eyes were heavy, lambent, cheeks pink with a warm wash of color, soft pink lips parted for her soughing breaths. She jackknifed upright, running her palms eagerly over his heated skin, and his breath sucked sharply into his chest.

"Mark," she breathed out shakily, and he ground his jaw as she flicked her thumbs over his hard nipples. Knowing he was on the verge of something explosive, he grabbed the bottom of her shirt and jerked it off over her head, forcing her arms up high. The second the cloth cleared her fingertips, she wrapped her arms around her breasts, nibbling on the corner of her plump lower lip as the flush on her face spread down the slender column of her pale throat, blooming prettily over the satiny skin of her chest and the mouthwatering mounds she was so preciously trying to hide from him. They bulged around her caging arms, and he wasn't sure whether the low rumbling sound echoing in his ears was a storm blowing in off the Pacific or his own cracking control.

"Don't hide from me," he grunted in a low, gravel-filled voice, pulling her arms away as she shivered, and the sight of her small, tender pink nipples nearly killed him. Her hands fluttered shyly at her sides, and he pinned them to the table with the firm press of his own, telling her without words to keep them there. Something primitive and savage stretched to awareness within him, snarling at the thought of her hiding from him. "Don't ever cover up in front of me, Mel," he demanded roughly, moving his hands to her shoulders and forcing her back against the table.

She shivered beneath the bright, revealing overhead light and what he knew was the purely feral look of hunger burning in his gaze, her firm breasts trembling, soft and beautiful, against her chest.

"Mark...the light," she whispered, staring up at the bright overhead ceiling fixture, while he flicked the button undone on her shorts, lowered the zipper and quickly gripped the thin cotton in his hands.

"No," he breathed out huskily, wrenching the shorts over her hips, then stepping back so that he could pull them down her legs. Her tiny scrap of pale pink panties immediately followed. "I want to see you — all of you — when I go down on you this time," he said gutturally, aware that his voice trembled with his need for her. With his hands on her knees, he forced them out wide at her sides and stepped back between them, knowing he couldn't have looked away from the breathtaking perfection of her naked cunt if his life depended on it. "I want every one of these gorgeous, pink little details up close and personal, knowing that they belong to me. *Only to me.* Right, Mel?"

"Yes," she moaned, arching beneath him, unable to remain still. She rode the surface of the table in a shimmying wave of need, looking like a primordial sacrifice, laid out and spread for his pleasure.

But first, Mark wanted hers.

Without any warning, he lowered his head and pressed his mouth to the hot, deliciously wet folds of her pussy with gentle avidity. He burrowed into her moist, succulent warmth, feeling drunk on her womanly scent and taste as it surrounded him, beautiful and sweet and pure. Fresh and utterly new, making him crave her in a way he'd never thought he could hunger for a woman.

Swirling his tongue lazily around her clit, he avariciously collected her honeyed juices. He moved lower, and the second his strong tongue stroked deeply, piercing her lush entrance, she came. He ate at her greedily, like he was starved...and he was. He claimed every seductive drop for his own, swallowing her into his mouth while his tongue stroked possessively through her folds, lapping into her tight, rhythmically pulsing entrance, marveling at the pure perfection of her. When he finally raised his head, he grinned wickedly as he gazed up at her damp, crimson face over the arc of her pubic bone. "Don't you know you're supposed to make me work for it, sweetheart?"

"Oh...um, sorry," she mumbled hoarsely, raising her head to stare at him down the shivering line of her torso.

"That's okay." He gave her a warm smile, tilting his head to the side as he studied the soft curve of her belly, the shallow indentation of her navel, stroking the quivering flesh with his palm. "But you owe me."

She blinked in owlish fascination. "I do?"

"Hell, yes," he groaned, moving up her body. His lips found the puffy swell of her right nipple, and he lustily drew it into the warm heat of his mouth, loving the low moan that shivered out of her as he suckled, pressing the hardened tip to the roof of his mouth, then working it hungrily with his tongue. His jaws opened wider, and he pulled more of that succulent flesh into his heat, wanting to swallow her whole. When she was writhing beneath him, arching up into the avid pulls of his mouth, he moved to the other breast, taking it with the same greedy urgency that he'd shown the first.

"You owe me, Mel," he drawled roughly, lifting his head to press his lips against the quivering point at the base of her throat where her pulse fluttered chaotically, "and I know exactly what I want."

His fingers found the tender flesh between her legs, all slippery and slick with her warm release. His head moved higher, claiming her mouth in a blistering kiss of carnal intent as his hand moved lower, seeking her demure entrance. Mark instantly pressed two thick fingers up into her, penetrating the tight sheath of her body, forcing her to stretch wide around him. She cried out into his kiss, a shocked, awakening sound of pleasure and pain, and he worked his fingers deeper, desperate to ready her for the heaviness of his cock.

It was Melanie who finally tore her mouth from his, her panting breaths pelting him sweetly in the face. "Damn it, do it!" she gasped at the same time that she reached down to grasp the waist of his shorts. "And I want to see you. *Right now.* This very second."

Mark moved back until he stood upright between her widespread thighs, her sweet, juice-covered cunt trembling and open, the tiny slit swollen and crimson from her recent climax. He locked his jaw as he stared at the way it breathed, slick with her cum, and toed off his trainers, shoving his shorts down until they fell to the floor. Melanie gasped a sharp, shocked little sound of surprise at the sight of his cock sticking out from the dark curls in his groin, and the male animal inside him wanted to throw back its head and howl with primitive pride.

Shaking his head at his caveman reactions to this woman, he fisted his hand around the wide base of his erection and looked down as he pressed forward, rubbing the fat, swollen head against the tender flesh of her slick, puffy pussy lips. His shaft was ruddy, thick and long and heavy with want. The round, plum-sized tip already glistened with fluid, the nestled slit leaking with lust for the woman spread open before him. The thick network of veins that crossed beneath the surface of his skin bulged beneath the biting pressure of his fist, and he knew he wasn't going to last worth shit once this started. Hell, just the sight of her made him want to jerk into the air, showering over the pearly pink folds of her sex, across the pale expanse of her belly.

But there was no way in hell he was coming anywhere but deep inside her. As deep into her as he could possibly get.

He had his wallet in the zippered pocket of his shorts and knew there was a condom inside. He *knew* he needed to reach down and get it out, slip it over the brutal ache of his erection—and yet, he couldn't move. He wasn't stupid. He'd never had sex before without one, but he didn't want that goddamn latex barrier between him and the liquid pull of Melanie's body. He wanted her to feel the burn of his cock as he penetrated her, wanted to feel the lush cream of her pussy as he crammed himself all the way inside. Wanted her gasping as each swollen, vein-ridged inch impaled her. Wanted to feel the lusty bite of her hot little cunt sucking him in, milking his cock.

"Talk about something surpassing your expectations," she murmured wryly, a bit breathless as she stared wide-eyed at his erection. Despite the pain shooting up from his balls, twisting into his gut, Mark couldn't help but laugh.

"I'm glad you like it."

"Like it," she grinned, reaching down to stroke her finger across the swollen glans, making his teeth grind so hard he wondered why they didn't crack. "Yeah, I definitely *like* it."

"Keep looking at me like that," he groaned, his gaze flickering back and forth between the provocative sights of her stroking his cock head and her pink tongue licking her bottom lip, "and it's going to be inside you before I get the rubber on."

"You want to wear...one?"

Her voice came so softly that he almost wasn't sure whether she'd spoken or he'd imagined those halting words. He didn't think it was possible, but the knot in his shaft grew thicker, his jaw locked tighter. "Honestly? *Hell no.* I've never had sex without one, so I know I'm safe...and I'm a big enough bastard to like the idea of you swollen with my baby. But I wouldn't do that to you so soon, Mel."

"I've never...had sex without a condom either...and I'm, um, on the Pill because I had some trouble with my cycles. So...um..."

He went so still, not even his lungs moved. "You're shitting me," he gasped.

She wrinkled her nose at his words, even while she smiled at the eagerness of his expression. Mark knew he looked like a kid who'd just discovered the magic of a hidden treasure map. "Um, no, I'm not."

"*Oh hell*," he groaned, already fitting the wet head of his cock to her crimson inner lips, both of them sucking in hard, sharp breaths at that first breathtaking, sizzling contact. "This is gonna be so fucking good, Mel," he gritted out through clenched teeth. "It's gonna blow my ever-loving mind."

She opened around him like a tight, hungry little mouth, deliciously wet and blisteringly hot against his naked flesh. He groaned a ragged, shuddering sound of ecstasy, and pushed deeper, shoving in an inch...and then a couple more as he moved over her. It was nearly impossible to work himself into her, her snug little body protesting his brutal penetration while her words pleaded for more.

Melanie pressed her open mouth to the sweaty skin of his shoulder, nipping him with her teeth. "I want to feel you all the way inside. Stop holding back."

He pulsed inside the tight clench of her tender sheath, wondering if his head was going to explode from the incredible pressure. It was like sinking into the ultimate sexual haven — pure, white-hot fantasy — the heat and grip of her snug muscles, the liquid heaven of her juices soaking him, urging him to pound her hard and fast and deep, until he'd ridden her through the table.

"Mel, stop," he groaned in a gritty voice, forcing himself to go slow as he fed more of his thick, hard dick into her. "I'm on edge here, honey, and you're tight enough to make me forget how small you are. I'm trying to get myself together." He breathed roughly, pushing another two inches into her, loving how the walls of her cunt parted for him, then sucked in around him like a fucking throat swallowing him down. "God, just give me a second."

Or two...maybe a thousand. Hell, he didn't think he was ever going to get his head on straight again. This wasn't fucking. This was some kind of teeth-grinding ecstasy that went so far beyond anything he'd ever known, he had no frame of reference. He was breaking her open, inch by inch, and he felt stripped bare by the sensation. Utterly at its mercy...and falling deeper every second. He shifted, and those sweet inner muscles clutched at him in a silken, voluptuous caress, making him curse hotly under his breath.

"You feel so good," she panted, her hands never stopping, moving over the hot skin at his nape, across the slick heat of his shoulders, even lower, clutching at his hard buttocks as she struggled to pull him deeper. He groaned and surged forward in a sudden, jolting thrust that buried more thick inches into her. A low, rumbling growl broke from his throat, and she cried out a sharp, keening sound of surprised pleasure, clutching at the slippery line of his spine, her short nails pricking into the bunched heat of his muscles.

"You have no idea how worried I've been, thinking I might never get here," he breathed out with his next restrained pull and thrust, his voice raspy and raw as his broad shaft cut through her wet heat like a knife, working into her one inch at a time, stretching, pulling her open. He lifted back and gripped her behind her knees, pulling them out wide, leaving her vulnerable and open, his head falling forward as he stared at the point where his body penetrated hers.

"Faster," she gasped. "Hurry, Mark. *Please!*"

"No," he muttered, suddenly releasing her knees to catch her wrists in the strong grasp of his big hands. He stretched her arms up high above her head and held them there, then savored every delicious, burning point of contact as he pressed his body against the gentle cushion of hers. The wet, delicate silk of her sex gripping him so impossibly tight, his chest cushioned against her breasts, the giving warmth of her skin, so silky and smooth it drugged him — all of it blew his fucking mind, and he suddenly feared where it could push him. She was delicate and soft, and he struggled not to let the primal instinct in his blood take over, riding her with everything he could feel breaking open inside him. Dark, sensual hungers for raging, explosive sex — the kind that would mark them both as owned, claimed, taken. The kind that sealed your fate, that you could never return from.

The kind that meant something.

That meant *everything*.

It'd taken thirty-six goddamn years, but he'd finally found the one who mattered, and it threatened to rip his hard-earned control right out of him, scraping him raw.

She didn't know what she was tempting him with — didn't understand just how far he could go with this thing. That fear of being too much for her, of scaring her off, kept twisting through him like a sickness.

Melanie stared up at him, her brown eyes shimmering and damp, liquid and soft. "You said you're in love with me," she murmured. "It's true, isn't it?"

"Yeah," he groaned, rubbing his mouth against the damp silk of her lips, taking her sweet breath into his lungs. "It is most definitely true, Miss Green."

"Then give me all of you, Mark. I promise you, I can take it, whatever it is you have to give — however you need to give it."

He wanted to believe her, but he'd been with women far more actively sexual than Mel, and even with them, he'd often had to hold back. He *should* have had himself on a damn leash, instead of forcing his way deeper into her, but there was no going back. His control was being systematically ripped away by need and lust and that sweet, aching clench in his belly that staggered him every goddamn time he saw her face. He was strung tight with a brilliant, blinding desperation to get into her and stay there forever. The wet heat of her body as it grew softer, accepting him, tempted him like manna—like the perfect sin—and he was helpless to resist.

"I told you," he grated out of a dry throat as she took another inch of him, "it's perfect. Like a skintight little glove. Damn, Mel, you're gonna suck the cum right outta me, sweetheart. Unbelievable."

"Then stop fighting it, Mark. I can feel you holding back and I hate it! I *want* you to lose control."

"What control?" he snorted, resting his forehead against the smooth heat of hers. He moved his head from side to side, sucking at air as he tried to claw onto some kind of restraint, but he could feel the violent urge to move...to fully penetrate and claim burning up from the core of his balls, pumping through his cock with a desperate urgency that would soon break him. "Shit," he cursed roughly, blindly searching for her mouth as a tremoring wave of hunger jolted through his system.

"I love you, Mark," she sobbed hoarsely against his lips, and he felt that burning ball of insatiable need explode, shattering apart inside him.

"Aw, hell," he gasped, every muscle shaking as he struggled to hold himself together. "Have mercy on me, Mel. I'll never forgive myself if I blow this."

"It's true." She smiled up at him, pulling her hands free of his slackening grip, then smoothing the dark line of his brows with her trembling fingertips, the cinnamon-brown of her eyes infinite and bright, pulling him in, sucking him under. "You take my breath away. I feel so empty without you, and I don't want to feel empty anymore, Mark. I want to feel like this, full of you, like you're everywhere inside me. I love you, and I want to know what it feels like to have the man I love go wild on me, over me, in me...*because* of me. Just trust me." And suddenly that smile turned wicked, the expression in her eyes one of such feral heat, he felt burned. "Trust me enough to know when I want to have my brains fucked out by the man I love. Come on, Mark, and show me what I do to you. Show me what you want from me."

A deep, guttural groan rumbled up in his throat, vicious in its intensity, and his muscles trembled from the impact of her words. "Christ, you've done it now," he growled...and that was it. Without direction from his lust-fried brain, he clutched her upper arms as his hips surged back, then powered forward, shoving the brutal length of his cock into the sweet, clenching depths of her pussy. Those tight inner walls clamped down, so deliciously strong, but he shoved through them, *hard*, separating her—penetrating her—cramming himself in with a wholly violent power until she'd taken him to the hilt. He didn't stop until his balls were jammed up tight against her ass and the fat, heavy head of his cock was lodged possessively against the mouth of her womb.

Her shocked scream echoed through the thickness of his head, but he couldn't rein himself in—and thank god, he didn't need to, if her words were anything to go by.

"*Oh god...again!* Mark, move...*now!*"

He was lost. Some kind of savage, terrifying snarl ripped out of his throat, and he couldn't control it. He *had* no control. Her words and the soft press of her mouth, the sweet clench of her cunt, all of it drove him over the edge and out of his mind. He shouted, pulling back, and then rammed forward with all his strength, until their groins slammed together and she'd taken every hard, aching inch of his cock again. He hammered into her, burying himself solid and deep again and again, while her soft sobs and cries for more filled his ear, and he couldn't stop. His hands, damp and shaking, moved to clutch at the soft swell of her sweet little ass, and he held her pressed between his lust and the ungiving surface of the table, fucking her with everything that he had.

He took her at her word and gave all that she'd asked for.

The table lurched across the Spanish-tiled floor, screeching and jarringly loud as it slammed into the wall. A distant part of his euphoria-dazed brain hoped like crazy her neighbors weren't nosy enough to come and investigate, because there was no way in hell he was stopping. His blood thundered in his ears, accompanied by the sexy sounds breaking from Melanie's throat, and he moved his arms under her legs, lifting them high as he reached up and curled his hands beneath her shoulders. Her eyes widened the second she realized how thoroughly he had her controlled, her body trapped in his unbreakable hold. He tried to smile to reassure her, but the muscles in his face wouldn't cooperate. Instead, he heard himself growling a deep, rumbling sound of absolute possession, while his body rode her in a hard, pounding rhythm, his heavy cock powering into her.

Then he felt that first exquisite contraction—that mind-shattering rush of liquid fire—and he knew she was coming.

"*Mark!*" she screamed, pulling him closer at the exact moment her climax shot through her, erupting with the earthy violence of a warm tropical storm, lashing him with sensation. He growled against the tender silk of her neck, roaring like a bull as he battered into her, no finesse or skill or smooth seduction—just a beast claiming his woman in the most elemental, brutally intense way he could imagine. And then he followed her over, trembling on his feet, every muscle taut and stretched to the breaking point, his head thrown back, chest heaving, while his body did its best to turn itself inside out. He poured into her forever, until it felt as if he'd given everything, all that he was, into her body. The thick, pounding pleasure of release pumped rhythmically through his blood to an ancient, primordial beat—her name shouted into the air, guttural and raw, laden with emotion. There was something so basic and primal and perfect about filling her with his cum, and it erupted from his body with jaw-grinding ecstasy until he felt battered and bruised, the knowledge that this one sexual encounter had surpassed the culmination of every erotic moment he'd ever experienced burning like a bright, incandescent light of truth in his passion-drugged brain.

When it was over, he released her shoulders and collapsed on top of her, his lips twitching with the exhausted twinges of a smile at the cute grunt of sound she made. Her sweet arms wrapped around him, stroking the slick heat of his back, holding him tightly.

Mark never wanted her to let him go.

When their breathing grew calm and their flesh went cool, Melanie stroked the long line of his spine, marveling at the feel of him still hard and full inside her. He lifted his head, staring down at her through lambent, sexy-as-hell eyes, and with a crooked smile, he asked, "What?"

"I was just thinking about what you said before. So...*this*...um, was what you thought would scare me away?"

He shrugged, color washing over the high cut of his cheekbones. "You look like the sweet lie-on-your-back, missionary-position, with-the-lights-off type, Mel. I was terrified. And I gotta be honest with you, sweetheart—this is *only* the beginning. I want to twist and turn your beautiful body into every position that's ever been imagined. Do things to you that will most likely shock you at first, but I can swear I'll make you love them. *All of them.*"

"Well," she laughed, "that's what I *was*, but *this* is what I've dreamed of, Mark. This is what I've spent so many months wanting...with you."

He leaned down and kissed her. A sweet, smiling kiss that curled her toes. "And you fit me just like I knew you would. Perfect. I'll never get enough."

"I'm glad you like it," she laughed, mimicking his earlier words, "since it's all yours."

"And this is all yours," he drawled, kissing the sensitive underside of her jaw as he shifted his hips, nudging his cock a fraction deeper. "Don't ever doubt it, baby. We may get kinky as hell with each other, but it's always going to be just the *two* of us."

Then his head cocked slightly to the side as he studied her out of slowly darkening eyes, and in that deep, whiskey-rough voice, he added, "Though I can't say that the idea of fucking you on my bar one night, after closing, with the windows open and the moonlight spilling all over this beautiful body, isn't hot as hell. Knowing that anyone could walk by and see us, see how wild I can make you, how hard I can make you come and scream and how gorgeous you look when you're getting fucked. When this sweet body is crammed so impossibly full of my hard dick, your mouth open and your face red, while rough little grunts of sound break out of you every time I pull back and then give it to you harder…deeper. Maybe even handcuff your hands behind your back, so you can't fight it. Can't try to cover your face or these perfect tits when someone walks by, watching, seeing all of it. Seeing just how thoroughly you belong to me. No," he rasped, his voice velvety soft, but savage in its intensity, "I can't say that I don't find that idea hot as hell, Melanie."

"Oh god," she whispered, her own voice low and throaty with thick, painful arousal, the visual image of his sinfully, sexually decadent fantasy pulsing through her body in a violent wave of desire, making her pussy ripple around him, clinging and hungry for exactly what he'd described.

"I know," he answered in a scratchy, almost breathless rumble. "Just thinking about it makes me feel the same way, sweetheart."

She moaned in response, something dark and voluptuous, rich and succulent growing inside her, everything going heavy and moist, like a smoldering knot of desire inside her body as she felt his cock give a sharp twitch. "Mark…he's…still hard."

His mouth twisted into a wicked, sexy smile, green eyes turning shimmering and bright. "Yeah, I know that, too. He's been hard all fucking week, pounding like a goddamn toothache because I wanted you and couldn't have you." He leaned down and rubbed his mouth over hers, and the touch of his silken lips felt like love.

"Is he, um, always like this?" she asked impishly, running the tip of her index finger down the hot side of his face, his silky stubble rasping against her skin.

"Well, I've never been known to bat only once at the plate, but this—you—hell, this is like winning the pennant. He might not go down for days," he drawled against her mouth, licking the plump pad of her lower lip before playfully nipping it with his teeth.

"Mmm...lucky me. I knew I was incredibly intelligent to fall for you."

"I hope you're ready to fall again," he groaned, pulling back and then feeding his heavy shaft back into the sweet, sensitive vise of her thoroughly, beautifully fucked little cunt, jabbing his hips in shallow thrusts to work the thick rim of his cock head back into the clenching hold of her body. "Do you have any idea how perfect you feel?" he asked huskily, loving the feel of being *in* her, of working himself into her precious, cum-slick pussy again and again. "What it feels like sinking into you, fucking you? How goddamn different it is from anything I've ever known before?"

Her head tilted back as the pleasure pushed up into her, heavy and full. "Do you have any idea how it feels to know I'm so wanted?"

"I know how it feels to be the one wanting you," he laughed roughly. With one warm hand on the back of her neck, he pulled her forward, tilting her face until she too was watching the slow, heavy cramming of his body into hers, his tempo still deliberate and controlled, making her feel every inch as it moved in and out of her grasping tissues. "Doesn't that tell you how much I want you?"

"Yeah, it's a nice visual," she agreed breathlessly, while her hands clutched the roped sinew of his forearms.

He pressed his lips to her temple. "Do you have any idea what you do to me? I could stay inside you forever, but I'm about to lose it again any second now."

"I can't wait," she answered breathlessly.

"If it's too much," he rumbled, "you'll tell me?"

"I told you before, I can take it."

"You'll tell me," he insisted, the words hard with command. Mel peeked at him from beneath her lashes to see his face damp with sweat, dark hair sticking to his temples.

"Fine," she muttered. "I'll tell you. Now do your best."

His big hands clasped onto the rounded curve of her hips, and he held on to her as the next thrust powered him in. Her body jolted and the next one he pulled her into, so that they slammed together, and he sank in even deeper, making her back arch as a keen sensation of being utterly filled ripped up through her body.

God, he's breathtaking, she thought, the air in her lungs literally catching at the provocative visual he made. His beautiful body gleamed, bronzed and sweat-slick, the long muscle and sinew starkly defined. Around the rugged features of his face, his dark hair was damp and wild, the sensual line of his lips parted for the low grunts that came with each perfect thrust of his body into hers.

Her gaze fell, and she made a low, purring sound of delight at the sight of the thick stalk of his cock gleaming wetly, coated in the slick heat of her cream and their recent climaxes, plowing its way into the tight clench of her inner vaginal lips. It stretched her open with a forceful, shoving motion that worked him in, fed him deeper, while the musky scents of sweat and slick, wet sex surrounded them. The air went thick around them, buzzing with the sizzling sound of mating and the harsh, soughing rhythm of their breath as it battered its way from their lungs.

"There's so much of you," she panted, gasping, her voice unusually husky and raw. He felt like a hot, thick force shoving into her, parting her walls, demanding that she make room for him—that she accept all of him.

"I want more. Let me feel this sweet little cunt rippling around me...pulling me deeper, so beautiful and hungry. Come for me, Melanie. I want to feel you come again, sweetheart." He lowered his head and nipped carefully at her rosy nipples, working the swollen peaks against the roof of his mouth with the flat of his raspy tongue, while his hips drove into her, powerful and possessive, relentless in their purpose.

When the orgasm hit her, it was so beautiful and cleansing and pure that she could do nothing but writhe beneath the thrashing wave of pleasure, smiling up at him, loving the stark look of lust and need and love etched into his fierce expression as he lifted his head to watch her.

"Damn, woman," he rumbled, "you are so gorgeous."

She gave a small, disagreeing shake of her head, unable to keep the shy smile from curling her lips. "No, I'm not."

"Yes, you are," he groaned, leaning down to take her mouth in another slow, sweet, wickedly suggestive kiss that had him claiming every part of her. "And I can prove it to you."

"How's that?"

"Like this." He gave a thick, grinding thrust, driving deep until he was pressed against that sweet spot that only he could reach, then held himself there. "No one else, Mel. No one else has ever made me feel like this before. If you want me, it'll be only yours for the rest of my life."

"All mine, huh?"

The grin spreading across his face was pure, wicked mischief. "Uh-huh, with certain conditions, of course."

Mel arched one brow. "And those would be?"

He ran his hand down the dipping swell of her torso, the touch of his body, both inside and out, making her arch in a voluptuous wave beneath him, her soft breasts swaying upon her chest in a provocative dance that seemed to capture his full attention. "All of this, all of you, is mine forever. No one else's. No one's to touch, to kiss, to stroke, to fuck, but *me*. Christ, you feel so *right*. I swear I never knew it could be like this."

"Like what?"

"Like I'm sinking into every part of you. And you holding me so sweetly, so wet and tight like you never want to let me go."

"I don't want to let you go. But," she laughed on a harsh burst of air, "I might not be able to walk straight after this."

He smiled this time—a slow, wicked smile of pure carnal intent. "It's okay, honey. I'll carry you everywhere you need to go."

And suddenly his strong arms were wrapped around her, one across her back, the other locking around her hips, holding her in place as he stood up, his cock driving impossibly deep, and began walking across her living room, heading for the dim hallway.

"Hold on, Mel," he soothed in a low, melting voice when she gasped. "Put your arms around my neck and hold on tight, baby."

"If this is how you plan on getting me around town, then my standing with the town gossips is going to skyrocket!"

He laughed, and she gasped at the resulting jolt deep inside her.

"You okay?" he asked, his deep voice sharp with concern.

"Yeah," she breathed, licking her lips, "you're just…um, big. But I can't help wanting more…and more." Her face burned with heat. "I never knew I was this greedy."

"Greedy? Hell, woman, I want to go tie you up to your bed and take you again, even harder this time. I want to ride you through your mattress, honey, and get so deep into you that you can feel me shoving into the back of your throat. So be as greedy as you want, angel. I love it."

She knew he was speaking figuratively in that funny, raunchy sex-talk of his that made her burn so freaking hot inside she felt like she'd explode...but he *was* so deliciously big, she couldn't help but giggle at the fact that he *did* reach deep inside her. Deeper than she'd thought a man could go, but there was no denying that she loved it.

Suddenly he turned, pressing her against the cool surface of her hallway wall. "What are you doing?" she asked drowsily, sifting her fingers through the damp silk of his hair, knowing she was staring up at him like a lovesick little fool, but too happy to care.

His smile was hard and full of mischief. "I'm losing control again—and nailing you to the wall, sweetheart."

"Ooh...I can't wait," she laughed. "I've never had sex against a wall before."

"Oh shit," he groaned, lowering his forehead to hers, "that isn't helping, you little tease."

"What?" she asked, turning her face to press a kiss to the warm, scratchy silk of his cheek.

"I'm trying to be cool here, but you keep saying stuff like that and it just drives me over the edge. And it's a hell of a drop on the other side, baby. You gotta try to help me hold on."

"Mmm...that's not what I want. I want you to fall over the edge. I want to push you over it, Mark. Just shove you right over the side." Her lips found the slight bump on the bridge of his nose and she pressed a tender kiss to it, just as she'd imagined doing the week before, when she'd watched him chatting with Roy in the street. "So what's the problem?"

"You have no idea what you're asking for—and you make me so fucking desperate for you that I just want to break you open. *Plus,* I'm a hell of a lot bigger than you are, that's what," he muttered, sounding adorably aggravated. "If we're not careful, you're going to be sore as hell. And shit, Mel, you really have no idea just what kinds of things I want from you."

Holding her stare, he slipped one warm hand over her bottom. With a raw, carnal fire smoldering in the green of his eyes, he deliberately stroked the blunt tip of one finger between her cheeks, then directly over the sensitive pucker of her ass, sending a hot, piercing stab of need through her sex that felt as wickedly good as it did odd and bold. "I'm not kidding when I say I'll want *all* of you. *Everywhere*," he rasped roughly, those sinful green eyes narrowed as he studied her beneath the thick fringe of his ebony lashes. "*Every* hot, tight, naughty little inch."

"Mark?" she said, shivering, stroking the long, tight tendons of his neck, following them down to the powerful curve of his wide shoulders. His body was a work of art, and she couldn't wait to watch it mature over the years. To know that it belonged to her, that it looked to her for its pleasures—all of them—no matter how fierce or raw or darkly sexual they might be. And god only knew she had a lifetime of fantasies saved up to enact on his poor bod.

"Yeah?"

"Let go. I'm not some fragile flower. Just because I've never had the kind of sex you're talking about, doesn't...doesn't mean I can't handle it...or that I don't want it." Tilting her head to the side, she sent him a slow smile, adding in a throaty whisper, "Maybe I just needed the right man to give it to me." Then she leaned forward and nipped his earlobe at the same time she flicked his left nipple with her thumbnail. Mel grinned, feeling the growl breaking out of him vibrate through the long, thick stalk of his cock, and quiver against the tender tips of her nipples pressed so deliciously against the powerful muscles of his chest. Then the erotic scrape of sound poured over her lips, and he moved in for a full, taking kiss.

"You asked for it, Mel," he warned roughly, using that one thick finger to carefully penetrate her ass, then working it steadily in and out, never going too deep, but letting her know *exactly* what he'd soon want from her. "You better be ready to take it."

"I'm ready," she gasped, nearly sobbing from the rich flood of satisfaction the next powerful stroke of his cock slammed through her system—the vicious pleasure only heightened by his finger fucking deliciously into her backside, each thrust suddenly taking it just that little bit deeper, until the biting sensation all but had her keening in sexual discovery. "Now...give it your best shot, Mark."

He growled again at her daring teasing, forcing his heavy cock balls-deep at the same time he forced his long finger completely into the fist-tight depths of her ass, and a sharp, breathless cry jerked out of her as the ecstasy crashed down on her, violent and earth-shattering, creating something within her that was brilliant and new. He held himself pressed deep, giving her the hard column of his cock to crash against, while his buried finger stroked knowingly against the tender, intensely sensitive tissues within that erotically forbidden hole.

"That's it, baby. Come for me, Mel. Let me feel how much you love my cock crammed so deep into this hot, perfect little cunt—how much you're enjoying my finger fucking you here. Christ, it's so fucking good. So tight and hungry and sweet, angel. I'm gonna kill myself fucking you, sweetheart."

"Mark," she cried out, and the next words that left her mouth took that last thread of his restraint and snapped it so violently that the aftershocks shuddered through him, making his legs shake, his damn knees nearly give, it was so powerful. "Mark...oh god, I want it now. I want...I don't know...I just want you to take me. Do it...whatever you want, damn it...just take me and do it!"

"You want it now, Mel?" he grated, the words harsh and ragged as he spoke them between the hard, heavy breaths that fought their way out of his lungs. "Do you even know what you're saying, angel? Because it won't be pretty and sweet. I want you too fucking badly for that."

"I trust you, Mark. You won't hurt me...and yes, I want it. I want everything that you want. Don't ever hold back with me. I love you, and that means all of you. Trust me," she pleaded with a shy, sexy smile, leaning forward to sink her teeth into the tender flesh of his lower lip—and he broke.

Shattered.

One second he stood pressing her against the wall, and then, without conscious direction from his brain, he found himself with her on the soft, white linens of her bed, her face and upper body pressed into the rumpled bedding. Her head was turned to the side so that she could see him, lush ass in the air, knees spread wide by his hard thighs...and her slender, delicate wrists trapped in the dominating grip of one big fist as he held her arms pinned forcefully against her lower back. Through narrowed eyes, he watched his throbbing, cum-slick dick slide through the swollen, thoroughly fucked lips of her cunt, coating himself in that rich, decadent cream she'd poured over him until he was glistening with it. He took precious seconds to appreciate the ruthlessly carnal view—her cunt so swollen and pink, dripping with her juices, rosy ass cheeks trembling from excitement, and then he pulled back and firmly gripped his other hand around the broad root of his cock. His big fingers bit down, making the full, blood-filled veins bulge, and with an animal snarl of possession, he pressed the fat, bulbous head against the tiny, innocent hole that he'd only moments before penetrated with his finger.

"*Mark, yes...*" she cried out at that first blistering contact, and she shivered beneath him, all hot, hungry woman, and his heart nearly burst from the rich swell of love rushing through him, filling him up, all his fears lost as he realized the acceptance she was giving him, offering so unconditionally. The eagerness and want for all his darker pleasures—his breathtaking little equal, in *everything*. No woman had ever come close to matching him so perfectly.

"Oh Mel, you look so damn hot like this, angel. This is going to be so fucking good," and he pressed forward, forcing the very tip of him against that incredible tightness, until she began blooming open for him, swallowing the head, all that puckered, tender flesh opening wider and wider. The strong, biting muscle bit down on him so perfectly, as the head slipped in, that he had to grind his teeth to keep from shoving in his entire length and hurting her past that sharp point of pleasure that he knew she was feeling. No, they'd have to work up to that, and he knew his wicked little innocent was going to love every second of it.

And god, he loved how it looked, this primitive taking of her. Her arms pinned against her back, trapped, the rosy cheeks of her ass spread apart, and that sweet little hole spread too, forced open as his dick crammed its way in, stretching her until he knew the biting, burning pleasure was being seasoned with sparks of pain that would only heighten the feelings instead of hurting her. Damn, but did he *love* the pure, raw eroticism of the visual they made, his heavy cock digging deeper and deeper into the tight, so incredibly fucking tight, little opening, her body sucking him up inside, squeezing down on him hard, while below her gorgeous cunt just kept creaming, spilling that delicious, syrupy sweetness that he could still taste on his tongue. Still feel in his throat—that he'd hunger to eat for the rest of his life…and would.

"Aw, Mel, you look so sexy, honey. So delicate and sweet. I wish you could see this. It's so gorgeous—my cock pumping into your tight, pretty hole. I can't believe you're taking it." He curved over her, whispering darkly in her ear. "But you like it, don't you, Mel? You like being fucked in this hot little ass. Love having my cock here, reaming into you, so hot and hard that you can barely breathe from how good it feels, don't you, sweetheart?"

"God, yes," she panted, her face cherry red and damp with raw passion.

Mark lifted the hand around his dick and brushed the heavy fall of her hair to the side, then pressed his open mouth against her neck, trailing wetly up to the sensitive place behind her ear. "I think deep down inside, I knew you would. Knew this beautiful body would belong to me just as thoroughly as your heart, if I could ever get lucky enough to convince you to take a chance on me. Knew you'd let me do anything I wanted to it, and that you'd love it. I'm so damn lucky to have found you, Melanie. I don't know what the hell I did to deserve you, but I'm smart enough and ruthless enough to do everything it will ever take to keep you. You're always mine. *Always*," he grunted, powering his cock into her with a suddenly powerful shove of his hips, sending more thick inches into her as her pretty hole completely swallowed the top portion of his heavy shaft, stretching that tight, tender opening wider, her whole body going crimson from the hard, grinding feel of having her virgin ass fucked for the first time.

"Yes, yes...always," she sobbed softly, her voice wrecked from the grunts of pleasure curling out of her—pleasure he could so easily feel riding the surface of her skin, rushing through her as she shimmied beneath him.

"Is this how you thought it would be?" he asked in a low, silken voice, his breath panting from his lungs as he hammered into her with short, jabbing thrusts that were working him in deeper and deeper, until she'd taken over half his long length, the scent of her cunt filling the air around them with hot, earthy perfume as she creamed her pretty pink pussy and the smooth inner surfaces of her thighs. It drugged him, made him out of his mind to take her with everything that he was, claim every piece of her for his own. "Did you ever think about having me here, Mel? What it'd feel like to have your tender little backside ridden and claimed by the man who owns it?"

"Yes. I...I dreamed about this," she cried out hoarsely, "but it feels so much better than anything I ever imagined. It feels wicked and sinful, but so possessive and intimate that I love it. I love knowing that you're the only man who's ever had me this way. The only man who ever will."

"Fuck, Melanie," he groaned, gritting the words through his clenched teeth as he began to pick up his tempo, her body jolting beneath him, slender hands still trapped helplessly against her back, so that he controlled everything, all of it, undone by her words. His heavy balls drew up so tight, he knew he didn't have but seconds left before he exploded. "I want you to come, Mel. I want your sweet pussy to gush without even having to touch it. Want it to flood and ripple from nothing but the feel of my cock fucking you *here*," he grunted, shoving in another thick inch, making her cry out a harsh, choking sound of pleasure.

"I want to," she sobbed, "Oh god, Mark, I want to come so badly. *Please*."

"You will, angel." He was getting rougher, more controlling, his darker cravings for dominant sex coming through, he knew, but she wasn't running on him or fighting it. No, she was gripping him with her inner muscles, begging with the low, throaty purrs tumbling past those bee-stung lips, her beautiful body blossoming into a carnal thing of want, desperate for everything he could give her. His perfect equal in all of it, everything, and it hurt so goddamn good, that burning, blinding ecstasy at having her and being accepted — all of him — that it nearly turned him inside out.

"Tomorrow we're going shopping, sweetheart, and I'm going to buy you a whole new play set," he growled, his heart as eager as his cock for all the years they had ahead of them to share and enjoy together — an entire lifetime. "A sweet, pretty plug for this tight ass that you'll wear for me, and before you know it, you're going to be taking *all* of me, Melanie. Every hard, aching inch of me will be drilling into you here. I'll fuck that beautiful cunt that I love so much, that I won't ever get enough of, and after you've come so many times you're boneless, I'm going to lift you up, fill that throbbing little pussy with a nice, fat dildo, and then I'm going to stuff you full, honey. I'm going to fuck your ass and make you pump your pussy with a big, hard cock. I'm going to take you so that

I can watch it all. Hold you spread over my thighs, and watch you screw yourself with your favorite new toy while I pound this sweet, tight ass full of me. And when I jerk into you, when I fill you full of cum, you're going to shove your toy deep, pinch your pretty little pounding clit, and you're going to come so hard that it blasts through you, Mel, hot and hard and vicious in how good it feels. So wicked and powerful that you'll pass out, angel, and when you wake up, I'll be right there, licking up all those slippery juices with my mouth and my tongue. I'll kiss your tender, ravaged body all better, drink down your warm, honeyed cum until you feel so soft and sweet that you melt in my arms."

"Oh god…Mark…it's happening," she cried out, and he could feel it. Could feel the tightening of her pussy through the thin membrane separating that sweet place from the gripping, tender channel that he was breaking open. That he was hammering with his cock now, until they were wet with sweat and burning with the fires of hard, raunchy fucking that seared them both.

"That's it, baby," he ground out through clenched teeth, watching her shatter as he used his free hand to reach beneath her and pinch one swollen nipple between his rough thumb and forefinger, pumping it in perfect rhythm with his cock. "Oh angel, you feel so good, I can't hold it."

She cried out, shouting and screaming and sounding like a woman who was experiencing the most intense, convulsive climax of her life, and it pulled him in, pulled the dark, deepening wave of pleasure out of him, until he jerked into her hard, the cum rolling up through his dick like an eruption. It pumped out of the fat, buried head of his cock in a vicious, pulsing, powerful wave that made him growl and grind into her, another inch shoving through that tight ring of muscle, and they shook together, trembling and slick as their bodies shuddered against the other, their cries raw and primal in the soft, heavy sweetness of the sex-scented air.

When the last ripple and pulse finally faded, Mark released her wrists, wrapped his shaking arms around her shivering body, and put up a valiant struggle to find his breath. "Oh god, Melanie, honey, that was incredible. I think you short-circuited my brain."

"I can't believe it was even better than my fantasies," she murmured softly, and he felt sublimely heavy with happiness as he laughed a deep, rich sound of male delight against her temple. A moment later, they fell onto the tangled sheets of her bed, his harsh breath in her ear, heavy body pressing her into the mattress, and as she sent him a wicked look over her smooth shoulder, they shared smiles of pure, unadulterated satisfaction…and sweet, everlasting love.

Later, after a sensual shower of eager, curious hands and pleasurable discovery that led to another frantic encounter that took them from the bathroom to the bedroom floor, and finally the bed again, they lay tangled in her sheets, their skin slick and warm, chests moving with slow, deep breaths as they struggled to find enough air.

"Your brother came by earlier," she murmured around a yawn.

His head jerked up from the pillow. "What?"

Melanie laughed out loud. "You know, you say that a lot. Why is that?"

"Because you're always shocking the hell out of me," he said with a quick kiss and a slow smile, before rolling to her side and asking, "What in the hell did Cain want?" His smoky green gaze narrowed. "He didn't ask you out, did he?"

She swatted at his chest. "No, you goof. You're his brother! Of course he didn't ask me out."

Mark snorted. "Mel, I could be the King of England and it still wouldn't stop Cain from going after my woman if he wanted her."

"He's stolen your girlfriends before?" she asked with stunned surprised.

"No," he snickered, "but then you're a hell of a lot more than my *girlfriend*. And...I know he thinks you're hot as hell."

"Really?" she smiled, knowing she was blushing at the thought.

"Yeah, and don't look so happy about it," he grumbled. "I'm going to be beating him off with a stick for years to come, until we find him his own woman."

"Well, to answer your question, he came to convince me to believe in you."

He snorted another arrogant sound of disbelief. "You're shitting me."

"Uh, no," she laughed, wrinkling her nose at his less than savory choice of exclamations, "I'm not."

His look clearly said he wasn't buying it.

"Honestly, Mark. He came by and tried to talk me into giving you another chance. He wanted me to find you and be honest about what I wanted from you, since he...he seemed to think you really wanted *me*."

He studied her out of piercing eyes. "And that's why you're here, Melanie?"

"Where?" she asked, sitting up, clutching for a corner of the sheet to hold against her breasts.

In one swift move, Mark had her tumbled to the bed, trapped beneath him. "In my arms, under my body, drenched with my cum." His voice came smooth and deep, like rich, thick honey.

"Of course not!" she said indignantly. "I'm *here* because I love you, you dolt. But it was terribly sweet of him to come over. He was so tense and anxious with brotherly concern."

"Now I know you're shitting me," he laughed, making that damn snorting sound again.

"You know," she murmured, "we have *got* to find you another expression, Mark. But no, I'm not *shitting you*, as you so eloquently put it. He really was worried for you."

"Well color me surprised and slap me stupid," he drawled. "I never would have believed it."

"Well, it's true. And don't you dare go throwing his concern back in his face."

He tried to disguise the wicked gleam of anticipation that had brightened his gaze with a look of utter innocence. "Would I do that?"

Melanie wasn't buying it. "What's your middle name?"

"Joseph."

"Then Mark Joseph Logan," she muttered, "you bet your fine ass you would, and I won't have it."

"Yeah?" he asked huskily, arching his brows. "This sounds interesting. Just what are going to do about it?"

His devilish humor was contagious. A slow smile spread across her face, so wide she could feel her dimples cutting grooves into her cheeks. "Hmm...I bet I can make it worthwhile."

His eyes narrowed, intent green gaze full of smoldering anticipation. "I'm listening."

She wet her lips, her cheeks burning with color. "It...uh, will probably involve lots of licking and sucking. And...*swallowing*."

"Yeah?" he rasped, twin dark spots of color burning strong on his cheekbones, his eyes heavy, lips parted and full. "I think you ought to start right now."

"I couldn't agree more," she laughed. Then her laughter faded, and she said, "I want to keep you satisfied, Mark. That night, I hated watching you walk away, knowing you'd be leaving me to go find some hot floozy who could satisfy your hunger. It ate away at me all week, wondering *what* you were doing. Wondering *who* you were doing it with."

"Won't *ever* happen, angel. This, my hunger," he grinned, all wicked mischief and carnal intent as he rubbed his granite-hard erection into the giving softness of her belly, "is all yours. I've got a one-item menu for the rest of my life, but there's a thousand different ways we can serve it up."

"Mark," she laughed, her eyes watering at his playfulness.

"I know, it's corny as hell," he smiled, "but you make me...*happy*." The word rolled off his tongue like the sweetest of promises, and she recognized the gift that he'd offered her—another tender insight into his soul that was all hers. "Happier than I ever imagined I could be, Melanie," he said huskily. "That's my only excuse. I can't help it."

All the significant things she wanted to say in return crowded into her tight throat—so Melanie settled for pulling his mouth down to hers, responding with a slow, love-filled kiss that said it all.

* * * * *

The day passed in a sublime, sexual lassitude that neither wanted to end. They stroked and hugged and rocked softly against each other, their bodies burning with the excitement of love and discovery, eager to touch and taste and learn.

"So," Mark sighed with soul-deep satisfaction hours later, rolling to his back and pulling her across his chest, while one big hand rubbed the back of her head, tangling her curls, "as soon as I can walk, I'll get Cain to start helping me get your stuff moved over to my place. I'd move in here, but my place is bigger and I don't wanna crowd you."

"Mmm...you better wait before you call him. I don't plan on letting you outta this bed for at least a few more hours."

"Maybe I should tell him to plan for tomorrow afternoon." He let everything he felt for her fill him up, until it felt as if it were pounding through his veins, and he knew she could see it, all of it, burning in his fiercely possessive gaze.

"Yeah, that sounds better," she said breathlessly. "We'll need to break for food by then anyway."

"Oh man, you're turning into an insatiable little sex maniac, aren't you?" he drawled with keen anticipation, reaching down to grope her sweet little bottom.

"You think so?" she asked with a brilliant, blinding smile, and he pulled her higher onto his chest until she draped his body like a blanket of warm, willing, wonderful woman. All his, and he was going to spend the rest of his life making her deliriously happy for gifting him with her love.

"I think you're amazing. And mine. And I'm madly in love with you. Would you like me to *tell* you all about it?" he asked with a teasing grin, knowing she was already hungry for him, and god only knew his cock was hard and ready to please, pressed between their bellies.

She arched one slender brow, her beautiful brown eyes shimmering with humor. "Are you going to let your body do the talking?"

He tsked playfully, shaking his head from side to side. "And here I thought you wanted a little less conversation from me, sweetheart."

"What can I say? I like your body language, Marky boy," she drawled with a cocky grin that would have made even an arrogant bastard like Cain proud. "Go ahead and *talk* to me some more. I'm all ears."

Mark threw back his head and roared with laughter...and then gave her exactly what she wanted.

Also by Joey W. Hill

☙

Behind the Mask (*anthology*)
Enchained (*anthology*)
If Wishes Were Horses
Make Her Dreams Come True
Nature of Desire 1: Holding the Cards
Nature of Desire 2: Natural Law
Nature of Desire 3: Ice Queen
Nature of Desire 4: Mirror of My Soul
Nature of Desire 5: Mistress of Redemption
Nature of Desire 6: Rough Canvas
Snow Angel
Threads of Faith
Virtual Reality

About the Author

I've always had an aversion to reading, watching or hearing interviews of favorite actors, authors, musicians, etc. because so often the real person doesn't measure up to the beauty of the art they produce. Their politics or religion are distasteful, or they're shallow and self-absorbed, a vacuous mophead without a lick of sense. From then on, though I may appreciate their craft or art, it has somehow been tarnished. Therefore, whenever I'm asked to provide personal information about myself for readers, a ball of anxiety forms in my stomach as I think: "Okay, the next couple of paragraphs can change forever the way someone views my stories." Why on earth does a reader want to know about me? It's the story that's important.

So here it is. I've been given more blessings in my life than any one person has a right to have. Despite that, I'm a Type A, borderline obsessive-compulsive paranoiac who worries I will never live up to expectations. I've got more phobias than anyone (including myself) has patience to read about. I can't stand talking on the phone, I dread social commitments, and the idea of living in monastic solitude with my husband and animals, books and writing is as close an idea to paradise as I can imagine. I love chocolate, but with that deeply ingrained, irrational female belief that weight equals worth, I manage to keep it down to a minor addiction. I adore good movies. I'm told I work too much. Every day is spent trying to get through the never ending "to do" list to snatch a few minutes to write.

This is because, despite all these mediocre and typical qualities, for some miraculous reason, these wonderful characters well up out of my soul with stories to tell. When I manage to find enough time to write, sufficient enough that the precious "stillness" required rises up and calms all the competing voices in my head, I can step into their lives, hear what they are saying, what they're feeling, and put it down on paper. It's a magic beyond description, akin to truly believing my husband loves me, winning the trust of an animal who has known only fear or apathy, making a true connection with someone, or knowing for certain I've given a reader a moment of magic through those written words. It's a magic that reassures me there is Someone, far wiser than myself, who knows the permanent path to that garden of stillness, where there is only love, acceptance and a pen waiting for hours and hours of uninterrupted, blissful use.

If only I could finish that darned "to do" list.

I welcome feedback from readers—actually, I thrive on it like a vampire, whether it's good or bad. So feel free to visit me through my website www.storywitch.com anytime.

Joey welcomes comments from readers. You can find her website and email address on her author bio page at www.ellorascave.com.

Tell Us What You Think

We appreciate hearing reader opinions about our books. You can email us at Comments@EllorasCave.com.

Also by Rhyannon Byrd

༄

A Bite of Magick
Against the Wall
Alpha Romeos
A Shot of Magick
Down and Dirty (*anthology*)
Half Wild
Horn of the Unicorn
Triple Play
Waiting for It

About the Author

Rhyannon Byrd is the wife of a Brit, mother of two amazing children, and maid to a precocious beagle named Misha. A longtime fan of romance, she finally felt at home when she read her first Romantica novel. Her love of this spicy, ever-changing genre has become an unquenchable passion—the hotter they are, the better she enjoys them!

Writing for Ellora's Cave is a dream come true for Rhyannon. Now her days (and let's face it, most nights) are spent giving life to the stories and characters running wild in her head. Whether she's writing contemporaries, paranormals…or even futuristics, there's always sure to be a strong Alpha hero featured as well as a fascinating woman to capture his heart, keeping all that wicked wildness for her own!

Rhyannon loves to hear from readers.

Rhyannon welcomes comments from readers. You can find her website and email address on her author bio page at www.ellorascave.com.

Tell Us What You Think

We appreciate hearing reader opinions about our books. You can email us at Comments@EllorasCave.com.

Why an electronic book?

We live in the Information Age—an exciting time in the history of human civilization, in which technology rules supreme and continues to progress in leaps and bounds every minute of every day. For a multitude of reasons, more and more avid literary fans are opting to purchase e-books instead of paper books. The question from those not yet initiated into the world of electronic reading is simply: *Why?*

1. *Price.* An electronic title at Ellora's Cave Publishing and Cerridwen Press runs anywhere from 40% to 75% less than the cover price of the exact same title in paperback format. Why? Basic mathematics and cost. It is less expensive to publish an e-book (no paper and printing, no warehousing and shipping) than it is to publish a paperback, so the savings are passed along to the consumer.
2. *Space.* Running out of room in your house for your books? That is one worry you will never have with electronic books. For a low one-time cost, you can purchase a handheld device specifically designed for e-reading. Many e-readers have large, convenient screens for viewing. Better yet, hundreds of titles can be stored within your new library—on a single microchip. There are a variety of e-readers from different manufacturers. You can also read e-books on your PC or laptop computer. (Please note that Ellora's Cave does not endorse any specific brands.

You can check our websites at www.ellorascave.com or www.cerridwenpress.com for information we make available to new consumers.)

3. *Mobility.* Because your new e-library consists of only a microchip within a small, easily transportable e-reader, your entire cache of books can be taken with you wherever you go.

4. *Personal Viewing Preferences.* Are the words you are currently reading too small? Too large? Too… ANNOYING? Paperback books cannot be modified according to personal preferences, but e-books can.

5. *Instant Gratification.* Is it the middle of the night and all the bookstores near you are closed? Are you tired of waiting days, sometimes weeks, for bookstores to ship the novels you bought? Ellora's Cave Publishing sells instantaneous downloads twenty-four hours a day, seven days a week, every day of the year. Our webstore is never closed. Our e-book delivery system is 100% automated, meaning your order is filled as soon as you pay for it.

Those are a few of the top reasons why electronic books are replacing paperbacks for many avid readers.

As always, Ellora's Cave and Cerridwen Press welcome your questions and comments. We invite you to email us at Comments@ellorascave.com or write to us directly at Ellora's Cave Publishing Inc., 1056 Home Avenue, Akron, OH 44310-3502.

Make each day more *EXCITING* With our

Ellora's Cavemen Calendar

www.EllorasCave.com

COMING TO A BOOKSTORE NEAR YOU!

ELLORA'S CAVE

Bestselling Authors Tour

UPDATES AVAILABLE AT
WWW.ELLORASCAVE.COM

Cerridwen, the Celtic Goddess of wisdom, was the muse who brought inspiration to storytellers and those in the creative arts. Cerridwen Press encompasses the best and most innovative stories in all genres of today's fiction. Visit our site and discover the newest titles by talented authors who still get inspired - much like the ancient storytellers did, once upon a time.

Cerridwen Press
www.cerridwenpress.com

Discover for yourself why readers can't get enough of the multiple award-winning publisher Ellora's Cave.

Whether you prefer e-books or paperbacks, be sure to visit EC on the web at www.ellorascave.com for an erotic reading experience that will leave you breathless.

Lightning Source UK Ltd.
Milton Keynes UK
UKOW04f1033011214

242449UK00001B/177/P